DEATH BY DAUBER

DONNA WALO CLANCY

DWC PUBLISHING

DWC
PUBLISHING

To all the older women out there in the world that enjoy life, just like Thelma and June.

1

"I told Kami to pick us up by five o'clock. If we don't leave by then, we will lose our regular seats," Thelma complained. "If I don't sit in my lucky seat, I won't win."

"Pish. You win all the time no matter where you sit," June stated. "Maybe she's already down in the parking lot waiting for us."

"I doubt it. She was just pouring a glass of wine when I last talked to her. My niece insists it relaxes her so she can find the numbers easier. If you ask me, it makes her overlook numbers and miss bingos. But who am I to say?" she said as she pressed the elevator button.

"Kami is definitely your niece. Loving the old vino runs in the family, doesn't it?" June teased.

"I drink wine for health reasons," Thelma insisted.

"Sure you do," June said, rolling her eyes.

Thelma Frost was just the type to say whatever she wanted to say regardless of what it was or who was around her when she said it. At fifty-nine years old, divorced since she was forty, she had learned to survive on her own, and part of that survival was speaking her mind. Thelma Frost was one feisty woman. The queen of feisty many would say.

Her bright red hair, which she insisted was her natural color, made her stick out wherever she went. She was in good health and worked part-time at the Sechuette Animal Hospital as their front desk receptionist. Thelma was a spitfire, and people rarely argued with her when she was making a point.

The two friends walked out into the lobby of the building. Because of a severe shortage of housing for people aged fifty plus in the area, the Falling Leaves Community Complex was built. Consisting of two three-floor buildings with an adjoining courtyard, the apartments were filled in the first month they were offered.

The courtyard contained several large maple trees that the buildings were purposely built around. Each year, the leaves showed off their beautiful autumnal colors making the area the favorite place of the residents to sit and enjoy the afternoon sun. As the air turned colder, the maples shed their leaves, hence the name of the complex, The Falling Leaves.

The friends lived in building B. Thelma lived in 212, and June lived on the floor directly above her in 312. They had been two of the original residents. They loved the carefree lifestyle of no maintenance, a full dining room if they chose not to cook for themselves, and many other amenities too numerous to track.

At the front door, they spotted Kami, leaning against her car, waiting for them. She looked up and pointed to her watch.

"And you said she wouldn't be ready." June snickered as she opened the door. "Maybe you should have a glass of wine before bingo. Then you wouldn't be so cranky."

"I don't need any wine. I just need my lucky seat," Thelma insisted, climbing into the passenger seat of the car. "And I'm not cranky!"

"Did I hear something about wine?" Kami asked as she slid into the driver's seat.

"No, just drive." June laughed.

The parking lot was packed. During the summer, the hall had twice as many people attending the nightly events, which led to more fights over seats. Visiting tourists didn't know what seats were claimed by the year-round regulars and would sit wherever there was an open table. A few of the die-hard players would stand behind a seated visitor until they got the hint and moved to another spot.

The three friends walked past the cashier and the long line of customers waiting to pay for their cards and headed to their regular table. Two strangers already had their cards spread out and were taping their paper strips together.

"I don't believe this. We're five minutes early, and someone is already sitting at our table," Thelma grumbled.

"It's fine. They're only in my space. I'll just move to the other side of Kami and sit there. I'm still facing the board, and you will have your lucky seat," June said, setting her bingo bag down on the table at her new spot.

"I just hope they don't crowd me," Thelma stated, loud enough for the two women to hear her. "I play a lot of cards and like my elbow space."

"You sound more and more like Agatha Tram every day," Kami said, shaking her head.

"I do not!"

"Yes, you do. For years we have made fun of Agatha and her ways, and now you are the carbon copy of her," Kami confirmed. "Speak of the devil…"

A loud commotion broke out on the opposite side of the hall. Agatha Tram was standing behind a young girl who was sitting in her regular seat and wasn't going to give it up. The older woman requested three times that the player move down two spots so she could have her treasured seat, and the girl countered by telling her to sit the same two places down. Agatha had sat in that exact seat since the first night that bingo started almost thirty years ago and wasn't going to sit anywhere else. She was furious, as she was wealthy and used to getting her own way.

Her husband, Robert, died many years ago in a plane crash while flying overseas on one of his many business trips. He left his widow very well off. The local newspaper, the Sechuette Gazette, was one of the few businesses that Agatha had decided not to sell. She loved to stir up trouble and could do so in her weekly gossip column by mentioning things that weren't entirely true. This had made her many enemies over the years.

A square-jawed woman with coal-black eyes that could stare straight into your soul, she had gray hair that was always drawn into a tight bun at the top of her head. Even though Agatha was only five foot two, she emitted an intimidating presence, and very few people had ever seen her smile. No one knew her exact age as it was a well-guarded secret by Agatha.

Wayne Spikeman, the caller for that evening, hurried over to defuse the situation before it escalated to the next degree. Anyone who had been in the hall on previous nights knew that if the person did not move willingly, Agatha would start to remove their belongings from the table and toss them onto another table nearby. Wayne offered the young girl a free dauber and a seat up near the caller if she would relent to the older woman's wishes.

Not happy about having to move, the visitor reluctantly agreed, and she and her friend took their new seats at the front of the hall, glaring at Agatha the whole time. The older woman settled into her favorite place. She proceeded to set up her space with her lucky charms and many different colored daubers.

"I give you five years, and you'll be raising a commotion just like Agatha if someone sits in your lucky seat." June laughed, taking her wallet out of her purse.

"Never!" Thelma insisted, emptying the contents of her bingo bag, and spreading them around to protect her space. "I'm not rich and uppity."

"I'm getting in line," Kami stated. "It's getting close to early bird, and I want my cards to be all taped and ready to go."

"I'll join you. Are you coming, Thelma?" June asked.

"In a bit. I have to check my daubers. Some of them are drying out, and the tops are splitting. I need to know what colors to buy when I am in line."

Thelma sat down and pulled a piece of scrap paper out of her bingo bag. She opened one dauber at a time, and after checking the sponge on the top, she then daubed the paper to see if it was worth keeping or she would throw them away.

"Excuse me. Can you help us out a bit? We have never played bingo before, and the order of papers is a little bit confusing," the woman next to her asked.

"Did you grab a program when you were in line?" Thelma asked.

"Yes, we have one right here," she answered, holding up a piece of paper.

"I'll put your strips in order, and then you can do your friends," Thelma stated, taking the pile of papers handed to her.

"These are the solid colors, and these are the border colors. The solid colors are played in the first half and the border colors after intermission," Thelma lectured. "If you want to play the early bird games, you have to find the worker selling them and buy them separately."

"Thank you for your help. Can I buy you a cup of coffee as a thank you?"

"Coffee is free, but thank you anyway." Thelma smiled, going back to her dauber testing.

Deciding that she needed a new green, purple, and neon orange dauber, she picked up her wallet and walked to the end of the line of people buying cards. As she was taking her money out of her wallet, someone bumped her from behind, almost causing her to drop everything. She turned and was face to face with Agatha.

"A 'sorry' or 'excuse me' would be nice," Thelma grumbled.

"I don't apologize to anyone," Agatha stated firmly.

"Yeah, we know," Thelma mumbled under her breath.

As they stood in line waiting to buy their cards, the young girl who Agatha had made move walked by them. She was so busy looking for the bathroom that she walked a little too close to Agatha and knocked the wallet out of the crook of the older woman's arm.

"Well, I never!" Agatha exclaimed as the girl kept walking.

"What goes around, comes around," Thelma muttered under her breath

Wayne rushed up, picked up the wallet, and handed it back.

"Don't think this will gain you any favors at work," Agatha said with a sting in her voice.

"I wasn't expecting any," Wayne admitted, quickly walking away.

Thelma felt one of those "I need to say something" moments welling up in her brain.

"You are a piece of work! You couldn't just say thank you to the man?" Thelma lectured. "Would it kill you to be nice once in a while?"

Agatha stared at the woman standing before her in line. No one spoke to her like that, let alone a red-haired nobody whom she only knew as the aunt of one of her employees. Yes, she had seen her at other bingo halls, but she had never engaged in conversation with her. They weren't of the same social status, not even close. Agatha had no friends as she genuinely believed no one else was good enough to be her friend.

"Never mind," Thelma said in disgust.

They stood in silence for the rest of the time they were in line. Thelma bought her cards and her new daubers and plopped in her chair when she got back to her table.

Agatha had set her cards down and was walking to the refreshment center when she stopped behind Kami on her way there.

"If you value your job, I'd tell your aunt to watch who she questions in the future," Agatha hissed.

Before Kami could utter a word, Thelma pushed her chair back and stood up.

"Are you threatening my niece's job?" Thelma demanded loudly.

"No, I am just offering her a bit of friendly advice," Agatha shot back.

Kami stood up next, towering over her boss.

"Whatever problem you have with my aunt has nothing to do with me or my job," Kami insisted. "I am good at what I do at the newspaper, and my job should not be called into question because you are having a tiff with someone else."

Agatha stormed off, upset that for the second time that night, she had failed to get the upper hand in a situation that she had been involved in.

"Well, that was interesting," June said, breaking the silence.

"I can't believe the nerve of that woman, threatening Kami's job," Thelma spouted.

"Don't worry, Aunt Thelma. I am too valuable to her to fire. No one brings in as much money to her newspaper as I do. She just likes to make everyone think that she is totally in charge and can't be questioned," Kami said, sitting down.

"Exactly what do you do at the paper?' June asked.

"I run the advertising department. Two people work for me, and we surpass our set quota of income every month. People trust me, and many times, I have ironed out problems between Agatha and clients of the paper. She knows she needs me, so her threats are just empty words," Kami stated.

"I don't know how you can work for that woman," Thelma protested. "She is just plain miserable."

"The pay is good at the paper, and the benefits are some of the best offered among local jobs. She may be miserable, but she does take care of her employees," Kami replied. "Even if she threatens us continually."

"That's why I love my job. No threats, just lots of animals to love and take care of. The people I do have to deal with are loving, caring people who worship their furry family members. And those who don't or can't anymore know we will find them good homes," Thelma said. "Speaking of which..."

"How many?" both June and Kami asked at the same time.

They looked at each other and burst out laughing. Both women knew when Thelma started with that statement that they were going to be asked to foster a rescued or abandoned cat or kittens. Ignoring their private little joke, Thelma continued.

"Do you remember Mrs. Greystone? She passed away a few months ago, and her kids don't want her two older cats. Tucker and Tommy are having a terrible time adjusting to the kennel and all its noises. It's so sad. They cower in the corner of the cage together and won't eat. They are beautiful, long-haired male cats. We are looking for somewhere for them to live until they find a permanent home."

"How old are they?" June asked.

"According to their records at the vet, Tucker and Tommy were brothers from the same litter and are thirteen years old. Mrs. Greystone took very good care of them. Their shots are up to date, and both are fixed," Thelma recited.

"I guess I could take them in," June suggested. "I just lost Poppy after having her for eighteen years, and the house is kind of quiet."

"Wonderful!" Thelma exclaimed.

"Excuse me again. We weren't eavesdropping, but we heard what you said about Tucker and Tommy. We just moved to the area and bought Mrs. Greystone's house. We would love to adopt the two cats and return them to the house they knew and loved," the woman closest to Thelma said. "I'm Wendy Small, and this is Mandy Beston."

Thelma stared at the woman, stunned at what she had just heard. This was the best solution to the cats' problem. To be able to return them to the home they knew and were comfortable in was music to Thelma's ears. She teared up at what had been offered by these two strangers.

"You would do that?" Thelma inquired.

"We sure would. Right before we moved away, my mother insisted on keeping my cat. We shared a house, and she was always home, where we worked and were only home at night. She swore that she couldn't get along without Penelope, so I left her with my mom as much as I didn't want to. But I know she loves the cat as much as I do, if not more, and she will be great company for her."

"Are you already moved into the house?" Thelma asked.

"We moved in last week. We also just rented the vacant building down at the end of Main Street. It is going to be the future home of Sechuette Tees," Mandy informed them.

"Is the house all unpacked? The cats would freak if there were boxes everywhere," Thelma asked.

"We are all settled in. The cats might look for Mrs. Greystone and be a bit confused when they can't find her. Still, I am sure they will settle in as they probably know every nook and cranny of the old house," Mandy answered, amused at how concerned the red-haired woman was for the cats. "Please, we would love to adopt them."

"It is settled. Can you come in Monday to the Sechuette Animal Hospital? I will waive the fees because you are keeping them together and returning them to their old home," Thelma offered.

"We will be there Monday," Wendy replied.

"Well, I guess that means I don't have two new visitors coming to my house," June chuckled, knowing that there would always be more animals to foster.

"If you really insist, I do have another two-year-old that needs fostering..."

Before anyone could say anything else, the caller took his seat behind the bingo board and started to make the weekly announcements. The hall became quiet as everyone concentrated on finding the numbers that would allow them to holler bingo. Kami won once, Thelma won three times, and June just donated money for the night.

"Before everyone leaves, I just want to remind you about the plaque dedication tomorrow before the morning bingo. I hope everyone will attend," Wayne announced.

"Not if I can help it," Thelma muttered as she picked up her bingo bag to leave.

"I have to be here, so you have to be here," Kami lectured. "Otherwise, you need to drive yourself to bingo."

"We'll be ready," June said.

"Fine, but I don't have to like it," Thelma insisted.

Tomorrow was Sunday, which meant the group played bingo twice, once in the mid-morning and once at night, both in the same hall but for different fund-raising groups.

2

The sun was shining brightly through the kitchen window. Zumbutt, Thelma's permanent roommate, was stretched out on the floor, enjoying the warmth of the sunbeams. The big black cat had come to Thelma as a foster six years ago and never left. He was the boss of the house and knew it. He had his private litterbox room and toys scattered from one end of the apartment to the other.

He won over Thelma's heart because of many reasons but mostly for his affectionate ways. No matter where she sat, he had to sit with her. He slept with her, and they ate their meals together. When Thelma was home, the cat was never more than three feet away from her.

Zumbutt had gorgeous eyes. They were the brightest blue eyes that Thelma had ever seen on a cat, and they were mesmerizing. When she was having a bad day, all she had to do was look in his big old eyes, and all her sadness disappeared.

He was also so easy going that no matter what foster Thelma brought into the house, it didn't bother the black cat at all. The cat seemed to sense that whoever it was visiting at the time needed love and attention as he did. He shared his toys, and many times, his cat house in the middle of the living room.

Several weeks into Zumbutt's foster period, Thelma discovered that the cat loved wine as much as she did. It didn't matter what kind of wine was in the glass, Zumbutt had to have his fair share, or he would pester his owner until he got it. She knew then that he was meant to stay with her, and from that day on, he was family and no longer a foster.

"How about some breakfast?" Thelma said, shaking the dry food box.

Zumbutt sat there, not pleased with the food she offered.

"Oh, I get it. You're too good for dry food. Wet it is then," she said, grabbing a can of food out of the cupboard.

She placed the bowl on the floor, and the cat sauntered over to check it out. After a couple of sniffs, he sat down and looked up at her. He let out a meow and walked away into the other room.

"Okay, be like that. You are not getting anything else. I know you like that flavor. You're just being difficult," Thelma announced. "You'll eat it when you get hungry enough!"

She sat at her kitchen table with her morning coffee and yesterday's mail. A manila envelope caught her eye first. There was no return address, and the postmark was local. She grabbed her letter opener and slit the top open. Dumping out the contents onto the table, she carefully looked over the items.

She picked up the handwritten letter that was unsigned. It stated that the two pictures contained in the package had to be protected at all costs and not shown to anyone else. They were evidence, and their existence had to be kept secret.

Evidence of what?

Thelma put down the letter and picked up the white envelope. Two Polaroid pictures fell out. They were black and white, and Thelma could tell they were taken quite a while ago. The first one showed a person lurking in a set of bushes. It had been taken from a reasonable distance away, and the face wasn't all that clear through the leaves.

The second picture showed a figure running away with what looked like a blanket in its arms. You couldn't tell if the figure belonged to a man or woman.

She set the pictures down and picked up the letter again.

The writer closed by stating that certain people wanted the pictures destroyed. The sender felt that Thelma would guard them and not reveal to a single soul that they were in her possession. Someday, she would understand just how important the pictures were.

She set the letter aside and picked up the pictures again. The face in the bushes had a slight familiarity with it, but Thelma couldn't place who or why.

Well, Zumbutt! Where can we hide these where they will be safe?" she asked the cat who had wandered back into the kitchen and returned to his food dish like she had predicted he would.

She walked to her bedroom but changed her mind thinking that would be too obvious and would be the first place that someone would look.

"I have the perfect place," she claimed, returning to the kitchen.

She enclosed both the letter and the pictures in a plastic bag and sealed it closed. Rummaging through the kitchen junk drawer, she found the roll of duct tape that she knew was there. After several grunts and groans, she was able to move the refrigerator far enough away from the wall to get her hand back there to tape the plastic bag on the back wall. She pushed the appliance back in place, figuring no one would ever think of looking there.

"I have no idea who sent this or what the pictures are of, but I think they are plenty safe where they are. Whoever entrusted me with them won't have to worry about anyone finding them," Thelma said to the cat as it rubbed up against her leg. "It's time to get dressed for bingo."

Kami had called and said she wasn't going to the morning session. There was an emergency at the newspaper. She had to handle that situation because Agatha was going to be at the ceremony. She would join them for bingo later at the night session.

Thelma would have to drive to the center instead, but she didn't mind. Her car was a good-sized SUV that June felt safe riding in. Several years ago, June had been involved in a bad automobile accident. She was not at fault as the other person ran a red light and hit her broadside. The car was stolen, and the driver ran from the scene and never held accountable for the accident.

June wasn't hurt too bad physically—bumps and bruises and one broken arm—but emotionally, she couldn't bring herself to get behind the wheel again. She also left her job at the real estate company because she didn't want to drive to the various properties to do the house showings. Her commissions over the years had allowed her to retire early and not worry financially. Instead, she chose to take a job at the nearby community college that she could take the bus to Monday through Friday.

It had taken almost six months for Thelma and Kami to get her to ride in a car again. June's license expired, and she never renewed it. She was content to either ride in the back seat of her friend's cars or to take the bus.

They met down in the lobby at ten o'clock.

"Are you ready to go listen to Agatha brag? Even though it was her husband who bought, restored and donated the community center to the town, she is going to take credit for the whole thing," June stated. "Luckily, they only slated five minutes for her to speak."

"That doesn't mean she will stick to her speaking time," Thelma replied. "You know how she is."

"We'll get our cards and then go out and listen to what she has to say. If she talks too long, we'll simply slip back inside to get ready for bingo," June commented.

"Sounds like a plan to me," Thelma chuckled, climbing into the driver's seat.

The traffic was bad as Sunday was turnover day in Sechuette. Tourists were leaving at the end of their vacation as others were for arriving for theirs. The community center was located on Main Street, in the middle of the downtown business district, behind the library. Thelma was cut off several times while driving down Main Street, which had June cringing in her seat. They finally reached the parking lot, and June couldn't get out of the car quick enough.

"I will be so glad when Labor Day gets here, and the town returns to its quiet little self," June said, reaching for her bingo bag.

"Four more weeks," Thelma replied. "Four more weeks."

In front of the building, Agatha was standing near a bronze plaque, getting her picture taken for her own paper. She stared at the two women as they walked by to enter the hall.

"That will be on the front page, no doubt," Thelma chuckled as she opened the door for her friend.

They got their usual seats and stood in line to buy their cards. As they were back at the table taping their paper strips together, Wayne announced that the ceremony was about to begin outside. He also assured everyone in the hall that several of the workers would be staying inside to watch over everything while people were gone.

The two women grabbed their purses and followed the rest of the players outside. They stood way over to the side, near the door, in case Agatha got long-winded, and they wanted to go back inside. Agatha still stood in front of the plaque, scanning the audience as if she were looking for someone.

Mayor Pike clapped his hands to get everyone's attention.

"I would like to welcome everyone here today to celebrate the thirtieth anniversary of the dedication of the Sechuette Community Center," he announced loudly. "Can everyone hear me up back?"

A chorus of yeses sounded, and the mayor continued.

"It was exactly thirty years ago to the day, on this very spot that Mr. Robert Tram dedicated this building and presented the deed to the town of Sechuette. I can truly say that this community center is the most used building in the area and that many people benefit from its use. Robert never wanted any group to raise money for the children of this town to pay rent to use the place. He had left an endowment for the taxes and repairs to the building," Mayor Pike recited. "We lost him too early in his life and those of us who were lucky enough to call him a friend miss him every day. Now, I will turn over the ceremony to his wife, Agatha Tram, who will dedicate the bronze plaque that has been set in place in Robert's name."

"Thank you, Mayor Pike," Agatha started. "Many of you that live here in Sechuette now never knew my husband. He was a caring, generous man who wanted to make people's lives better."

"Unlike Agatha," Thelma whispered to June.

"Yes, we lost Robert too early in his life, but he taught me many things before his accident. He taught me how to be business savvy and how to stand up for myself. He also taught me that there are times in life when we become responsible for things that we have no prior knowledge of and must help in any way we can to make things right."

Thelma stared at Agatha. Was she trying to tell her something? Did she send the pictures and the unsigned letter? Agatha glanced over to the area where Thelma and June were standing.

"She did send the envelope," Thelma muttered under her breath.

"Are you talking to me?" June asked.

"No, just thinking out loud," Thelma replied.

"I would like to finish up by thanking the mayor and the town selectman for this beautiful bronze plaque dedicated to my husband. I'm sure he is watching from above and smiling in appreciation. May the community center see many more years of service, and the town always remembers my husband fondly," Agatha said, tearing up. "Now, let's go play bingo."

"That is a side of Agatha that I am sure many people around here have never seen," June said, astonished that the town's newspaper owner had a soft side.

Thelma was still trying to figure out if it was indeed Agatha that sent her the envelope. As much as she couldn't stand the woman, she would try to talk to her in private after bingo concluded to see if she was right and if she was, what the pictures were supposed to represent.

"Thelma! Did you hear what I said?"

"I'm sorry, June. My mind wanders sometimes. What were you saying?" she asked as she opened the door.

"Have you ever heard Agatha talk like that before?"

"Maybe her husband was the one thing in her life that she truly loved, and now she misses him," Thelma replied.

"Are you actually feeling sorry for her?"

"No, all I am saying is that everyone has a weakness, and maybe losing her husband was hers."

"I never thought of it that way. I guess you could be right," June admitted.

Agatha walked by the two women on her way to get her cup of coffee that she always got right before the early bird started. Thelma and Agatha's eyes met, just for a split second. There was a fear in the rich woman's eyes that Thelma had never seen there before. She was always in control and sure of herself, but not today.

What was Agatha afraid of? Who was she afraid of? It must have something to do with those old photos. She knows something, and Thelma would find out just what that was after bingo.

The morning session of bingo went by quickly. This time it was June's turn to win, and Thelma waited almost every game but never got to holler bingo. They packed up their bingo bags, and Thelma turned around looking for Agatha, but she had already left.

I'll talk to her tonight.

"Shall we go get some lunch?" June asked.

"Sounds good to me. Where do you want to eat?"

"The summer is almost over, and I haven't had a single fried clam yet. Let's go to The Seafood Shanty and eat out on the deck overlooking the water," June suggested.

"I could use a large order of their onion rings," Thelma admitted, climbing into the car. "And a big fat lobster roll."

"We have two hours before we have to be back. I'll text Kami and tell her to meet us at the hall later," June stated, pulling out her phone.

"I wonder what the emergency was at the paper. Agatha didn't seem too worried about it," Thelma said, turning the car toward the pier.

"I'm sure Kami will tell us," June replied. "I just hope it was nothing too bad."

The woman ordered lunch at the window and went to pick a picnic table close to the water to sit. A short time later, a waitress delivered their food.

"Oh boy, I think I ordered way too much food," Thelma complained as she looked at her overstuffed lobster roll and her hearty serving of onion rings. "This coffee milkshake will fill me up even more."

"You can always bring what's leftover to work tomorrow for lunch," June suggested, diving into her pile of fried clams. "Me, I'm going to eat every one of these clams before I leave this table."

As they ate, enjoying the afternoon sunshine, it became apparent that the couple a few tables away were fighting about something. The man slammed his fist on his table, which made all the other patrons eating around them jump.

"I will not give in to blackmail," the woman stammered.

"Keep your voice down," the man commanded.

"I will not. I have kept quiet for twenty-five years, and you can't expect me to be silent anymore," she replied, glaring at the man she was sitting with.

He lowered his voice and said something close to her ear. She ran away from the table, not looking back. His face showed his displeasure as he grabbed a handful of fried scallops and left the rest to go chase after her.

"Do you know either of them?" Thelma asked her friend.

"No, I've never seen them before now," June replied.

"Tourists," Thelma said, shaking her head. "I am so full I don't know if I can move."

"He left an untouched jumbo shrimp cocktail," June noticed.

"Are you thinking of going and helping yourself to it if he doesn't come back?"

"Oh, he's not coming back. They just left in that green car," June stated, eyeing the shrimp.

"Seriously? Are you really going to take the food off that table?"

"It IS jumbo shrimp," she insisted. "That's twenty-five dollars going to waste."

"At least wait until I leave for the car before you go steal it," Thelma requested.

"I'm joking with you." June chuckled.

Even if June had been serious about stealing the shrimp, she lost her chance when three seagulls landed on the table and started eating what was left behind. The waitress ran to the table to shoo them away, but they were staying put and not giving up their prize.

People were laughing as the persistent birds flapped their wings and screeched to scare the waitress away when she came near them. Giving up, she returned to the pick-up window and watched them while they gobbled down the food that had been left behind.

"Can't fight the gulls! Anyone who lives here knows that," Thelma said, laughing. "It looks like that one is really enjoying your shrimp cocktail."

"What a waste of all that money," June mumbled.

"Are you done? I would like to swing by the newspaper and see if Kami is okay," Thelma said, standing up.

"I'm ready. I ate every clam but left a few fries. Now I need a nap," June commented as she went to throw the trash in the barrel. "I'll catch a catnap in the car when you go into the paper."

They drove through the center of town and noticed a back-up of traffic on the side road that led to the cul-de-sac where the newspaper building was located.

"It might be quicker to park at the community center and walk over," June suggested. "I wonder what is going on to cause the traffic jam?"

"I don't know, but I aim to find out," she answered, pulling into the parking lot at the center. "Are you coming with me or staying here?"

"Wake me when you get back," June said, closing her eyes.

Thelma hurried down the sidewalk. Traffic was at a complete standstill. An ambulance was attempting to work its way down the street, and cars were pulling up on front lawns to let the vehicle by. A police cruiser followed shortly after the ambulance. Thelma quickened her steps. Once the cars passed the road that led to the newspaper, the traffic thinned out. That told Thelma one thing...the action was at the paper, and she was afraid more than ever for her niece.

Thelma was met at the front door by Deputy Cameron Elder. He held up his hand to prevent her from entering the building.

"Cameron, I need to get in there. Kami is working, and I need to know that she is all right," Thelma demanded, pushing his hand away.

"You can't go in right now. This is an official crime scene, and no one goes in or out without Sheriff Morse's okay," he stated formally. "To ease your mind, Kami is okay. She is in her office being questioned by the sheriff."

"What happened here?"

"I don't know exactly yet. All I do know is that Betsy Lee was attacked down in the file room," he whispered. "But you didn't hear it from me."

"Hear what from you?" the sheriff asked as he exited the door.

"Nothing, sir," Cameron stammered.

"Go help your brother fingerprint the place," Sheriff Morse ordered, shaking his head.

"What's going on, Clayton?" Thelma asked the sheriff.

"It seems when Betsy went down to the basement to get a file for a story she was working on, she was whacked on the head from behind. She doesn't know how long she was out and never saw the person who did it," he answered.

"Is my niece all right?"

"She is fine. Kami was up in her office and never even knew her co-worker had come to work ahead of her. She found Betsy on the floor when she went down to get advertising contracts of a client disputing past bills and what she was being charged. And no, the client was not present at the time. Kami called 911 immediately," Sheriff Morse replied. "She locked herself in her office and stayed on the phone with my dispatcher until we arrived. There was no one else moving around in the building that she could see."

"Can I talk to her?" Thelma asked.

"She'll be out when my deputy is done fingerprinting her. We need her prints to rule out any that are hers. Meanwhile, you need to go over and sit on the bench out of the way. The paramedics will be coming out soon to transport Betsy to the hospital," the sheriff requested.

"Is Betsy okay?"

"She's going to need stitches, but I think she'll be fine after some rest."

"Is there anything missing from the file room?" Thelma asked, thinking if Agatha did send her those pictures that could have been what the thief was looking for.

"We can't tell yet. The place is a mess. We need Agatha to help us figure that out. We've called her, but she hasn't returned our calls. Kami said she doesn't use the research files so she wouldn't know if anything was missing or not," he answered, still blocking the door. "I have to go back inside."

Thelma resigned herself to the fact that the sheriff wouldn't let her enter and that she would have to wait on the bench. She plopped herself down, letting out a sigh of relief that her niece was okay.

Where is Agatha, and why isn't she answering her phone?

The paramedics came through the front door with Betsy on a gurney. Her eyes were closed, her head was wrapped in gauze, and she was strapped down for the ride to the hospital. Thelma rushed over and asked the woman if there was anything that she could do for her.

"My phone is in my purse in my office. Please call my husband and have him meet me at the hospital," she requested.

"I will," Thelma assured her.

They loaded the gurney into the back of the ambulance and left.

"I already called Henry," Sheriff Morse said, walking up behind Thelma. "I couldn't find Betsy's purse anywhere in her office, or anywhere else, for that matter. I think the intruder took it with him."

"Him? You know it was a *him*?"

"No, I don't know it was a *him*. I was just using that as a general reference," Sheriff Morse replied. "Don't be sticking your nose in where it doesn't belong, Thelma Frost. I've warned you before."

"That could have been my niece leaving on that gurney. Something is going on at this newspaper, and I'm not going to wait around for Kami to be the next victim," Thelma advised him.

"Stick to bingo and let me handle the law enforcement around this town. Am I making myself clear?"

Before she could respond to his bingo comment, a black limo came tearing up and screeched to a stop in front of the building. The chauffeur opened the rear door so that Agatha could exit. She walked briskly to where the sheriff was standing.

"What's happening here, Sheriff Morse?" she demanded. "I got this ridiculous phone message that I couldn't make head nor tails of asking that I come to my paper on a Sunday when it's not even open for business."

"Betsy has been attacked and is on her way to the hospital," Thelma blurted out before the sheriff could reply to Agatha's question.

"Excuse me? Betsy wasn't even supposed to be at work today. Kami...where is Kami?" Agatha asked, temporarily losing her composure. "She was supposed to be here working this morning so that I could attend my husband's plaque ceremony."

"Why was it so important that she work this morning?" the sheriff asked. "There is no Sunday paper that goes out."

"Two clients were coming in from out of town and they could only meet to sign contracts today," Agatha stated. "Their advertisements are a large chunk of our holiday budget, and Kami is the one who knows them best and what they require for their new contracts to be signed for the coming year."

"I will need their names and phone numbers," he said.

"Kami has all the information you need. Is she okay?"

Thelma opened her mouth to say something, and the sheriff glared at her. She took that as a signal to be quiet and sit on the bench again, even though she had many questions that she wanted to ask Agatha. Thelma would have to corner the woman at bingo later that evening for the answers that she needed. She watched them walk away and disappear through the front door.

Sheriff Morse had a way about him. He had been born and raised in the town and knew everyone. About six feet tall, he had let himself slip out of shape as the years had passed. Because of his beer belly, he played Santa each Christmas at the town celebration. He was a fair man, with good morals, and he maintained a definite line of good and bad that you should never cross. His actions and appearance would scare anyone dealing with him for the first time.

The locals knew him best by his deep reverberating laugh and his bright blue travel mug with a teabag topper hanging out of the cover that he always had with him. He had been the sheriff for thirty-one years and had easily won reelection since the first year he took office.

In Thelma's eyes, he had one main flaw; he hated bingo. He considered it a mindless way to pass the time and a huge waste of money. His wife, Ellie, played three times a week and usually sat a couple of tables away from Thelma and company. She always complained that her husband lectured her every time she went out the door to play. He just wouldn't accept the fact that people enjoyed playing bingo.

Sitting on the bench once more, she glanced around her. It was not very often that she had the time to sit and appreciate her little town. The cul-de-sac where the newspaper building was located overlooked the town center and the town piers. Looking down from where she was, she could see most of the area in all its summer splendor.

Main Street consisted of all the little mom and pop shops that you would expect to see in a small town. A pharmacy with a soda fountain, an old fashioned five and dime, and a coffee café that served the locals year-round. Mixed in among the decades-old shops were shops that sold the technology and consumer products of the current times. Old and new, it all blended harmoniously together to form her beloved town of Sechuette.

Thelma's favorite shop had always been Dreams of Candy, a penny candy store at the end of town. Many Saturdays, she would take Kami there so she could spend her allowance on red string licorice. While there, Thelma would buy a pound of her favorite penuche fudge. To this day, Thelma would indulge herself every few months or so and buy a box to keep in her desk at work. The prices had gone up over the years, but at least the store was still there.

Sechuette Harbor was one of the most beautiful places in the state of Maine. Small cottages lined both sides of the land out to the inlet. Some had been built when the town was incorporated back in 1858 and had been passed down generation to generation.

Behind the cottages, newer, larger-sized mansions had been custom built by the current owners. They only used them as vacation homes during the summer. The water views were spectacular and did not come cheap. Anyone born and raised here could not afford the "Hill Area" as it was referred to by the locals.

The inner harbor consisted of four two-sided piers. Three of the piers housed commercial fishing vessels that worked out of the area year-round. The fourth pier housed privately owned boats. Slip fees would be paid to the town at the beginning of each new season by the summer occupants and locals to house their recreational boats. Names were submitted for a lottery so that everyone had an equal chance of winning a slip.

At the end of each pier were restaurants and small shops that catered to the summer population. Some of the best dinners served on the pier used seafood fresh off the boats. The daily specials always depended on what came in on the boats on that day.

It was high tide, and the boats were leaving with the tide to go out to catch their quotas. It was a beautiful sight to see, the sun shining off the brass fittings of the boats as they sailed away. The nets, hanging high on their riggings, swayed side to side as the boats made their way to the open ocean past the breakwater.

Thelma closed her eyes. The warmth of the sun and the smell of the surrounding flowers, coupled with her full stomach, made her sleepy.

"Aunt Thelma, are you okay," Kami asked.

"Kami! The question is, are you okay?" Thelma exclaimed, her eyes snapping open.

"I'm fine. Sheriff Morse told me that you were out here waiting for me. How did you know something happened here?" Kami asked, sitting down next to her aunt.

"June and I came back from eating on the pier, and I saw the traffic backed up behind the community center. I just had a feeling and had to come to check on you," she answered, grabbing hold of her niece's hand.

"Ahh, that feeling. You and that feeling." Kami chuckled. "Did you walk up here?"

"Yes, I did. You can give me a ride back to bingo, that is, if you are done here."

"I'm done. Bingo starts in half an hour, and we have probably lost our table," Kami replied.

"I have a secret weapon. June stayed behind, and I'm sure she went in to save the table when I didn't come back right away," Thelma stated. "Are you going to tell me what happened here?"

"I will, but we need to get to bingo first," her niece insisted, pulling her aunt toward the employee parking lot. "Let's go!"

The parking lot at the center was full, so Kami dropped her aunt off at the front door and went to park across the street at the pier parking.

June had been standing at the front door watching for them and ran out when she saw Thelma climb out of the car.

"What happened? How come you were gone for so long?" June demanded in one gush of words.

"Kami is going to tell both of us once we have our cards and are settled into our seats," Thelma replied. "All I know so far is Betsy Lee was whacked on the head from behind in the file room."

"Is she okay?" June asked, concerned for her old classmate.

"She is at the hospital getting stitches."

"I wondered why she wasn't here yet. She usually beats us here on Sunday nights. Wait a minute...it's Sunday, so why was she at work?" June inquired.

"I don't know. That is one of the first things I'm going to ask Kami or Agatha; whoever I can get to first," Thelma said. "Let's get inside. I need to buy mine and Kami's cards, so we will be ready to play when they start to call the early bird."

"Relax. I bought everyone's cards and taped them all. You owe me forty dollars, and Kami owes me thirty-two," June answered, smiling.

"You are the best!" Thelma said, hugging her best friend.

"What did I miss?" Kami asked as she walked up and saw the two women embracing.

"Oh, nothing except the fact that my best friend bought us our cards and taped them together, so we are ready to sit our butts in our chairs and play bingo," Thelma claimed happily.

"Thank you, June. This mess at the paper screwed everything up. I didn't even get to eat lunch. I guess I'll have to get something here," Kami stated, pulling money out of her back-jean pocket. "Here's the thirty-two I had set aside for playing tonight."

"You just put that money right back in your pocket," Thelma instructed her niece. "You have had a tough day, and I will pay for your cards tonight. Besides, consider it pay for all the questions that I am going to pummel you with all night long."

The three women took their seats. Kami left to order some food from the refreshment area. Thelma turned around just in time to see

Agatha running in the door to her table. Someone had placed a dauber and a cup of coffee at her spot to prevent people from sitting there. She stopped short behind the chair to stare at the items on the table. She then looked around in shock that someone would have done this for her.

"Well, I'll be," Thelma mumbled.

"Everyone deserves to have someone be nice to them once in a while," June whispered.

"Did you...?"

"Maybe, maybe not," she replied, tearing open one of the doors on her fifty-cent rip-off ticket. "Look! I won five dollars."

"You never cease to amaze me, my friend." Thelma smiled.

"Make sure you have your early birds daubed. Tonight, we are starting with all the even numbers covered," Wayne announced from the stage. "The Sechuette High School boosters wanted me to announce they will be holding their annual Labor Day on the Green this year. The proceeds will be used to buy the marching band's new uniforms."

"That's a worthy cause," Thelma stated, sipping her coffee.

"It is a worthy cause, and they nailed me to man the cotton candy booth again this year. Last time, I was picking spun sugar out of the hairs on my arms all day." Kami laughed, sitting down with her food.

"That looks good," June stated, glancing at Kami's food. "What is it?"

"Pulled pork in BBQ sauce with a scoop of coleslaw on top," Kami answered. "Do you want to try it?"

"No, I'm good. I ate enough fried clams this afternoon to fill a bathtub," she answered. "But thank you anyway."

"Now, before bingo starts tell us what happened at the paper today," Thelma insisted.

"I don't know what to tell you. I didn't even know that Betsy was at work until I found her in the basement," Kami replied.

"Do you know what files she went down to get?"

"No, I don't. According to the sheriff, whoever was in the file room must have been down there a while. The place was torn up," Kami said in between bites of her sandwich.

"How did the intruder get in? Isn't the building alarmed?" her aunt asked.

"Yes, and the alarm was on when I got there for work."

"That's really strange," Thelma pondered. "Unless Betsy reset the system when she was inside, not knowing that you would be coming to work, too. But it wouldn't account for the time before she arrived if the thief was there as long as the sheriff thinks. Maybe the person was in there all night. He could have entered on Saturday when the place was open for business and hid somewhere until everyone had gone for the day. Does the place have cameras?"

"No, Agatha never thought that we needed them. That might change now."

"So, they don't know what the thief was after?" June inquired.

"No, not yet. As for the story that Betsy was working on, it had something to do with an event that happened here in town twenty-five years ago. She and Agatha were working on an anniversary piece for next weekend's paper."

"But you don't know what the story was about?" Thelma asked.

"I have no idea. That's not what I do at the paper. They write the stories, and I get the advertisers to fork over their money," Kami stated, biting into her juicy pickle.

Before Thelma could press for any more information, Wayne turned on the fan for the ball machine and began the early-bird game. Questions were put on the back burner while the players concentrated on their cards and the numbers called.

Kami and June joked around while they daubed numbers, but Thelma had to concentrate on the game because she played twice as many cards as the others did. The two women got laughing about a joke shared between them, and Thelma shot them a look.

"Shhh!" a lady said to Kami and June from the next table over. "We're trying to play here."

"Sorry," Kami mumbled.

Intermission arrived without anyone at the table winning a thing. Thelma stood in line at the refreshment table, waiting for her turn to pay for her triple chocolate cake and vanilla ice cream. She watched Agatha head to the ladies' room like she did every intermission before they called the door prizes.

"Here," she said, shoving a ten in Kami's hand. "Pay for my stuff and get yours. I have to go to the bathroom."

Thelma entered the bathroom. No one else was in there except for the one person whose shoes she could see under the first swinging door. The toilet flushed, and Agatha exited the stall. She looked surprised when she saw Thelma standing near the sink.

"You sent me those pictures, didn't you?" Thelma asked as Agatha washed her hands.

"I have no idea what you are talking about."

"Yes, you do. I saw you look at me when you made your speech earlier today. What are the pictures of? Who are the pictures of?"

"Look, I can't talk now...people might be listening. Guard those pictures with your life. You are an intelligent woman, and I trust you immensely to do the right thing if something happens to me. I can't say anymore right now," Agatha whispered. "Please, be careful."

She rushed out the door before Thelma could ask her anything else.

Be careful? What has she got me involved in that I have to be careful?

As the door closed, she could hear the caller reading off the numbers of the weekly door prizes. Amy Spikeman, the caller's niece, pushed open the door as Thelma was reaching for it.

"Hello, Ms. Frost. Have you yelled bingo yet tonight?"

"Not once. How about you?" she asked the young woman.

"No. You would think with the caller being my uncle. I could win once in a while," she joked.

"I was sorry to hear about your mom," Thelma said.

"Thanks. She's at peace now. The last two years had been hard on her. She thought she had the cancer beat, but it came back," Amy said, sadly.

Well, again, I'm sorry. If you need anything at all, just call either me or Kami."

"I will," she said, heading into a stall. "Right now, I'm doing okay."

"Where were you? I was going to send in the Calvary when I saw Agatha come out of the bathroom, and you didn't. Did you two have another argument?" Kami asked her aunt. "Is my job on the line again?"

"No, of course not. We didn't even speak," Thelma replied, knowing she had to lie. "I was just talking to Amy Spikeman about her mom."

"Such a sad situation losing her mom so early," June stated.

"Kami, aren't you and Amy the same age?" Thelma asked.

"No, Amy is twenty-six, two years older than me. I didn't know her very well, growing up as her mom moved to Peckett, and she went to school there. We do sit together at bingo occasionally. She is a nice person. Did you know that she was adopted?"

"I didn't know that," June replied.

"It was a closed adoption, but Amy can get the files any time she wants to, now that she's over eighteen. But she has no interest in finding her biological mother."

"She may someday," Thelma commented.

"Take out your intermission sheets as we will be starting in a minute or so," Wayne announced. "I will be right back after I get my soda."

"Soda, right." Thelma snickered.

The players settled down, and the second half of the night passed quickly. Thelma won two, fifty-dollar games and attributed it to her lucky seat. They were cleaning up their table and chatting at the end of the night when June noticed Agatha leaving without cleaning up after herself.

"Are we all ready to go?" Kami asked, placing the trash bag on top of the table after they finished chatting.

A scream echoed in the hall.

"What the heck was that?" June asked.

4

"Come on," Thelma said, heading for the entrance hall where the scream came from.

Wayne and Thelma reached the doorway at the same time. Down the far end of the hall, outside the bathroom door, Ellie Morse, the sheriff's wife, was sitting on the floor, trembling. Everyone rushed forward to see what was wrong.

"Ellie, are you okay? What's the matter?" Wayne asked the tearful woman.

"In the bathroom," she squeaked out in a weak voice.

"Thelma, go see what she is talking about, please," Wayne requested, kneeling next to Ellie and taking her hand.

She opened the door slowly, not knowing if someone was still in the bathroom. Shoes that she recognized as Agatha's from their previous encounter in the bathroom that night were sticking out from under the door of the last stall. Taking a piece of paper towel, she crumpled it up and used it to open the door. Sitting on the floor in between the wall and the toilet was Agatha Tram.

Her eyes were closed, and her face was covered in round green circles made by a bingo dauber that lay at her side on the floor. Thelma reached to check for a pulse. She could feel the beat of a faint pulse and yelled to Wayne to call for an ambulance.

June pushed the door open to look in to make sure Thelma was okay. She saw Agatha on the floor and turned to keep Kami away from the door so she wouldn't see the condition of her boss.

"Is she...?" June whispered.

"No, but she is barely breathing," Thelma replied. "Don't touch anything. This wasn't an accident."

"Kami go out front and wait for the ambulance," June requested, closing the door.

"Wayne, call the sheriff," Thelma directed from behind the closed door.

Thelma sat on the floor next to Agatha. She didn't want her to be alone even though they weren't friends. She reassured her that help was on the way and to hold on. A short time later, June was opening the door for the sheriff.

"Is she alive?" Sheriff Morse asked, standing over the two women.

"Barely," Thelma replied, standing up. "Your wife found her and is really shook up."

"Wayne took her into the main hall and made her a cup of tea. I will talk to her shortly," the sheriff stated. "You haven't touched anything, have you?"

"No, not a thing. I used a paper towel to open the stall door."

"Did you see anything or anyone?"

"We were in the bingo hall, cleaning up our table when your wife screamed. Wayne and I were the first ones to get to her. I can't speak for Wayne, but I didn't see a soul except for Ellie crumpled to the floor."

The paramedics entered the bathroom door and asked the sheriff and Thelma to move aside so they could do what they had to do. They felt for a pulse and then hooked her up to their portable machines to check her vitals. They asked the sheriff to give them a hand in pulling her out from between the toilet and the wall.

Once in the center of the floor, the paramedics could check out the older woman more thoroughly. The back of her head was bleeding profusely from an injury that looked like it had been caused by hitting the plumbing when she fell backward.

"Do you think she fell or was pushed?" Thelma asked, watching the medics apply gauze and a wrap to Agatha's head wound to try to control the bleeding.

"I would venture to say that whichever way it happened, the person with Agatha was in a fit of anger for them to daub her face like that," the sheriff surmised.

"We are ready to transport the victim to the hospital," the paramedic stated, opening the door.

June, Kami, and a small crowd of the remaining bingo players were standing outside the door, waiting to see what was happening. The sheriff asked that the hallway be cleared so the gurney could be taken out to the ambulance.

"Is that Agatha?" echoed through the crowd.

"If anyone saw or heard anything relating to the incident, please stay in the main hall so my deputies can take your statements," the sheriff requested as the crowd began to disperse. "And please, no one leaves the building until you give one of my deputies your name and phone number."

"I saw Agatha hurry out of the hall without cleaning up her table. She always cleans up after herself, and I thought that was strange at the time," June offered.

"How much time passed before you saw her leave, and when you heard my wife scream?" the sheriff inquired. "Hold on a second. Deputy Elder, as you take names, check their hands for green dauber ink. If anyone has neon green ink on their hands, detain them in the hall. Tell your brother to do the same."

"Now," the sheriff said, returning his attention to June. "Can you estimate the time?"

"I would say no more than five minutes. We cleaned up, discussed who was going to drive to Tuesday night bingo, and picked up our bags to leave," June answered. "We were still standing next to the table when we heard the scream."

"Deputy Martin, seal off the entire area with crime tape. Heck, seal off the entire building. That far door leads to the bar area, which leads to outside. Anyone could have left by that rear exit without being noticed," the sheriff declared.

"You women can leave. I will add your names to the list. Thelma, thanks for staying with Agatha. I know you're not close, and it was a kind thing to do," the sheriff said. "In this town, she has more enemies than friends. This is not going to be an easy one to figure out."

"Sheriff, while I was sitting with Agatha, I did notice that her purse and bingo bag were nowhere in the bathroom. You can check her car, but I don't think she had time to go out and come back in," Thelma stated. "I think the person who did this to her took them."

"Are you saying that you think this was just a case of simple robbery?"

"Could be. She tends to flash big wads of cash around, and there are a lot of tourists around this time of year," Thelma insisted. "You never know who may be watching you."

"Thank you for your observations. We'll take it from here," the sheriff said, walking toward the bar area. "Martin, check out behind the building for any sign of a discarded bingo bag or purse."

"I think we have been dismissed," Thelma said, frowning.

"It's time to go home, Aunt Thelma. We all have work in the morning, well most of us do anyway," Kami replied, looking at June. "I'll have to go in early and inform the staff about why both Agatha and Betsy aren't there."

"You be careful," Thelma warned her niece. "I don't want to be visiting you in the hospital next."

"I will, I promise," she said, hugging her aunt and leaving to walk to her car.

"Home, James," June joked.

"I'm really worried about her," Thelma said, watching her niece walk away. "It seems that everything that happened today is somehow tied to the newspaper."

"Kami is a smart girl. She will be careful. Besides, you insisted that she take those self-defense classes last year, and I bet she could whoop any person that threatens her," June assured her friend. "I wouldn't want to tangle with her."

"I can still worry about her," Thelma insisted.

"Yes, you can. You are her aunt, and you are entitled to do so," June agreed, linking her arm in Thelma's and leading her to the car.

Arriving home, Thelma decided to take another look at the photos that had been entrusted into her care for safekeeping. It had stuck in her head that something was familiar about the face in the bushes, but she still couldn't figure out what. Sitting at the kitchen table, she stared at the face in the picture but still came up with nothing. She returned the plastic bag to its hiding place and went to bed.

Thelma arrived at work the next day in a better mood after a good night's sleep. The first thing she did each morning was walk to the big cage in the corner of the reception area and say good morning to Crocker. This bright green parrot had been abandoned on the steps of the animal hospital two years prior. He knew many words and phrases and was quite the conversationalist. It was decided that he would stay at the hospital and become the mascot for the place.

"Good morning, Crocker!" Thelma said, standing next to the cage with the bird's food.

"Good morning," the bird repeated.

"Do you want your breakfast? Does Crocker want his banana?" Thelma asked, sliding open the cage door.

"Waaak! Crocker want a banana!" the bird squealed, dancing around on his perch.

"You are just so darn cute," she said, handing the bird a third of the banana in her hand.

"Darn cute," repeated Crocker, grabbing the piece of fruit with his beak.

He hopped to the end of the perch, then grabbed the fruit from his beak with his claw. While he happily munched on his breakfast, Thelma filled his corner tray with the quarter cup of pellets that he ate each day. She refilled his water and closed the cage door.

"I guess I'll have to clean the bottom of your cage tomorrow morning," she told the bird. "We'll be too busy to get to it today."

Thelma took her seat behind her desk and turned on her computer. While she waited for it to boot up, she put her lunch in the bottom desk drawer and flipped open the lid on her travel mug. Today was surgery day, which meant that a steady stream of owners would be going in and out. That, on top of the daycare being full because of vacationing tourists, Thelma and the staff would be kept hopping all day.

Lizzie and Tracy, both vet techs, arrived at work with coffee in hand. Each girl was in her third year of vet school and worked at the hospital to gain extra credits for her degree. They were terrific with any type of animal brought into the hospital, even the nine-foot boa that Thelma would not go near.

"Good morning, ladies," Thelma said, smiling. "We have a full schedule today. Are you ready?"

"This is my third cup of coffee. I am good to go," Lizzie answered, holding up her cup and laughing.

"Great! The first patient will be arriving in twenty minutes," Thelma informed them.

The day was busier than even Thelma expected it would be. She usually went to lunch around one, but not this day. The first chance she had to look at the time was when her stomach grumbled, and she realized it was a little past two.

"Pam, I'm going to my car for a few minutes to eat some lunch," Thelma said to the other receptionist. "Will you be okay?"

"Go! It may be the only chance you have to get out of here," she answered. "I'll be fine."

She grabbed her lunch out of the drawer and headed to the rear parking lot where the employees parked. As she fumbled with her keys, she heard her name being called. Turning, she saw Kami coming toward her with two small dog carriers.

So much for lunch.

"Hi, Aunt Thelma," Kami said, setting the carriers down and hugging her aunt.

"What do we have here?"

"This is Wags and Wiggles. They are Agatha's two papillons. They are very friendly and so loveable."

"And how may I ask did you end up with them?"

"The maid called Sheriff Morse this morning to inquire what she should do with the dogs. The sheriff called the newspaper and asked if anyone could take care of the dogs until Agatha returns home. If she does," Kami answered, sticking her finger through one of the cage doors to pet the dog. "I offered to bring the dogs here to board them."

"That's a great idea... except for one thing. We have no available space for them right now with all the vacationers boarding their dogs," Thelma stated.

"I was worried about that very thing, so I talked to my dad this morning to see if I could keep the dogs in my rental house for a short while," Kami replied.

"I bet that went over well," Thelma said, knowing her brother did not favor having animals in his rentals.

Allan Frost, Thelma's younger brother, owned Frost Realty. He had started his business at twenty-two years old with one rental and now, at fifty, owned a multi-million-dollar real estate business. Allan owned most of the rentals in town, or he represented the person who did own them.

Kami rented a small house on the edge of town. She was renting to own and had been living there for almost three years. It had two bedrooms, two bathrooms, but more importantly, a fenced in yard that the dogs could go outside and be safe.

"Actually, word has spread around town about what happened to Agatha last night, and he agreed to let me babysit the dogs," Kami replied. "I was kind of shocked, too."

"How long before you own the house and can keep the pets you want?" Thelma asked. "I can't believe I am related to someone who dislikes animals so much."

"It's not that he dislikes them. It's just some people allow the animals to destroy the rentals they are in. So, it's easier for Dad just to say no animals allowed," Kami stated, defending her dad. "He has Sammy, his golden. Contrary to what you believe, he does like animals."

"I guess. I'm really sorry that we have no room, but I'm sure they will be good company for you while you babysit them," her aunt said, peeking through the cage doors. "They are cute."

"I hope Agatha doesn't mind that I took some of the food she had at her house for them and some of their toys. I took the afternoon off to bring them home and let them acclimate to their temporary housing."

"I don't think she'll mind. She'll be happy that someone is taking care of her babies. She loves those dogs more than her money," Thelma stated. "How is Agatha?"

"The sheriff said that she is still unconscious but holding on," Kami answered. "They have no leads as to who did it."

"Did he say if they found her purse or bingo bag?"

"He didn't say, and I didn't ask," Kami replied. "Okay, I am going to head home and get these two babies settled in. Call me if you hear anything about Agatha."

"I will. You do the same."

"Love you," Kami said, picking up the carriers.

"Love you, too."

Thelma sat in her car, mindlessly munching on her sandwich. She knew all these events had to be tied to the pictures that Agatha had given her. What were the images off, though? She decided, on her next day off, she would make a trip to the newspaper and find out what story Betsy and Agatha had been working on for the upcoming weekend's paper. She then wrapped up the remainder of her sandwich, threw it on the passenger's seat, and went back to work.

For the rest of the day, she was chained to her desk, processing files, and printing bills. Her mind wandered a few times, trying to remember what happened in the town twenty-five years ago that was so impor-tant. If she couldn't remember what it was, it couldn't have been that major an event.

At five o'clock she shut down her computer and said goodbye to Crocker, who was busy ringing the bell in the corner of his cage. There was no bingo tonight, so Thelma would spend a quiet night at home with Zumbutt.

"I need wine," she announced to no one as she pulled out of the parking lot.

She had just arrived at the package store when her cell phone rang.

"Hello."

"Thelma, this is Sheriff Morse. Agatha has regained consciousness and is asking for you. She won't talk to anyone else or make a statement until she sees you. Can you come to the hospital?"

"I'll be there in fifteen minutes," she agreed.

"Great. She is in room three-fourteen in the north wing. You will see Cameron Elder stationed outside the door."

"See you shortly," Thelma said, hanging up.

RIDING IN THE HOSPITAL ELEVATOR, Thelma's curiosity was peaking. Cameron greeted her outside the room and opened the door to let her enter. Agatha, looking pale and older than usual, slowly opened her eyes when she heard the door. The nurse had just finished checking her vitals and was recording them on the erase board hanging on the wall opposite the bed.

"The sheriff will be right in," Cameron said as he closed the door.

"She's very weak and can't speak much," the nurse informed Thelma. "Please don't stay too long as she needs her rest."

Agatha waved Thelma over to the side of the bed. She grabbed her visitor's hand and beckoned her to come closer so she could speak to her.

"Agatha, how are you feeling?"

The patient looked at Thelma with sorrowful eyes. She tried very hard to talk, but nothing came out. She waited for several minutes and tried again. This time, sporadic words came out.

"Help... my...goddaughter," she whispered. "Pictures..."

"Who is your goddaughter?" Thelma questioned.

"Help... her." Agatha sighed, closing her eyes.

Thelma stood there waiting for more information, but Agatha never opened her eyes again. Loud alarms started to go off on the machines that surrounded her. Nurses rushed into the room and ordered Thelma to leave.

Sheriff Morse, Deputy Elder, and Thelma waited anxiously outside the room while a steady stream of medical personnel hurried in and out of the door.

"What did Agatha have to talk to you about?" Sheriff Morse asked Thelma.

"She wanted to know if Betsy was all right," Thelma answered, staring at the door to Agatha's room so she wouldn't have to look the sheriff in the eye.

"Thelma Frost! Do you seriously expect me to believe that was what Agatha wanted to talk to you about? Give me a little credit here. What is so important that she could only tell you? You aren't even friends," the sheriff said, indignantly.

Thelma remained silent. She knew she should give the pictures to the sheriff. Whoever assaulted Agatha had to be looking for those pictures. But as long as Agatha was alive, Thelma would keep her secret as she was asked to do.

"Look, all I know is that Agatha is worried about her friend. She doesn't want her to end up in the hospital again," Thelma replied. "Agatha asked me to keep an eye on Betsy if she doesn't make it."

"I don't believe you. If you are withholding evidence, and she told you who did this to her, I will charge you with obstruction of justice. This is not one of your detective novels. This is real life. We have someone out there on the loose who did bodily harm to another individual. If you even have an inkling to who it is, you had better tell me now," Sheriff Morse demanded.

"I have no idea who did this to Agatha, and if I did, I would tell you," Thelma replied, this time telling the truth as she did not know the identity of the man in the picture.

The doctor exited Agatha's room and stopped in front of the group.

"I'm sorry. We did all we could. Do you know the name of a family member that we could call for arrangements to be made?" the doctor requested.

"Agatha doesn't have any living family that I know of. Her husband died many years ago, and her sister passed just recently. You will probably have to call her attorney with any questions," the sheriff answered.

"Thank you. And again, I'm sorry," the doctor said, closing his file and walking away.

"It's not fair," Thelma mumbled, tearing up.

"No, it's not. As much as Agatha wasn't liked in this town, she didn't deserve this," the sheriff agreed. "Deputy, this has turned into a murder case, and we need to step up our investigation."

"I need to call Kami. She is going to be so upset," Thelma said, excusing herself from the group before the sheriff could ask her any more questions.

She changed her mind and decided to see her niece in person and not deliver the news over the phone. Thelma sat in the car and cried. She didn't know why she was crying as Agatha was not a good friend; she wasn't even a friend at all. Maybe it was because of the way her life ended. She had been robbed of the many more years she could have lived.

And now, Thelma found out that Agatha had a goddaughter. But who was she and why did she need help as Agatha requested? There seemed to be more questions than answers, and with Agatha dead, they might never be answered. Thelma dried her eyes and drove out of the hospital parking lot.

Pulling into Kami's driveway, she could hear the two dogs yapping out in the back yard. The tears welled up again, knowing that with Agatha gone, they were now orphans. They would be so confused, never seeing their beloved owner again. A face peeked over the fence.

"Aunt Thelma, what are you doing here?" Kami yelled over the dog's barking.

Kami picked up the dogs so that her aunt could enter through the gate without them getting out. She noticed her aunt's red eyes.

"Agatha?" she asked, setting the dogs down.

"She died about half an hour ago. I guess her head injury was just too much for her body to handle," Thelma said, quietly. "I was there when she passed."

"You were there?"

"Agatha asked to see me before she would talk to anyone else. I think she knew her time was slipping away, and she needed to ask me about something that she needed to have done."

"Why would she ask for you? You weren't even friends," Kami asked in disbelief.

"I wish everyone would stop saying that! Agatha entrusted me with something very important, and maybe it was this *something* that got her killed. Maybe we weren't friends out in public, but she needed someone to confide in, and I stepped up even with our differences," Thelma stated.

"I'm sorry. I didn't mean to upset you. Have a seat at the picnic table, and I'll get us a glass of wine," Kami offered.

"Make it a big glass," her aunt instructed.

Thelma sat at the table, and the dogs jumped up on the bench next to her. They were sniffing her hand and cocking their heads as if they could smell their owner but couldn't see her.

"You don't understand, do you?" Thelma whispered to the dogs. "We have to find you a new permanent home now. I wish I could take you home, but they don't allow dogs in the building I live in. I know, stupid rules."

Kami returned, setting the wine glasses down along with her cell phone. Thelma could tell that she had been crying. The dogs left Thelma and jumped up on the bench next to Kami. Wags and Wiggles laid down near their new friend, sensing something was wrong. Twenty minutes passed while the two women sat in silence, drinking their wine.

"Who is going to make Agatha's arrangements?' Kami asked.

"I would assume that her attorney will do everything seen as she had no other family," her aunt replied. "She might have made other arrangements. I don't know."

"I called Betsy at work while I was inside. She and Wayne were the only two left in the building. We are going to call a staff meeting tomorrow morning at nine, even though I'm sure everyone will already know as fast as gossip travels around this town."

"Can you meet me in your office at eight?" Thelma requested.

"Why?"

"I need to know what story Agatha and Betsy were working on for this weekend's paper. I'm sure the story files are in one or the other of their offices," Thelma replied.

"Does this have something to do with what Agatha asked you to do?"

"I'm not sure, but it might. I don't want to involve you because I am afraid for your safety," Thelma admitted. "Will you meet me there?"

"Sure. Be at the front door at eight, and we'll check together. Betsy might even be in that early and can lead us to the files without us searching."

"What are you going to do about the dogs?" Thelma asked.

"They have nowhere to go now that Agatha is gone. After you leave, I'm going to call Dad and tell him I want to keep them permanently. They are such love bugs and so well behaved. Besides, this house will be mine next year, so if I want to keep the dogs, I don't see why I can't."

"I hope he agrees. They are obviously comfortable with you, and I wouldn't have to find them a home that would keep them together if they stayed here," Thelma stated, draining the last little bit of wine in her glass. "Call me later and let me know what he says."

"I will, and if not, I'll see you first thing in the morning," Kami said, standing up. "Come on, girls, let's go get you some supper."

Thelma watched the two dogs follow her niece into the house. She made up her mind right then and there that if her brother told Kami that she couldn't keep the dogs, she would get involved and fight for Kami and her new fur babies.

After stopping at the liquor store to get her wine, she drove home, knowing that she would have to stop at June's apartment and tell her that Agatha had died. June was not the kind of person who handled sad news very well. Thelma knocked on the door, and it flew open.

"Agatha's dead," June blurted out.

"I know, I was there. News sure travels fast around here," Thelma said. "Can I come in?"

"Sure," June answered, stepping aside so her friend could enter.

"How did you find out so quickly?"

"I guess he didn't get a hold of you. Agatha's attorney wants to talk to you, Kami, and Betsy tomorrow," June answered. "Betsy called here looking for you."

Thelma pulled her cell phone out of her purse. She had put it on vibrate while she was in the hospital and never turned the ringer back on. There were four messages on her phone—three from someone named Hanson Beckworth and one from her brother Allan.

"What was the attorney's name?" Thelma asked.

"Um," June said, glancing at a pad of paper on the kitchen counter. "Hanson Beckworth from Portland."

"Why would Agatha's attorney be calling us?" Thelma pondered.

"I don't know, but Betsy said it was important that he get in touch with you."

"It's too late to call him tonight. I'll call him first thing in the morning," Thelma stated. "I'm going home. Zumbutt hasn't had his supper. He's probably ripped the place apart, seeing as I'm so late." Thelma laughed.

"Good luck with that. Lunch tomorrow?"

"I'll let you know as soon as I know what's going on," she answered, closing the door to the apartment.

Zumbutt met her at the door, meowing loudly. She reached down to scratch behind his ears, but he backed away and then slowly moved forward to smell her hand.

"Oh, you smell Wags and Wiggles. Don't worry. They live somewhere else," she told the cat. "Do you want supper?"

The cat followed her into the kitchen and planted his butt in front of his bowl, watching her every move. After she fed him, she showered and got ready for bed. Thelma crawled in between the covers with the cat settling himself in on her pillow above her head.

Tuesday mornings were Thelma's time to sleep in. Most days, she was up at six, but on Tuesdays, she would lounge in bed until eight or so. Shortly after eight, her cell phone went off.

So much for me time.

Grabbing the phone off her nightstand, she looked at the caller ID. It was the attorney who had been trying to get a hold of her the previous night.

"He didn't waste any time moving in after Agatha's death, did he?" she asked the cat who had jumped down off the bed. "Hello."

"Hello. Is this Thelma Frost?"

"Yes. Who am I speaking to, please?"

"My name is Hanson Beckworth. I am, ah, was Agatha Tram's attorney. I must have a meeting with you, your niece, Kami, and Betsy Lee as soon as possible. I was hoping that you had some open time today to meet. I have spoken to Miss Frost and Mrs. Lee, and they can meet this morning at eleven if that is okay for you."

"What is this about?"

"I am not at liberty to discuss this unless all three of you are together. Can you make it at eleven o'clock? Betsy offered the use of the conference room at the newspaper if you can make it."

"I will be there."

"Great! I will see you then. Thank you. Goodbye."

Thelma strolled to the kitchen where she could hear the cat meowing for his breakfast. She fed the cat, started the coffee maker, and headed to the bathroom. She was getting dressed when her phone rang again. This time it was Kami.

"Good morning," Thelma answered cheerfully.

"Good morning to you, too, Aunt Thelma. Did you get a call from a Mr. Beckworth?"

"Yes, I did, and I agreed to meet with all of you at eleven. Do you have any idea what this is about?"

"No, I don't, but what I do know is that you were supposed to meet me here at eight."

"I totally forgot. Duh! I'll be there in fifteen minutes," her aunt replied.

"I'll be in my office, and I found the files that you wanted to look at."

"What is the story about?"

"You'll have to come here to find out. And bring coffee."

"I'll be there bearing gifts," Thelma laughed. "Bye."

The Coffee Café was buzzing with talk of Agatha's death. It wasn't just a case of assault anymore. Now it was murder. Thelma stood in line, waiting to order, listening to all that was being said around her.

"Word is that it was a robbery. You know how much cash Agatha always carried around with her," one woman said. "I'll be locking my doors from here on out, let me tell you."

"The sheriff said they hadn't found her purse yet," another woman added.

"I'll have my regular and one for Kami," Thelma ordered.

"I wonder what will happen to Agatha's estate and the newspaper," the first woman said. "She has no family, you know. No kids and her husband died before she did."

Listening to that last statement got Thelma thinking about what Agatha had said on her death bed. "My goddaughter...help her."

What if she does have a goddaughter? Would she inherit everything?

"Thelma! Earth to Thelma. You're holding up the line. That will be four dollars," Cassie said, waiting to be paid.

"I'm sorry. Lost in thought, I guess," she replied, handing her a five. "Put the rest in the tip jar."

Thelma arrived at the paper, and the employee parking lot was almost empty. Kami was standing in the foyer, taping a piece of paper on the window of the front door. She spotted her aunt and waved. Grabbing the coffees, Thelma walked up to the front door and stopped to read the notice posted on the door.

"Closed until further notice," Kami stated, opening the door. "Or at least until we figure out what is going to happen to the paper."

"I wondered why the employee parking lot was so empty."

"Betsy sent everyone home on a one-week vacation," Kami replied. "Paid, of course."

"Agatha would have a fit." Thelma chuckled.

"I told you we have great benefits here. One of which is four weeks paid vacation a year. It's not very often we get a vacation in the summer around here."

"I guess even Agatha had a good side," Thelma said, passing a coffee to her niece. "Now, where are those files?"

"They are in my office. We have just enough time to go over them before Mr. Beckworth arrives for our meeting. It's funny. In all the years I worked here, I never heard Agatha mention this particular attorney."

"Maybe he was her personal attorney and had nothing to do with the business side," Thelma suggested, following her niece into her office.

"Could be. I'm sure with all her money and businesses, she must have had more than one attorney on retainer," Kami replied, walking to the rear of her desk. "That's strange."

"What?"

"I know I left the file right here on the blotter on my desk, and it's not here."

"How long has it been since you were in your office?" Thelma inquired.

"I called you from here about half an hour ago. I went down to the copy room to make copies of the closed notice, and walked around, taping them to all the doors around the building."

"Who else is in the building?"

"I'm not sure exactly. Eight or ten others," Kami answered. "Let me call Betsy and see if she took the file to do some more work on the story."

Thelma walked out in the hall while Kami made her call. Several people she knew from bingo waved goodbye as they exited out the front door. None of them were carrying anything as they left.

"Betsy didn't take the file," Kami said, frowning. "That means someone was watching me and saw me put the file down on my desk and helped themselves to it when I left."

"What was in the file?" Thelma asked.

"I didn't read through the *whole* thing. The part I skimmed over had something to do with a kidnapping that happened in this town twenty-five years ago. A six-month-old baby girl was taken from her stroller in the park," Kami replied.

"I remember that now. She disappeared into thin air and was never found. Do you think the original files are downstairs?"

"I have no idea. The place is still torn apart from the break-in when Betsy was attacked," Kami answered. "Maybe she pulled the originals before the break-in and knows where they are."

"Let's go ask her," Thelma suggested.

Betsy was busy shuffling through a pile of papers when they entered her office. She looked perplexed as she stopped here and there to read something. She looked up and smiled as the women walked up to her desk.

"Did you find the files?" she asked.

"No, we didn't," Kami replied. "I can't believe someone that works here is a thief. If they wanted to look at the files, all they had to do was ask."

"Maybe they didn't want you or anybody else to know they were interested in them," Thelma suggested. "Betsy, do you have the original files from twenty-five years ago?"

"Unfortunately, I don't. Agatha had them in her safe, and I don't know if they are still there or not."

"Does anyone else have the combination to the safe?" Thelma asked.

"I do, but the attorney requested that the safe be left as is until he arrives and makes an inventory of the contents," Betsy informed her. "Mr. Beckworth will be here shortly. I will request that he open the safe to see if the originals are still in there."

"Good. Someone doesn't want those files seen or this story written. I think Agatha died because she got too close to the truth," Thelma declared.

"You really think it had something to do with the story we were going to run this weekend?" Betsy asked.

"I do," Thelma confirmed.

"Hello!" echoed down the hall. "Is anyone here?"

"That sounds like Mr. Beckworth. Come with me," Betsy said to Kami and Thelma.

The trio walked toward the front door, where a man in a three-piece black suit was waiting. He looked to be in his early thirties, was good looking and about six feet tall, give or take a few inches. He smiled when he glanced at Kami.

"Betsy, so good to see you again," he said, hugging her. "And you must be Thelma and Kami. Can we move right to the meeting as I am due in court at two o'clock?"

"The conference room is this way," she replied. Would you like some coffee?"

"No, thanks. I've been up since four this morning and have had enough coffee to last me a week." He laughed.

The conference room was empty. The foursome sat at one end of the table at the attorney's request. He pulled papers and legal documents out of his briefcase and organized his thoughts before he started to speak.

"First, let me say how sorry I was to hear about Agatha's passing. I have been her attorney for almost five years now, and I had nothing but admiration for her. Many people had one reason or another for disliking her. Still, I was fortunate that I got to see a side of Agatha that not many others got to see."

"Um, excuse me," a voice interrupted from the door to the room.

"Was it Wayne? Can't you see we are in a meeting here?" Betsy snapped.

"I know, and I apologize. I just wanted to let you know I shut down all the presses and locked everything up downstairs," he said. "The mail has been sorted and delivered to everyone's desk. I'm going home now."

"Thank you. When we know what is going on with the paper, we will call you," Betsy stated stiffly.

"Okay. I guess I'll go home and bother the Mrs.," he mumbled as he turned and left.

"That man makes me crazy. I don't know what it is about him, but he gives me the creeps. It's like he's always watching me," Betsy mumbled. "I'm sorry, where were we?"

"As I was saying, Agatha had a decent side that not many people saw. She wanted to take care of the people that were loyal to her. As such, the paper has been left to Kami Frost and Betsy Lee."

"Excuse me?" Kami questioned.

"Agatha trusted you and Betsy to run the paper. It was one of the few businesses that she kept after her husband died, and she wanted the paper to continue even though she is gone. You each have a fifty percent share of ownership in the newspaper."

"I don't know what to say," Betsy stammered.

"Agatha knew that the locals hated her Friday social column, but she so enjoyed keeping people on their toes. She used to say that her column was the only thing that stirred things up in this humdrum town and kept it interesting to live here. She wanted you to know that it would be okay with her if you discontinue that particular column," Beckworth informed them.

"This is a lot to take in," Kami stated. "I never expected to own a newspaper."

"Of course, there is also a monetary amount for each of you. This is not for business use; it is a thank you from Agatha for being loyal to her and working as hard as you did for her. A check for one hundred thousand dollars will be issued to each of you once the estate is settled."

"I don't know what to say," Betsy repeated, reaching for a tissue box in the center of the table.

"I know Agatha isn't even buried yet, but she wanted this arrangement settled immediately so the paper would continue to be published. There will be an official reading of the will at my office once all the legal matters have been satisfied. What do you think? Do you want to continue with the paper as Agatha wished?" Beckworth asked.

Kami and Betsy looked at each other. Neither said anything right away as if they were waiting for the other one to speak first.

"Do you ladies want to go into another office and discuss this between yourselves?" the attorney asked.

"I think that's a good idea," Kami replied, standing up. "Let's go to my office."

The two women left, and Thelma sat there looking at the attorney.

"No offense, but what am I doing here?" Thelma asked. "I don't work at the paper."

"No, you don't, but you were working for Agatha in another way. Or should I say working with her," he stated, sitting down next to Thelma. "I know she asked you for help with her goddaughter."

"You know about that?" Thelma asked.

"Anything that is said in this room in the next few minutes cannot leave this room. Is that clear?"

"I have kept Agatha's secret so far and not even told my niece," Thelma insisted.

"So, no one else knows that you have the pictures?"

"No, no one."

"Do you know what you have in your possession?"

"All I know is that she told me to keep the pictures secret and not tell a soul that I have them," Thelma replied. "What are the pictures of?"

"Twenty-five years ago, Agatha's goddaughter was kidnapped from the park here at the elementary school. At first, the police thought because the baby was Agatha's goddaughter, she was taken to be exchanged for a large ransom. The call never came, and the child was never found. After a while, the case grew cold, and the police moved on."

"They stopped looking for her?"

"They assumed she had been murdered. The police stopped looking, but Agatha never gave up. Over the years, she hired private eyes to keep looking, but they never found anything. And then, two months ago she received an envelope in the mail."

"The pictures?"

"Yes. The typed note that accompanied them said that the pictures were of the kidnappers. The writer of the note said she took the pictures herself and that she had kept them hidden all these years as a safety measure to protect herself. Personally, I think she can't live with the guilt of what she knows anymore," Beckworth said, pulling a full file folder out of his briefcase. "This is copies of all the original paperwork from the case."

"I thought the originals were in Agatha's safe."

"They were up until three days ago when I removed them."

"Why me? Why did she send the pictures to me?" Thelma inquired.

"She often said that you were one of the few people in this town that stood up to her, and she admired you for that. Agatha also knew that you considered yourself an armchair detective, and she trusted your instincts. She never forgot that you figured out who stole the statues from the community center. The police refused to help her anymore, so she turned to you."

"I almost gave the pictures to the sheriff."

"Please don't do that. At least not right now. We don't know who was in on the kidnapping, and Agatha didn't trust anyone, not even the police," he stated. "In her will, she left almost everything to her goddaughter. She truly felt that you would be the person to find her so she could inherit what was rightfully hers."

"Are those files for me?"

"Yes, but I would prefer that you put them in your purse so that no one sees you leaving with them," he said, pushing the folder closer to her. "I have the originals locked up in a safe in my office."

Thelma picked up the folder and carefully squeezed it into her purse.

"Good thing my purse is not any smaller than it is," she said, zipping it up.

"I know this is a lot to ask of you, especially after the events of the last few days. Please don't tell anyone that you have the files or what you are doing. I think Agatha was killed because someone found out that the pictures had been sent to her. If you don't want to do this, I would totally understand," Beckworth stated.

"It won't hurt to look over the files. Especially after what she has done for my niece," Thelma replied. "She really didn't trust the local police?"

"Over half of the current police force was on duty when the baby was kidnapped. She never believed that they tried their hardest to solve the case."

"The sheriff is a good man. I can't believe Agatha thought that."

"She did. This is for you. Agatha wanted you to have it for any expenses that you may incur. And she felt it was a fair sum to pay you for your work after all the money she paid to the other detective agencies," the attorney said, handing her a sealed envelope.

"This wasn't necessary. I'll do my best to figure it out," Thelma said, tucking the envelope in the front pocket of her purse.

"Figure out what?" Kami asked as she and Betsy entered the room.

"We were talking about Agatha's dogs. But I think we already have a home for them," Thelma said, smiling at her niece.

"Thank you, and Agatha thanks you," Beckworth said, shaking Thelma's hand.

"Yes, they will be staying with me," Kami confirmed.

"Great. Agatha would be so pleased. Now, what is your decision on the paper?" Beckworth asked.

"We talked it over and have decided to give it a go," Betsy stated.

"We would like to keep the paper closed for a week as we first planned. That way, we will have a chance to go over Agatha's books and her files. We need to see how she ran things behind the scenes."

"Agatha told me that you two ran the paper in her absence when she left on business trips. I have the utmost confidence in both of you. Congratulations."

"This is so weird. I always wanted to work at a newspaper, but never imagined that I would own one," Kami said.

"You both will do great," Thelma declared. "Now, if you don't need me anymore, I would like to go to lunch with June."

"Here is my business card if you need to get in touch with me," Beckworth said, handing Thelma a fancy looking card.

"Bye, all."

She left the office looking over her shoulder at her niece. Kami would now take her place in the business community as the co-owner of the local newspaper. Her college degree in finance would make her an asset to the partnership. Betsy, a top-notch editor, would be responsible for the written stories. They would make an unbeatable team.

Sitting in the car, she called June and told her she would pick her up in fifteen minutes for lunch. June said she would be waiting out front. Next, her curiosity getting the better of her, she pulled out the envelope the attorney had given her. Peeling it open, she pulled out a cashier's check for twenty thousand dollars.

Wow! I think I will become a professional private eye if they make this kind of money.

She tucked it back in her purse, thinking to herself that she would not cash it unless she found Agatha's goddaughter. But at the same time thinking that it would be a nice addition to her retirement fund.

"Where do you want to go to lunch?" June asked as she climbed in the car.

"I was thinking that we haven't been to The Lotus Palace for a while. How's that sound to you?"

"Chinese food sounds excellent. I think I will also have one of those pineapple drinks with the little parasol in it," June replied.

"Only one drink, or you'll never be able to see your numbers at bingo tonight," Thelma lectured.

"How was your meeting with the attorney?"

"I have so much to tell you, and so does Kami. I think I will let her tell you her news tonight," Thelma replied. "Kami is going to keep Agatha's two dogs."

"Your brother okayed it?" June asked in disbelief.

"Kami will soon own the house so he won't have a say in it." Thelma smiled.

"Did she win the lottery or something?"

"Something like that."

"I can't wait until tonight. Tell me now. It has something to do with Agatha, doesn't it? Did she leave Kami some money?"

"Okay, I will tell you, but you have to act surprised when Kami tells you tonight at bingo. Agatha left the paper to Kami and Betsy, fifty percent ownership each. She also left them a cash bonus for being loyal and working so hard for the paper," Thelma explained.

"Wow! Makes me wish that I had worked at the paper," June stated.

"I don't know if she did something for everyone that worked there or not, but she obviously trusted Betsy and Kami to keep the paper going, or she wouldn't have left it to them," Thelma replied.

"I hope they drop that Friday social column. So much hate and discontent stemmed from the trash that Agatha called an informative town listing. I am glad that my name never appeared in her writing," June stated.

"What is she going to write about you? That you go to bingo too much?" Thelma laughed.

"I guess I do lead kind of a boring life, don't I?" June sighed.

"How would you like some excitement in your life?" Thelma questioned.

"Thelma Frost! What have you got yourself involved in that you need my help?"

"I'll tell you while we eat, but you have to solemnly swear that you won't breathe a word of what I tell you to anyone else. The attorney asked me to keep it to myself, but you are so helpful when I need to bounce ideas off someone, and a second set of eyes is always good."

"The attorney? You mean Agatha's attorney? I wondered why they wanted you at the meeting. Does he want you to find the person who killed Agatha? Shouldn't that be left up to the police?" June asked, not leaving any time in between questions for her friend to answer.

"Slow down, woman." Thelma chuckled. "Let's get a table as far away from everyone else as we can, and I'll explain everything."

The hostess seated the two women at a table in the rear of the restaurant. It was a hot summer day, and most of the tourists were at the beach, so the lunch crowd was thin. There wasn't anyone eating closer than twenty feet to them.

They each ordered a lunch special, and June ordered a Pineapple Passion Punch. Thelma ordered her usual glass of wine. As they ate, Thelma explained to her friend about the situation that she was tasked with by the attorney. June was shocked that Agatha had a goddaughter and that she had been the baby that was kidnapped twenty-five years ago.

Thelma left out the part about the pictures that she had in her possession as she didn't want to put her best friend in danger. She swore June to secrecy and requested that they would only discuss the case in the security of either of their apartments. They finished eating and requested doggie bags to take the unfinished food home with them.

"Kami is going to pick us up at five," Thelma informed June as she stepped out of the elevator. "I'll see you then."

Once in the safety of her apartment, she poured herself a glass of wine and took the files out of her purse, setting them on the kitchen table. She looked around for the cat, who usually met her at the door, but Zumbutt was nowhere to be found.

"Zumbutt, where are you?"

She heard a faint meowing coming from down the hall near the bedroom. Calling out the cat's name as she walked, she finally located him locked in the bedroom closet.

"How did you get in there?" she asked the cat, snuggling him close.

He rubbed up against her face and meowed. She looked around her bedroom, and nothing seemed to be out of place. She set the cat down and returned to the living room, the cat right on her heels. Everything seemed to be just like it was when she had left earlier.

Entering the kitchen, she had an overwhelming urge to check to see if the pictures were still behind the refrigerator. Still, something in her gut told her not to. She poked around the shelves in the kitchen, and that was when she made a frightening discovery.

6

small video camera had been hidden among the coffee mugs on the top shelf above the sink. It was placed in such a way that it could film the whole kitchen area and into the living room. She reached to turn it off but withdrew her hand at the last moment, thinking that it might bear the fingerprints of who placed it there.

Thelma placed a bowl over the camera to block it from recording anything going on in her apartment. Two towels were thrown over the bowl to muffle any noise. She fed the cat and walked into the bathroom to call the sheriff. Stopping halfway through dialing, she knew she had to come up with some explanation of why this happened as she had promised Agatha's attorney secrecy in the matter. But this break-in showed a level of desperation that Thelma hadn't counted on. She could genuinely be in danger.

Someone already knew that she was helping Agatha and was watching her. She didn't know if that scared her more or made her madder that they had the nerve to enter her apartment. And why did they lock the cat in the closet? It's not like Zumbutt was a dog that was going to bark or attack someone he didn't know.

"They had to check in at the desk downstairs," Thelma said to the cat who had wandered into the bathroom. "I'll be right back."

Robbie was behind the desk in the lobby. He had worked there since the buildings opened and knew everyone who resided there. He smiled as Thelma approached.

"Hi. Is your cable working now?" he asked.

"Excuse me?"

"Your cable. The guy came to fix it earlier, and I let him in. He showed me the work orders, and you weren't here. The orders said you gave permission to let him in to complete the work," Robbie explained.

"Have you ever seen this guy before?" Thelma asked.

"No, I haven't. Why? Did I do something wrong?" he asked fearfully.

"There was nothing wrong with my cable. Was he wearing a uniform with his name on it? Would you recognize him if you saw him again?"

"I didn't notice a name. He was wearing the normal gray jumpsuit with the local cable company logo on it. Should I call the police?" Robbie questioned, fidgeting uncomfortably. "I'm so sorry if I screwed up and let someone in that shouldn't have been there."

"I'll call them, thanks anyway," Thelma stated, taking a seat in the lobby.

"Clayton, this is Thelma Frost."

"Hello, Thelma. What can I do for you?"

"I need you to come to my apartment building. No lights or sirens, just quietly so you don't attract attention. It would be nice if you could come in your own car and not a cruiser."

"I was just on my way home, but I will swing by. Are you okay?"

"I'm not sure yet. I need your help. It's really important," she replied. "I'll wait in the lobby for you."

She hung up the phone and sat staring out the windows, scanning the area around her building. There were many bushes and cars that someone could hide behind without being seen.

"Am I going to lose my job?" Robbie asked, sitting down next to Thelma.

"I won't say anything to the association, but the sheriff may want to talk to you at some point. In the future, don't ever let anyone in my apartment if I'm not there regardless of what they say or what paperwork they show you. Okay?"

"I promise. I will never let anyone into anyone's apartment from here on out," Robbie promised, happy to still have his job.

"Before you go, did you put Zumbutt in the bedroom closet?"

"No, but I bet the cable guy did. When I opened the door, he was not happy to be greeted by a cat. He said he was allergic to them and despised them. Is Zumbutt okay?"

"He's fine."

"I would never have forgiven myself if something happened to your cat," Robbie replied.

"I have to go," Thelma said, standing up as the sheriff walked toward the front door.

"Thank you for not having me fired," Robbie said, returning to his seat behind the reception desk.

"Clayton, come in," Thelma said, unlocking the door for the sheriff. "Please, follow me up to my apartment."

"What is going on, Thelma? What have you got yourself involved in now?"

"Not down here," she instructed him.

Outside her apartment door, she requested that the sheriff be quiet and not say anything as they entered the apartment. She would explain why once they got inside. Leading the sheriff to the kitchen, she had him stand in the little nook to the side of the sink out of the camera's sightline. He gave her a funny look as she held her finger to her lips and then reached up to move the towels off the upside-down bowl.

He shot her a quizzing look but kept silent as requested.

Picking up the back side of the bowl closest to the wall, she beckoned him to look underneath. His face scrunched up like he was trying to figure out what he was looking at. She set the bowl back down and motioned for him to follow her. Once they were in the bathroom with the door closed, she spoke.

"Someone entered my apartment today under the pretense of fixing my cable. I would never have known that the guy had even been here if he hadn't locked Zumbutt in the bedroom closet and forgot to let him out," Thelma whispered.

"Why would someone want to film you?" the sheriff inquired. "You're not telling me the whole story."

"I will but not here."

"Are there any other cameras?" the sheriff asked.

"I don't know. I haven't had a chance to look."

"The first thing I need is plastic bags. Do you have any?"

"In the kitchen."

"We need to take the camera down, but we need to do it with the bags so we don't smudge any fingerprints the suspect may have left behind. When we move the camera to shut it off, whoever placed it there, they'll know it's been found."

"They aren't going to be happy going through so much trouble to plant them," Thelma replied.

"Let's shut the one in the kitchen down and then search the apartment for any others they may have left," the sheriff instructed. "Are you ready?"

"Let's do this. It really makes me mad that they have invaded my personal space," Thelma frowned.

They returned to the kitchen, not speaking a word between them. Thelma handed the sheriff a plastic bag, and he positioned himself in the nook behind the camera for a second time. Working together, Thelma tilted the bowl so the sheriff could hit the button on the camera to shut it off. He then enclosed everything, including the attached wires, into the bag and set it on the table.

Thelma started to say something, and he signaled her to be silent. She followed him as he walked around the apartment, looking for more cameras. A second one was found in the living room behind some pictures and a third in her bedroom.

The sheriff placed the bags containing the cameras on the kitchen table, looking over each one as he did. Neither of them had spoken a word in over half an hour. He turned to face Thelma and motioned for her to follow him out into the hallway. Once there, he pulled out his cell phone.

"Elder! I am at Thelma Frost's apartment at the Falling Leaves Community Complex, building B. I need you to bring the radio frequency detector with you and get over here pronto," Sheriff Morse instructed the deputy. "We'll meet you in the lobby."

"Do you think there may be more cameras?" Thelma questioned.

"No, I think we got all the cameras. It's listening devices that I want to check for," he replied. "Let's talk down in the lobby."

As they rode the elevator down, Thelma could feel Sheriff Morse's eyes burning a hole in her. How was she going to tell him the whole story without telling him about the pictures that Agatha had sent to her? Maybe she should turn them over. They were evidence in a kidnapping, after all. Besides, she trusted Sheriff Morse even if Agatha hadn't.

"This way, Thelma," the sheriff ordered when they exited the elevator.

They sat on one of the leather couches near the front door. He stared at her, waiting for her to speak, but she didn't say anything, not knowing where to start.

"Well? What are you mixed up in now?"

"Let me start by saying that I didn't go looking to be involved in this. I was pulled in by Agatha," she stated.

"Agatha asked for your help?"

"Yes, and I am going to be blunt here. Agatha didn't trust the police here in Sechuette. They had disappointed her many years ago, and she never forgot that," Thelma replied. "So, she asked for my help in a matter that was close to her heart."

"And what would that matter be?"

"Her goddaughter's kidnapping that took place twenty-five years ago," Thelma claimed.

"Why would she bring that up now? We did everything that we could to find that child when it happened but to no avail. After three years passed with no new leads, it became a cold case."

"Agatha received some new evidence that had to do with the kidnapping," Thelma said, still wrestling with whether she should release the pictures in her possession.

"What new evidence? If she had something to help us find her goddaughter, why didn't she call me?" the sheriff asked.

"I told you, she didn't trust you or any of the other police on the force back then. When you gave up, she kept searching. She hired private eyes and various agencies and never gave up on the idea that someone would find her."

"Elder is here. We can finish this after we sweep your apartment."

Thelma stayed in the kitchen with the cat. At the same time, the sheriff and the deputy swept her entire apartment for listening devices. Nothing was found in addition to the three cameras. The cameras were given to the deputy with instructions to return them to the police department, log them into evidence and then dust them for fingerprints. The deputy left, and Sheriff Morse sat down at the kitchen table.

"Shall we continue?" he asked, pushing aside the file of evidence, not realizing what he had in front of him.

"I would love to, but Kami will be here in fifteen minutes to pick June and me up for bingo. Can I come to the station before I go to work in the morning?"

"I know, you can't miss bingo," he said, rolling his eyes. "Don't you think that this is a little more important?"

"Yes, I do think this is important, but I also have to take into consideration what Agatha requested of me. I do know whoever did this won't dare come near the building again since the cameras have been found. Maybe you should go talk to Robbie before he leaves for the day. He let the man in and could probably give you a good description of him," she suggested.

"I know how to do my job, Thelma. I expect you in my office no later than nine in the morning. Be ready to tell me about this so-called evidence that Agatha told you about—regardless of her request," he ordered.

"I'll be there," she promised.

After the sheriff left, Thelma walked around the apartment, trying to decide where to hide the files from the attorney. Still not feeling totally safe in her own apartment, she decided to put them back in her purse and keep them with her wherever she went.

She needed to make sure the pictures were still in their hiding place. Still afraid that someone could be watching, she pretended to be looking for something on the top of the refrigerator. As she moved things around, she peeked to the back, and to her relief, the bag was still taped to the wall. In the morning, she would make copies of them at the library before she turned the originals over to Sheriff Morse.

Kami and June were waiting for her in the lobby.

"You're late. I don't want to hear a single complaint if someone has taken your seat," June lectured as Thelma approached them.

"You won't. I have so much to tell you," Thelma gushed. "But I'll tell you in the car, not here in the open."

On the way to bingo, she told them about the hidden cameras and how the deputy swept her apartment for hidden listening devices. June was immediately worried about her own safety. Still, Thelma convinced her that she was okay, and the intruder had only gone to Thelma's apartment.

"All this has to do with Agatha and the newspaper story?" Kami asked.

"I believe so," her aunt agreed, not telling neither of them about the pictures for their own safety. "Not to change the subject, but I feel really, really lucky tonight."

"I think all my luck was used up earlier today," Kami announced, smiling.

"And why would that be?" June asked, pretending that she didn't know about Kami's good fortune.

"Agatha left Betsy and me the newspaper! Isn't that exciting?" Kami gushed.

"You own the newspaper now?" June asked, smiling. "I hope you get rid of that terrible Friday column of Agatha's."

"She gave us permission to do just that, and Betsy and I agreed that would be the first change that we would implement," Kami replied. "Aunt Thelma told you already, didn't she?"

"Well, maybe she mentioned it," June admitted.

"That's okay. I am so excited about this new venture. Betsy and I work so well together, and I hope things will go smoothly throughout the transition."

"I'm sure they will, honey," June said. "I have the utmost confidence in you and your abilities to take the newspaper to greatness."

"Let's not go overboard." Kami laughed. "It's just a small hometown paper, but it does have a good size readership which triples in the summer tourist months."

They pulled into the parking lot at the lodge. Kami drove around looking for an available space and finally found one at the far end of the lot.

"Thelma! Isn't that the green car that was on the pier yesterday? Why is it parked around the back of the building?" June asked as they walked toward the front door. "Those are usually spaces for members only."

"I don't know," Thelma answered. "You got a better look at the car than I did."

"I really think that's the car," June insisted.

They entered to a full hall. Their spots were already taken because of Thelma's tardiness, so they had to sit a couple of tables further away from the number board. As they stood in line to buy their cards, June grabbed her friend's arm.

"I was right! Look over in the corner behind the stage," June exclaimed.

7

"What are you talking about?" Thelma asked.

"The guy that was eating on the pier. He's over near the stage talking to Wayne Spikeman," June replied. "Take a couple of steps forward, and you can see him."

"It is him," Thelma stated. "You know just because they had a spat on the pier doesn't mean that they are bad people. Everyone has disagreements with their other half occasionally. I do wonder how Wayne knows them, though."

"Maybe they are visiting him, you know, on vacation," Kami offered.

"Could be," June agreed, moving up with the line.

Thelma stepped up to the register and handed the cashier her the weekly registration card. She paid the cashier and followed her card packets down the line to the end of the table, where she picked them up and headed back to her seat. Glancing at the stage again, Wayne and the mystery man were gone.

Arriving late, the three women didn't have much time to tape their strips together and get their early-bird games marked. They knew it was going to be a long night after just the first game. A woman that none of them knew hollered bingo and didn't have it.

"Bingo liar," reverberated throughout the hall when the mistake was announced.

"Boy, tough crowd in here tonight," June whispered.

"Good thing I didn't drink any wine before I came. I sure don't want to make a mistake and face the wrath," Kami said, changing her dauber color for the start of the next game.

Intermission arrived without anyone at the table winning a thing. Thelma decided to get cake and coffee before the second half started.

"Anyone want anything from the kitchen?" she asked her friends.

Neither wanted anything, so Thelma left to stand in line by herself. Searching around the hall looking for the mystery man, she didn't see him anywhere, but she did see his woman friend sitting in the corner of the room by herself. Foregoing the food, she headed for the table where the woman was sitting.

"Hello. Excuse me for the intrusion," Thelma said as the startled woman looked up from her rip-offs.

"Do I know you?"

"No, you don't. I was on the pier the other day when you argued with the man that you were eating lunch with. I just wanted to make sure that you were okay," Thelma explained.

"Oh, that was my husband, and we argue like that a lot," she replied. "I'm fine, really."

"Are you here on vacation?" Thelma pushed on in her questioning.

"My husband is visiting his step-brother. I'm soaking up the sun while we are here," she smiled.

"Well, welcome to our little town. I hope you enjoy your time here," Thelma replied. "Good luck this next half."

"You, too."

Thelma noticed that Wayne had been watching the two women from behind the curtain of the stage. He did not look the least bit happy that Thelma and the woman were talking. She returned to her table and pulled out her intermission strips.

"Where are your cake and coffee?" June asked.

"I was standing in line when I spotted the woman that was on the pier," she stated.

"She's here in the bingo hall?" June asked.

"Yes, she is, so I went to talk to her. She informed me that her husband and her fight like that all the time. She also told me that her husband is here visiting his stepbrother," Thelma informed her friend.

"I can't believe you just walked up and started talking to her," June said, shaking her head in disbelief.

"I told her I was checking to make sure that she was okay after witnessing the fight on the pier," Thelma said. "Funny thing though, Wayne was watching us and didn't look happy that I was there speaking with her."

"Guess it was just a husband and wife thing," June admitted.

"Normally, I would agree with you," Thelma started to say.

"Here we go." Kami sighed.

"Hush, you! June, do you remember what the woman said as she stood up to leave the pier?" Thelma asked.

"No, nothing in particular."

"She said that she had kept quiet for twenty-five years and she couldn't be silent anymore. Isn't it funny that the kidnapping also happened twenty-five years ago?"

"If she said that they fight all the time, maybe she was just telling him that she wasn't going to be quiet anymore and was going to start standing up for herself," Kami offered.

"But she also said something about not giving in to blackmail," Thelma added.

Before they could discuss things any further, Wayne started up the bingo ball machine to mix up the balls. He also called the numbers of the intermission drawing winners for the four door prizes. When looking to see who won, Thelma noticed that the woman she spoke to was gone.

During the second half, Thelma looked up several times to catch Wayne staring at her. He was starting to give her the creeps, and for the first time, she was glad that she lived in a secured building, even after the day's mishap. She didn't say anything to Kami or June about what she felt as June was already skittish enough, and he worked at the newspaper with Kami.

As soon as the last bingo had been verified, Wayne disappeared from the stage.

The night ended with Kami winning two fifty-dollar games and not having to split them with anyone. Thelma blamed her losses on not sitting in her lucky spot. June promptly lectured her about it, agreeing not to say anything because it was her fault they were late. They cleaned up their table and left.

Zumbutt met her at the door. After she made sure the door was securely locked, she proceeded to the kitchen where she poured herself a large glass of wine. Still feeling a little weird about someone being in her apartment, she sat at the table, looking at the spot where the camera had been and took a big drink of her wine. Zumbutt jumped up on the table, waiting for his share of the drink.

"Here you go," she said, tilting the wine glass in his direction.

The cat stuck his whole face into the wine glass and happily lapped up the red wine. Thelma smiled as she watched him drink. He was a strange cat, but she loved him anyway.

"Okay, I think you've had enough," she said, taking the glass away.

He placed his paw on her hand as if telling her he wasn't done and wanted more. She gave in and allowed him to drink a little bit more before she picked up the glass and walked into the living room. She sat in her favorite recliner, sipping the remaining wine and trying to decide just what items she was going to turn over to the sheriff.

Zumbutt jumped up and tucked himself in between her leg and the chair. He stared up at her and began purring when she ran her hand over his sleek black fur.

"How do I get myself mixed up in these things?" she asked the cat. "I'm all for a good mystery, but these people are playing rough. I'm just glad he didn't hurt you. I don't know what I would have done if something had happened to you. It was bad enough that he locked you in the closet."

They sat together for the next half hour. Thelma closed her eyes to think as she continued to pat her furry roommate. She hadn't even looked over the files that the attorney had given her from Agatha. She decided she would keep those to herself for now. After all, the sheriff only asked for the evidence that Agatha had received, which meant that all she had to give him was the pictures.

Finishing her wine, she gathered her purse with the files still in it and went to the bedroom with the cat right behind her. The pictures were safer where they were for the time being. The cat was already asleep on the spare pillow when Thelma crawled into bed. She set the alarm on her phone for seven as she wanted to get an early start in the morning.

Zumbutt was patiently waiting for his breakfast when Thelma entered the kitchen. She turned on the coffee pot, fed the cat, and sat at the table, waiting for the coffee to brew. She was staring straight ahead when she suddenly realized she didn't have to go to the library to make copies of the pictures.

"Sometimes, I wonder if I really have a brain," she said to the cat who had finished breakfast and was cleaning his face. "Kami gave me that beautiful printer that makes copies."

Reaching behind the refrigerator, she grabbed the manila envelope that was taped to the wall. She poured her coffee and sat down to look at the photos again. She was sure these were pictures of the kidnapers from twenty-five years ago. Otherwise, why would someone send them to Agatha? Putting on her readers, she took a long hard look at the face in the bushes.

The man couldn't have been any more than thirty years old. His face was round and clean-shaven. Dark straight hair fell over his forehead. His eyes were dark and close-set. There was just something familiar about this man that Thelma couldn't place.

The second picture showed the same man still hiding in the bushes. This time, in the background, another person with their back to the camera was running away, clutching a blanket. The second person must have been who took the child from the carriage and ran to a waiting vehicle while the man in the bushes acted as a lookout.

Thelma refilled her coffee and then went to the printer to make copies of the pictures and the letter that accompanied them. She made three copies of each. Placing one set in an envelope and taping it behind the refrigerator, the second set was added to the files in her purse. Holding the third set of copies in her hand, she began to feel guilty about breaking her word to Agatha even if she was no longer alive. Agatha begged her not to let these pictures out of her possession.

She changed out the originals with the copies in her hand. Thelma decided to give the sheriff a set of copies instead. She never told him exactly what she had for evidence. She felt better keeping the originals just in case Agatha was right about her distrust of the Sechuette police.

The third set was hidden in Thelma's bedroom. They were rolled up and stuffed into a shoe at the bottom of the closet. She hopped in the shower, singing while she lathered up. She didn't do that very often, but she felt good inside knowing that she was keeping her word to Agatha.

"Be a good cat," she said to Zumbutt, who followed her to the door to say goodbye. "I'll be home after work. We'll have some more wine while I peruse the files."

Fifteen minutes later, she pulled up in front of the police station and parked. She walked up to the front desk and requested to see Sheriff Morse. The deputy called him on the phone and was instructed to show Thelma to his office.

"Thelma, have a seat," he offered as he closed the door behind her. "Now that we won't be interrupted, please tell me what is going on."

"I received a letter in the mail. It had no return address," she started, placing the envelope on the desk and pushing it toward the sheriff. "The letter inside also had no signature."

She waited for the sheriff to put on a pair of gloves and open the envelope. He pulled out the letter and the pictures, looking them over carefully and then returned his attention to Thelma.

"How do you know these were sent from Agatha?"

"The day she dedicated her husband's plaque at the community center, she said something in her speech. It was to the effect that sometimes we are given the responsibility of something important that we have to take care of, looking directly at me when commenting. I put two and two together. Agatha admitted that she sent them to me when I confronted her in the bathroom at bingo that night."

"And she believed that these were pictures of her goddaughter's kidnapping?"

"Look at them. Someone lurking in the bushes while another man runs away with a blanket. What conclusion would you come to?" Thelma inquired.

"Did Agatha ever find out who sent them to her?" the sheriff asked, not answering her previous question.

"No, she didn't. That's why she asked for my help. She knew I liked mysteries and was impressed when I figured out who stole the statues from the community center last summer," Thelma replied.

"You said that she didn't trust the police department here. Did she give you any details about why?"

"She felt that years ago, many leads were brushed under the rug and not followed up on. There are still four men on the force to this day that worked the case, yourself included," Thelma stated. "She never said so, but I believe she thought someone on the force was in on the kidnapping and shielding whoever pulled it off."

"That's not good. It's a no wonder she didn't trust us," Sheriff Morse admitted.

If you don't mind me asking, who were the parents of Agatha's godchild?" Thelma asked, knowing the information would probably be in the files she had received. Still, she wanted to make the sheriff feel included in what she was doing. She had to earn his trust.

"The parents were Carol and Hunter Bohannon. Hunter was Robert Tram's business partner, and Carol was Agatha's best friend. Their daughter's name was Amelia Bohannon, and she was six months old when she was taken," he replied. "It was sad. A park full of people and no one saw a thing."

"Was everyone that was there that day interviewed?" Thelma asked.

"As far as I know. I wasn't the sheriff then and was not in charge of the investigation. It wasn't until the following year that I was elected sheriff, but by then, the case had gone cold."

"Do you think these pictures are enough to open the case again?" Thelma inquired.

"They are kind of grainy, but I will have one of the officers send them to the lab to try to clean them up and then run facial recognition on them. We will try our best for Agatha," he replied.

"Thank you. Now, is there anything else? I have to get to work," Thelma said.

"One more thing. Has anyone else, but you touched these pictures?"

"Not while I have had them. I can't tell you what happened to them while Agatha had them," she lied, knowing they were copies. "Why?"

"We need to dust them for prints and exclude yours," he stated.

Thelma hadn't thought of that. The originals probably have many fingerprints on them, including those of whoever sent them to Agatha. These copies wouldn't even have Agatha's prints on them. How was she going to explain that? She would have to admit that she had the originals at some point.

"Can I go now?"

"Yes, just stay in touch with me if you find out anything. I never thought I would hear myself say this, but maybe we can work together and find Amelia."

"I will," she said, feeling guilty that she hadn't given him the originals and that she might be impeding progress on the case.

She drove to work, her mind trying to justify one way or the other what was the right thing to do regarding the original pictures. Thelma wanted to keep her word and keep them safe. Still, fingerprints on the originals might lead the police to who had sent Agatha the new evidence. If she had just told the truth at the beginning, she wouldn't be in this mess. Tonight, she would go through the files and pretend that she found the pictures. But then she would have to turn over the files, too.

Note to self. Make copies of everything in the files and call the attorney to tell him she was going to turn them over to the police and why.

Thelma pulled into work and noticed the entire parking lot was empty. She walked to the front door, where a note was taped to the window. It stated that the place would be closed until further notice because of a reported gas leak.

It's nice they let me know.

She looked in the window and noticed that Crocker's cage was empty. Walking around to the back of the hospital, total silence met her ears. All the kennels were empty.

This must have happened yesterday while I was off.

Walking back to her car, she pulled her cell phone out of her purse to check yesterday's messages. Concentrating on her phone, she didn't notice a figure sneaking up behind her. A cloth sack was thrown overhead, and before she could react, her purse was ripped from her arm, and she was thrown to the ground.

8

helma ripped the sack off her head and scrambled to her feet. She looked around and spotted a male figure with her purse in his arms, running into the adjoining parking lot, disappearing in between the parked cars. She searched the ground for her cell phone, which she dropped when the sack had been forced over her head. Siting on the hood of her car, she called 911.

Not knowing if the assailant would come back, she hid behind her car and waited for the sheriff. Two cruisers flew into the parking lot and stopped on either side of Thelma's car. The sheriff and two deputies exited the vehicles. He motioned for Thelma to join them.

"What the heck is going on?" the sheriff asked. "Are you all right?"

Thelma explained that she showed up for work, and no one else was here. She showed the sheriff the sign on the door.

"That's strange. Our office wasn't informed of any gas leak in this area. Hold on. I need to make a call," he said, walking away and pulling out his cell phone.

"Which way did the guy go?" Deputy Elder asked.

"He went over that way through the parking lot," Thelma answered.

"And all he took was your purse?"

Suddenly Thelma got a sick feeling in the pit of her stomach. The files from Agatha's attorney were in her purse. She wondered if this was just a purse snatching or what the thief was after all along. But how could he have known that the files were in her purse? The sheriff returned from his phone call.

"I just got off the phone with my friend at the gas company. They have no record of a gas leak being reported for this location."

"But everyone is gone, even the animals have been evacuated," Thelma insisted.

"Can you call someone and get them down here. We need to find out exactly was happened here yesterday," the sheriff requested.

Thelma called Tracy, one of the vet techs, and asked her to come to the animal hospital. She agreed once she found out there was no danger.

"Did you get a good look at the guy?" Sheriff Morse asked.

"No, he shoved that bag over my head and threw me to the ground. By the time I could stand up and take the bag off my head, he was too far away for me to see him. He was about my height and skinny."

"I thought you didn't see him?" Sheriff Morse asked.

"I didn't see him close up. But when he was behind me, he had to reach up to put the bag over my head. I could feel his arms on my back. When he was running away, I could tell he was slightly built and was wearing a black or dark blue ski cap hiding his hair and face," Thelma answered.

"And he stole your purse?"

"He could have been in the other parking lot, and this was a crime of opportunity. He saw you here by yourself and came after your purse," the deputy suggested.

"I seriously doubt that," Thelma mumbled.

Tracy pulled into the lot and hesitated when getting out of her car. The sheriff walked over to assure her it was safe.

"What is going on, Thelma?" she asked.

"That's what we are trying to figure out," the sheriff replied. "What can you tell me about the gas leak?"

"We received a call at noon that someone had called the gas company and reported smelling gas in the back parking lot."

"Who called?" Sheriff Morse asked. "I mean, who called you not who called the gas company to report it."

"It was a man named Edgar from the gas company. He told us to clear out and remove the animals. He said they would send a crew out to check for leaks, and we were to stay away from the area until the gas company called back to tell us it was clear to return," Tracy explained. "Luckily, we only had eight dogs staying with us, and we transferred them to Dr. Haven's kennel at her house."

"Where is Crocker?" Thelma asked.

"I took Crocker home with me," Tracy answered.

"The gas company never received a complaint and had no idea what I was talking about when I called them," Sheriff Morse stated.

"What!" Tracy exclaimed. "So, who called us, and why?"

"I think someone wanted everyone away from here so they could attack Thelma," Sheriff Morse stated. "The bigger question is, why?"

"But how did they know she would even be here if everyone was told to stay away?" Tracy asked.

"They didn't. They took a chance, an elaborate chance," Morse replied. "Thank you for coming down here to talk with me. The gas company is going to send someone down to check things out and will let you know what they find. I'm sure it will be nothing, but better to be safe than sorry."

"I will call you as soon as I learn anything," Thelma told Tracy.

"As frustrating as this is, at least we can expect to be able to continue our work here," Tracy said, hugging Thelma. "I'll be at home if you need me."

Tracy left, and the sheriff sent the deputies to look in the parking lot area where the thief escaped. He crossed his arms and stared at Thelma. She knew that he wasn't done with her and was waiting for the lecture that she knew was coming her way.

"You didn't tell me everything this morning, did you?" the sheriff asked. "Do you realize what danger you could be in?"

"I'm starting to," Thelma muttered.

"Well?"

"All right. I may have left a few things out and stretched the truth about other things," Thelma admitted. "I was only trying to honor my word to Agatha."

"Agatha is dead, and you may be too if you don't start to work with me here. Thelma, do you trust me? I know Agatha didn't, but do you?"

"I do."

"Then what is the problem?"

Before she could answer, Deputy Elder returned with Thelma's purse dangling from his nightstick. He set the purse on the hood of the cruiser.

"I found this on the ground," the deputy stated. "Is it yours, Thelma?"

"It's mine."

Sheriff Morse pulled some plastic gloves out of his utility belt. He opened the purse and held it in front of Thelma, warning her not to touch it.

"Can you tell if anything is missing?" he asked.

"Yes, something is missing," she answered, feeling sick.

"Your wallet is there. Why wouldn't the thief take your wallet?"

"Because that's not what he was after," Thelma replied.

"All right. Start at the beginning. Just what was he after?"

"Agatha's attorney gave me copies of all the files that she had collected over her years of searching for Amelia. There were also copies of the pictures that she had received in the mail. I had them in my purse to keep them with me after what happened at my apartment," Thelma replied. "The thing is, I can't figure out how he knew they were in my purse."

"Were they copies of the same pictures that you gave me earlier today?" Morse asked.

"Yes, but that was the part I kind of fibbed about. I have the originals that Agatha received in the mail. I made copies and gave them to you thinking that would be keeping my word to protect them at all costs."

"The thief must have hoped the originals were in the folder," the sheriff surmised. "What else was in the files?"

"I don't know. I was going to sit and go through them tonight after work," Thelma admitted.

"Does the attorney have the originals so he can make another set of copies?"

"Yes, he does. I suppose I have to call him to let him know what has happened so he can be on his guard, too." Thelma sighed. "He's going to think I am such an idiot for losing the files."

"I need the original pictures to check for fingerprints," Morse stated, frowning. "There's no sense in using the copies you gave me. You have wasted the department's time and taxpayer dollars. I should have you arrested for obstruction."

"If you follow me back to my apartment, I will give them to you," Thelma said, trying to appease the sheriff. "If you return my car keys to me out of my purse, that is."

A crew from the gas company pulled in as they were getting ready to leave. Sheriff Morse talked to one of the men before he got in his cruiser. The gas truck drove around to the back of the animal hospital as Thelma left the parking lot.

She pulled in at her apartment building with the sheriff in tow. Zumbutt met them at the door. Sheriff Morse scratched the cat behind the ears and then followed Thelma to the kitchen. He walked to the window and looked out over the area behind the building. He noticed a hill directly across from the window that would give someone a great vantage point to see into the apartment.

"Where are the pictures?" he asked, donning another pair of gloves.

Thelma walked to the refrigerator and pulled it forward. She reached into the space and ripped the taped plastic bag off the wall.

"Clever hiding place," the sheriff said as she handed him the envelope.

He opened it, glanced at the pictures, but didn't touch them.

"I think your friend sat on the hill out there with a pair of binoculars. He saw you put the files in your purse and knew you had them with you," Morse stated. "I'm going to have Elder check out the area. Meanwhile, I highly suggest that you get yourself some curtains to block any further intrusions into your privacy."

"I know you need my purse for fingerprinting, but can I have my wallet back seen as the guy had no interest in it and probably didn't even touch it?" Thelma requested.

"Follow me down to my car, and I will give it to you," he agreed.

"Good. The first thing I am going to do is go to the department store and buy some curtains."

Sheriff Morse locked the pictures in the console of the cruiser and handed Thelma her wallet. He decided to check out the hill area while he was there. Thelma sat in her car, watching him as he surveyed the area and placed several things in evidence bags. He took out his cell phone and snapped several pictures of the ground where he was standing, and then he left without so much as a wave to Thelma.

I think after I buy myself some curtains, I'll see if Kami wants to go to lunch.

Thelma purchased two sets of yellow curtains with purple and yellow butterflies. She also decided to get a new purse since she didn't know when she would be getting her other bag back from the police. Feeling a little better that both windows in the kitchen would now be covered with non-see-through curtains, she drove to the newspaper to see her niece.

A sign on the front door stated the paper would be closed on Friday and Saturday for Agatha Tram's wake and funeral services. Kami wasn't in her office, so Thelma wandered around looking for her. Betsy was at her desk, and Thelma poked her head in and asked if she knew where her niece happened to be.

"Last I knew, she was heading for the mailroom. The daily mail hasn't been delivered yet, and she went to find out why," Betsy replied.

"Isn't that where Wayne works?"

"Yes, he's been in the mailroom as long as I can remember. The mail is always sorted and delivered by eleven a.m. every day. That's why it's strange that we haven't received it yet."

"I'll go find her," Thelma said. "Which way to the mailroom?"

"Go to the end of the hall, turn right and go down the first set of stairs that you come to. At the bottom of the stairs, turn left. The mailroom will be straight ahead."

"Do you have any meetings or anything important today? I was going to ask Kami to go out to lunch with me," Thelma asked, stopping at the door.

"No, nothing that I know of anyway," Betsy answered. "Have fun."

Thelma followed Betsy's instructions and found the mailroom with no problem. She swung open the door and let out a gasp. Kami was face down on the floor, and the room had been ransacked. Wayne was nowhere in sight.

9

"**K**ami!" Thelma screamed as she ran toward her niece.

She turned her over and noticed a trickle of blood running down the side of her face. Her niece groaned as she was coming to.

"Stay still. I am calling 911," Thelma told her.

She made the call requesting an ambulance. Propping the door open, she yelled for help as loud as she could. Several people from other departments came running.

"Someone go to the front door to show the paramedics where the mailroom is, please," Thelma requested. "And get Betsy on your way by."

"Aunt Thelma," Kami mumbled, attempting to sit up.

"Just stay put. The ambulance is on the way," her aunt ordered. "What happened?"

"I came down to check on why the mail hadn't been delivered yet. I'm waiting for some important contracts, and they were supposed to come in today. When I opened the door, the place was a mess, and I couldn't find Wayne anywhere."

"Did someone attack you?"

"No, I feel foolish. I slipped on some papers that were on the ground and whacked my head on the sorting table when I went down."

"We're still going to have the medics check you out when they get here," Thelma insisted.

"I'm fine, really. I'm going to have a whopper of a headache, though," Kami said, holding her head.

"Kami, are you okay?" Betsy asked, rushing into the room. "Where's Wayne?"

"I'm okay, and I don't know where Wayne is."

"If something happened to him, it looks like he put up quite a fight. This place is a mess," Betsy stated, looking around. "I'd better call the sheriff."

The paramedics arrived and checked Kami over. They cleaned up her head wound and bandaged it, claiming she didn't need stitches. They wanted to take her to the hospital for x-rays just in case, but she declined. Picking her up off the floor, they guided her to a chair and stayed a little while longer to make sure she had no dizziness or blurred vision. She said she was fine and asked one of the workers to get her a bottle of water and two aspirins out of the first aid kit in the breakroom.

The paramedics were packing up to leave when Sheriff Morse walked into the room. He stopped to speak to one of them. Walking up to Kami and Thelma, he shook his head and frowned.

"You two women are going to keep me busy," he stated. "And not a good busy either."

"I slipped on some papers that were on the floor," Kami started to explain. "It was an accident. I'm don't know what happened to Wayne or where he is."

"Did you see or hear him before you fell?" Morse asked.

"I walked in, and the place had been destroyed. I called out for Wayne but got no answer. Stepping forward, I slipped on the flyers that were on the floor. That's the last thing that I remember," Kami replied.

"Well, it looked like Wayne put up a good fight," the sheriff observed.

"I said the exact same thing," Betsy stated.

"Don't touch anything until my guys photograph the whole area. Is there a back-way out of here?"

"Yes, the loading dock is just around the corner over that way," Kami answered. "And there is a fire exit door, but if someone opened it, the alarm would have gone off."

"Wayne's car is still next to the loading dock where he parks it every morning when he is off-loading the mail," one of the other workers informed the sheriff.

"That would indicate he didn't leave on his own," Morse commented. "We can fingerprint the loading dock area, but I don't know what good that would do. So many people go in and out over the course of a day it would be pretty much useless."

"I did notice there is a cell phone on the counter. Could that possibly be Wayne's?" Thelma inquired.

Cameron Elder walked in, carrying a camera and evidence bags.

"Elder, bag that phone. It might tell us who Wayne Spikeman was talking to before he disappeared," the sheriff ordered. "Take pictures of the whole area."

"Are we done here?" Thelma asked. "I'd like to take my niece to lunch and let her relax a little."

"Yes. Just keep everyone out of the area while we finish up here," Morse requested. "Did you get any security cameras installed in the building since the last incident?"

"No, but under the circumstances, I think we will have them installed as soon as possible. Don't you agree, Betsy?" Kami asked.

"I wholeheartedly agree. Something funny is going on around here, and we need cameras to protect ourselves. I'll go to my office and call Sechuette Security and Alarms and make an appointment for them to come to the paper," Betsy said, turning to leave.

"Thelma, stay out of trouble if that's even possible," Morse said. "Kami, I'll be touch if we learn anything about Wayne."

"Thank you. I'm worried about him. He's not well-liked because he's a loner, but he's a great employee. This mailroom has always run smoothly under his management."

"Come on, Kami. Let's get some lunch," Thelma said, taking her niece's arm and leading her out the door.

"I hope you bought some new curtains," the sheriff said as they left the room.

"New curtains?" Kami asked, looking at her aunt.

"I'll explain later."

They were sitting at the restaurant, waiting for their lunch when Thelma's cell phone rang. She looked at the screen, and it was Agatha's attorney.

"I need to take this call. I'll be right back," she told Kami. "Order me another root beer, please."

The attorney was not happy when he found out that the files had been stolen or that cameras had been planted in her house. He felt better when he found out that the pictures were safe, and that Thelma had given them to the sheriff. He always believed that Agatha should have turned the pictures over to the police, but he couldn't convince her to do it. She warned him to be careful because now the thief knew who he was. Promising to be careful and to send another set of copies to Agatha and one to Sheriff Morse, he hung up.

Back in the restaurant, Kami was eating her lunch that had arrived while Thelma was taking her call. The waiter came back to the table to deliver the root beer and gave Kami a folded piece of paper.

"A gentleman asked me to give this to the older lady at the table," he said.

"I will see that she gets it when she returns," Kami assured him. "Who sent it to her?"

"I don't see him anymore," the waiter said, looking around. "He was standing near the entrance to the bar."

Kami was going to open the note just as Thelma returned to the table. Instead, she handed it to her aunt.

"What's this?" her aunt asked, sitting down.

"I don't know. The waiter delivered it and said he was asked to give it to the older lady at the table. No offense, Aunt Thelma."

She read the message and jumped up.

"Which waiter gave this to you?"

"The one standing at the register. Why? What's wrong?" Kami asked, alarmed.

Thelma hurried over to talk to the waiter. He pointed toward the bar, and they went in together. Thelma returned to the table a short time later.

"What is going on?" Kami asked.

Thelma held open the folded note. In the center of the paper in large, handwritten block letters was the message, MIND YOUR OWN BUSINESS BEFORE YOU DISAPPEAR TOO!

"Do you think the note is referring to Wayne?" Kami asked.

"I would have to say yes," Thelma agreed. "I'm going to wrap this is my napkin, and after we are done eating, we'll stop at the police station and give it to the sheriff."

"You can eat after all that has happened today?"

"You don't know the half of it, my dear," Thelma said, picking up her fork. "And yes, I can always eat."

Over lunch, Thelma told her niece about the fake gas leak that was called into the animal hospital and how it was a setup to rob her when she showed up for work. She also explained what the sheriff meant about the curtain comment that he made as they left the newspaper. An hour later, they dropped the note off to the sheriff at the police station and were driving back to the newspaper. Thelma dropped her niece off at the front door with a word of caution and drove home.

Zumbutt was happy to have his mistress home during the day. He brought her a catnip toy and dropped it at her feet. She tossed it up the hall, and he went flying after it. This went on until the cat got bored and wandered into the living room to stretch on the windowsill in the sun.

Thelma called June and told her she wasn't going to bingo that night. It had been a tough day, and she wanted to stay home and relax with a glass of wine and the new mystery that she had bought when she was shopping earlier. Changing into a comfortable sweat suit, she put up the new curtains in the kitchen and stepped back to check them out.

No one is going to be looking into this kitchen again.

The buzzer near the front door went off as Thelma was pouring her wine. She pressed the button and said hi. Jimmy, the night receptionist at the front desk, informed her he had just signed for a package, and he wanted to know if she wanted him to bring it up to her. She said she'd be down to get it instead.

"Hi, Jimmy. How're things?" Thelma asked, approaching the front desk.

"Quiet, just the way I like it," he answered with a smile.

"I mean, with your girlfriend. Have you popped the question yet?" Thelma teased.

"Not yet. Her birthday is next month, and I think I'll ask her then," he said shyly.

"Good for you! You make sure you let us know where to send the wedding gifts," she replied, taking her package from him.

"Awe, Miss Frost, we don't need any gifts. We've been living together for five years now and already have all the house stuff we need," Jimmy insisted.

"Psssh! Everyone needs to receive wedding gifts when they get married. Besides, it's a great excuse for me to go shopping," she said, smiling. "Let me know what happens."

"I will. No bingo tonight?"

"Taking the night off for a change. I hope the night stays quiet for you."

Thelma took the box back to her apartment and opened it at the kitchen table. June's birthday was this coming weekend, and she had ordered a new deluxe bingo bag with all the accessories as her friend's bag was worn and falling apart in places. The bag was a blue, white, and orange paisley print with eight pockets around the outside to hold all June's many-colored daubers. It came with four fluorescent daubers, a roll of invisible tape, twelve plastic squares to place over a number to keep track of where you were, and a lucky holder for your admission card. Thelma would hide thirty dollars inside the bag for a free night of bingo on her. Draping the bag over her own arm, Thelma decided that June would look great parading it around the bingo cruise that they would be going on together next spring.

I may have to order one of these for myself before the cruise. In purple, of course.

Thelma put the bag back in the box and hid it in her bedroom. June would randomly show up to visit, and she didn't want her present sitting out in the open for her to see. She returned to the kitchen to find the cat up on the table, drinking her wine.

"You couldn't even wait for me to share it with you?" she asked the cat, laughing.

Thelma reclaimed her glass and sat in her recliner to watch the news. Zumbutt settled in on her lap. The events at the newspaper made the headlines, and the sheriff stated in an interview that, as of now, they had no leads on the disappearance of the mailroom employee. A knock on her front door made her leave the comfort of her recliner. She checked through the peephole to see who it was.

"June, you didn't go to bingo?" she asked her friend when she opened the door.

"No, Kami called and asked if I wanted to go with her, but she wasn't sure what time she would get out of work, and we probably would have missed the first few games. So, I passed on going."

"You have got to get your license again, my friend," Thelma said, moving aside so she could enter the apartment.

"You know how I feel about that," June insisted. "Someday, but right now, I just can't get behind the wheel again. I still have nightmares about the accident."

"It wasn't your fault, June. You did nothing wrong," Thelma replied. "He was the one who ran the red light."

"I know, but they never caught him, and I have vivid nightmares that he hits me for a second time. It wakes me up out of a sound sleep almost every night." She sighed. "Enough. I didn't come here to discuss my driving. Did you get the legal announcement in the mail from Agatha's attorney about the reading of the will?"

"I have to admit, with all that happened today, I haven't checked my mailbox downstairs. I walked right by it when I came home."

"When is it?"

"The end of September."

"Well, at least that gives me some time to find Amelia Bohannon," Thelma said, pouring her friend a glass of wine.

"Amelia Bohannon? Is that Agatha's goddaughter's real name?"

"Yes, it is. Her mother was Agatha's best friend, and her father was Robert Tram's business partner. The attorney told me some of the background information on the case."

"By the way, why didn't you go to bingo tonight?" June asked.

"Sit down. I have so much to tell you. I take it you didn't see the news tonight?"

"No, I was just leaving work when Kami called me to tell me you weren't going and that she would be late. I ran to the grocery store and came home."

Thelma explained the day's events for a second time to June, who sipped her wine slowly, upset about what was going on around her.

"Why do you think that I got a notice to go listen to the reading of the will? I wasn't friends with Agatha, and she didn't ask me to help her like she did to you," June asked, setting her glass down on the coffee table in front of her.

"Maybe she found out that you saved her seat that night and appreciated it," Thelma suggested.

"How would she have known that? And that happened just recently," June replied. "She wasn't the kind of person who rewarded people for kind acts."

"I don't know. Maybe she asked those that were sitting around her that night. And you know, I think Agatha was just a lonely person after she lost her husband and goddaughter. Maybe she didn't get close to anyone else, fearing that she would lose them, too."

"I don't know..."

"Look what she did for Betsy and Kami. She gave them the newspaper for all their loyalty and hard work."

"I can't believe I am sitting here listening to you stick up for Agatha. Two weeks ago, you were making fun of her like everyone else in this town," June said, shooing the cat away from her wine glass.

"I know, but sometimes you don't know what battles people are fighting in their own world. Are you up to going through the files with me when I get the new set from the attorney?" Thelma asked, trying to change the subject. "I could use a second set of eyes."

"I don't know. It seems anyone who is involved in this mess is either threatened or has something happen to them. I'm not as brave as you are," June stated.

"At least think about it," Thelma insisted. "Now, how about some more wine and a game of Scrabble. You still owe me four dollars from the last time we played. This could be your chance to get even."

"Last time you cheated," June replied.

"I did no such thing. I can't help it if I know all the little words that no one else knows."

"All right. Two dollars a game just like before," June agreed.

The next three hours were spent at the kitchen table drinking wine and playing the board game. Zumbutt kept jumping in the top of the box and batting around the little square tiles. Thelma would set him on the floor, but minutes later, he would return. June took the other half off the game box and placed it next to the one containing the tiles. The cat jumped in and curled up, purring as he went to sleep.

At ten-thirty, the game was packed away, and June left two dollars more in the hole. Thelma threw the empty wine bottle in the recycle bin, shut the lights out, and went to bed. She lay in bed, patiently waiting for the cat to get settled on the pillow next to her head. She allowed her mind to wander to what June had said about anyone close to the kidnapping or looking into it.

She was afraid for her niece at the newspaper. In the morning, she would call Kami to see if they had decided to run the article on the twenty-fifth anniversary of the kidnapping. Hopefully, with everything that was going on, she and Betsy had canceled the front-page story.

Zumbutt finally started purring, which was a sign he was ready to fall asleep, and Thelma wasn't far behind him.

Thelma was sitting at the table the next morning, enjoying her cup of coffee when she got a text message. Tracy from the animal hospital messaged her to tell her the gas company cleared the property for use again. The day would be spent bringing the animals back and rescheduling some of the missed appointments from the previous day. They wanted to know if she could come in for a couple of hours, even though it was supposed to be her day off. She sent a message back saying she would work from nine to two.

"Well, I guess I'm going to work today," she said to the cat who was eating breakfast. "You'll have to keep yourself busy while I am gone and no crawling up the new curtains in the kitchen."

Half an hour later, she left for work. It was nice to see the parking lot of the hospital full and to hear the barks of the dogs coming from the kennels in the back of the building. Crocker had been returned to his cage and was squawking at everything. Thelma gave him his piece of banana, which quieted him down for a short while.

The phone rang off the wall keeping Thelma busy rescheduling canceled appointments and making new ones. She never took a lunch and was glad when two o'clock finally arrived. June was at work until four, so Thelma decided to take the new mystery that she never got to read the night before and go sit on the beach for a couple of hours.

Setting up an umbrella over her beach chair, she buried her toes in the cool sand and started reading. The anxieties of the previous day melted away as she dug her toes deeper and deeper into the sand, and the cool ocean breezes brushed against her face. Her book, a cozy mystery, the first in a new series that she had been dying to read, kept her attention until a frisbee crashed into her umbrella.

"I'm sorry, lady," a teenager said, retrieving his frisbee. "We'll move further down."

Thelma smiled, remembering the days when she and friends spent the summer days on the beach. They would get there early in the morning and not return home until supper was being served. Thelma always tanned beautifully, but June would burn to a crisp at the start of every summer. Then, as they all got older, summer jobs replaced the time they used to spend together on the beach. After graduation, June was the only friend that Thelma had stayed close with over the years.

She set the book down on her lap and stared out over the ocean. It was on this beach that she had got her first kiss. Henry Paxton was the class nerd. He loved science, but more important to Thelma was the fact that he loved to read and spend time at the library. She would go to the library on Saturdays just so she could see him and talk to him. He wasn't much into girls, and Thelma couldn't really remember if he kissed her or she kissed him, but it was her first kiss none the less.

Whatever made you think of Henry Paxton after all these years?

Placing the book in her purse, she stood up, folded the chair, and closed the umbrella. Back at the car, she threw everything in her trunk except her purse. She brushed the sand off her feet and put on her shoes to drive home.

As she drove away, she was sad to think that today had been the first day that she had spent any time with her toes in the sand, and it was the middle of August. The summer was almost gone. Thelma reminded herself that this was the busiest part of the tourist season. More than likely, she wouldn't find a parking spot no matter what day it was unless she arrived later in the day like she had today.

Thelma purchased a beach sticker for herself and Kami every May. It seemed like a total waste of money for Thelma because each year that passed, she went to the beach less and less, but she bought them anyway. Kami went to the beach almost every day that she had off from work, and having the sticker saved her from paying the exorbitant daily fees that the tourists paid.

Thelma was stopped at the front desk when she entered her building. She had another package that Jimmy had signed for when she was out. The return address showed it was from Agatha's attorney.

"I've been waiting for this," she said to Jimmy. "Thank you for signing for it for me."

"Any time. Bingo tonight?"

"Yes, June and I are going. Kami's working again. This new job is going to take a lot of her time," Thelma complained. "I hope owning the newspaper is worth it."

"Kami owns the newspaper? Wow! Aunt Agatha must have trusted her to leave her the newspaper. It was her baby," Jimmy stated.

"Did you say Aunt Agatha?"

"Yes, she is... or was my aunt."

"Exactly, how are you related to Agatha?"

"She was my stepdad's sister. I guess we were only related by marriage, but we still called her Aunt Agatha. You know Tom Hill? He's my stepdad."

"I went to school with Tommy. I didn't realize that you were related. I didn't know he was related to Agatha either."

"Few people do. My stepdad was much younger than his sister. My last name is Bell. My real dad died when I was young and when my mom married Tom, she took his last name but not us kids. She asked him to adopt us, but he never would. I guess it's a good thing he didn't because he wigged out about ten years ago, and no one knows what caused it. One night he left for work and never came home again," Jimmy said, shaking his head.

"Is he still around?" Thelma asked.

Yea, he's in the area somewhere. I never bothered to find out where after he left us. He broke my mom's heart, and I never forgave him for that," Jimmy replied angrily. "I see him once in a great while, but we ignore each other."

"So, Agatha's maiden name was Hill. Did she have any other siblings?"

"Yes, she had an adopted sister, but she just recently died. Why?"

"I'm just gathering information," Thelma answered.

"Gathering information for what?"

"Your aunt asked me to try to find her goddaughter," Thelma replied before she realized that she had said something that she shouldn't have.

"Amelia. You're going to try to find Amelia Bohannon?"

"I'm going to try. I made a promise to Agatha that I would do my best," Thelma stated. "You have to promise not to tell anyone what I just confided in you."

"I won't say a word. Aunt Agatha had searched for Amelia since the day she was kidnapped, and I always hoped that she would find her before something happened."

"Before something happened?"

"Yea, she wasn't a spring chicken anymore," Jimmy answered.

"Yes, I guess you're right," Thelma agreed.

"Please let me know how things are going...in the search I mean," Jimmy requested.

"I will. Just keep quiet about what I'm trying to do."

"I promise."

Thelma walked into her apartment and stood in the hallway. She had the new copies of all Agatha's files and had to find somewhere to secure them in her apartment. Zumbutt strolled up the hall and planted himself in front of her, looking up and meowing loudly to get her attention.

"Hello, big guy," she said, reaching down to pick him up. "How was your day?"

He meowed as if to answer her and rubbed his nose against hers. She carried him to the kitchen, placed the cat on the floor, and threw the files on the table. Thelma opened a fresh can of wet food and fed the cat. She poured half a glass of wine and watched the cat eat.

"I really wish I wasn't going to bingo tonight," she said to the cat. "Now that I have the files, I would love to stay home and read through them."

The cat looked up as she spoke but was more interested in his food than his owner's words. Deciding that the same place that she hid the pictures was a safe place for the files, she took out the roll of duct tape from the junk drawer. She taped the envelope containing the files to the wall behind the refrigerator.

Changing out of her scrubs, she grabbed her bingo bag, said goodbye to the cat, and left to meet June in the lobby. Her friend was kneeling on the floor, picking up the contents of her bingo bag that had spilled when the handle ripped in two.

"Doesn't this tell you something?" Thelma asked as she approached her friend.

"What? Tell me what?"

"That you have way too much stuff in that bag of yours," Thelma teased, helping her friend pick up the ink daubers that had rolled away.

"No, what it tells me is this is a piece of junk, and I need a new one," June insisted, standing up. "I think I'll go online tomorrow and order a new bag."

"No, you don't need to do that. All you have to do is sew the handle back together," Thelma stated, afraid that her friend would ruin her birthday surprise. "It's still got lots of wear left in it."

"Do you want to trade, mine for yours?" June asked, holding up her ratty bag.

"Not tonight. We need to get going, or we will lose our lucky seats," Thelma replied, dodging the question.

"Just what I thought. You don't want it either," June mumbled, following her friend out the door.

The parking lot was overflowing with cars. The two friends were forced to park on the pier across the street from the community center.

"I have never seen it this busy," June stated as they waited for the light to change so they could cross the street.

"I wonder who's going to be the caller tonight with Wayne still missing," Thelma commented as they crossed the street. "I hope it's not Lucy. She's a terrible caller."

The line to buy cards snaked all the way out into the outer hall. The women looked at each other as they squeezed their way through the doors to the main hall.

"We'll never get our seats tonight," Thelma complained, turning to June.

"Oh, yes we will." June smiled. "Look!"

Kami waved at them from their regular table. She had bought their cards and saved their spots by laying them out at each of their seats.

The women hurried to the table, grateful that they weren't going to have to wait in the long line.

"What are you doing here," Thelma asked her niece, sitting down in her lucky chair.

"After I talked to June, Betsy and I had a meeting. We decided that even though we had the responsibility of running the paper now, we weren't going to let it run our lives like Agatha did. We are going to work our regular hours and still have a life after those hours," Kami replied.

"I am so glad to hear you say that. Does have a life include dating?" June inquired, smiling. "And thank you for getting our cards. That line is awful."

"I got here at five when the hall opened and was fourth in line. I had a feeling it was going to be crowded, so I bought your cards, too," Kami said, ignoring June's last question about dating and taking the money from her for her cards.

"You were right. I've never seen it this busy," Thelma agreed, digging around her purse for money. "Do you know who's calling tonight?"

"Unfortunately, Lucy is calling," Kami answered, rolling her eyes. "We'll be here until midnight."

Thelma finished daubing her early-bird strips and decided she was hungry. She didn't tell Kami and June what she was up to when she went to the kitchen and ordered three steak and cheese subs with peppers, onions, and extra cheese. Balancing three sodas, she walked carefully back to the table and set the drinks down, not spilling a drop.

"Supper will be delivered in ten minutes," Thelma announced.

"What are we having?"

"You'll see when it gets here. It's a surprise," she answered, smiling.

They chatted about the paper and the events that had occurred over the last twenty-four hours. June bought a handful of rip-offs and won ten dollars.

"You are so lucky with those games," Kami said. "I'm lucky if I break even on them."

"I wish I could peel off a special number for the thousand-dollar drawing a little more often," June commented. "Now, that would be lucky!"

"Here is your supper," announced a waitress carrying a large round tray.

As she bent over to place the first plate in front of Kami, she let out a scream, dropped the tray on the floor, and pointed toward the door.

$\mathcal{E}$veryone in the hall turned to look at where the waitress was pointing.

"Kami call the sheriff," Thelma ordered as she left the table.

Before anyone could reach her, Betsy Lee fell to the floor unconscious. Several of the bingo volunteers ran forward to help. Thelma felt for a pulse. Betsy was still alive.

"I had Kami call the sheriff. Maybe we should call 911, too."

"Good idea. Let's get her into the office and off the main floor," one of the men suggested.

Kami followed them to the office and watched as Paul placed Betsy on the leather couch at the back of the room. Thelma could see from the door that Betsy had blood on her head and a piece of rope hanging from one wrist. Her clothes were dirty, and her shoes were missing.

Betsy groaned and slowly opened her eyes. She panicked, not knowing where she was and started thrashing her arms around, trying to hit Paul, who had carried her into the office.

"Betsy! You're at the bingo hall. You're among friends. Calm down," Kami shouted, trying to get her attention so she would stop fighting those who were trying to help her.

"Kami! Watch out!" she yelled, covering her head.

"Betsy, I'm right here. I'm fine," she said, balancing herself on the edge of the couch and taking her co-worker's hand.

"They're coming for you. You need to hide," she rambled.

"Who is, Betsy? Who's coming for me?" Kami inquired.

"Where is she?" the sheriff demanded, entering the office before Betsy could answer her.

The paramedics followed right behind the sheriff.

"Everyone needs to clear out," the sheriff announced.

"Thelma," Betsy groaned. "You have pictures…"

Thelma looked at the sheriff. Now the threats made against Kami were making sense. Whoever did this to Betsy wanted the pictures that Thelma no longer had in her possession. The danger that her niece was in just became real.

"Paul, start calling the games. We'll take Betsy to the ambulance out through the kitchen. Thelma, stay put!" Sheriff Morse ordered.

"But I have cards to play that I already paid for," Thelma protested. "I'll not be a happy person if I miss a bingo."

"Someone else can play your cards for you. This will only take a few minutes," the sheriff insisted. "Kami, you can go."

"I'll watch your cards until you get back to the table," Paul offered as he was leaving.

"Thank you, Paul. Hopefully, I won't be long," she said, frowning.

The sheriff escorted Thelma over to the far corner of the room.

"We found fingerprints on the pictures that you gave us. One set was Agatha's that we matched to the ones her insurance company had on file. There are other prints on the pictures. You need to come to the station in the morning so we can print you and dismiss yours."

"My prints should already be in the system. I had to have them taken when I applied for a CORI to work at the elementary school's after school program," Thelma replied.

"How long ago was that?" Morse asked.

"I don't know. Maybe ten years ago."

"I'll look into it. We also ran the face in the bushes through the face recognition program and found nothing."

"I'm really concerned for my niece. Betsy said they were coming for her. They want the pictures that they think I still have. How are we going to protect her?" Thelma lamented.

"The paper is closed for the next two days. Kami needs to have a security system installed at her house. Maybe you should suggest that she stay at your apartment with you until we catch whoever is behind this," Morse suggested.

"Oh, she won't like that at all. And she has Agatha's two dogs now."

"Maybe you should stay with her then. I'm sure your cat would be fine on his own at night as your apartment is in a secured building."

"I'll talk to her."

"I'll make sure a cruiser goes by her house a couple of times each shift to keep an eye on her," the sheriff stated.

"Thank you. I appreciate that."

"BINGO!" a male voice yelled from the hall.

"That was Paul. He won on my cards," Thelma claimed, straining her neck to look out the office door into the hall.

"Go, go play your game," Morse said. "I'll let you know if I need a new set of prints from you."

Thelma hurried to her table, where Paul promptly handed her seventy-five dollars for winning the double bingo on the early-bird game. She tried to tip him for watching her cards, but he wouldn't take it, claiming they weren't allowed to accept tips according to state rules. Instead, she promised him a six-pack of beer next time she saw him. He agreed, thanked her, and wandered off toward the kitchen.

Thelma sat down, but her mind was not on playing bingo. She missed daubing numbers here and there that Kami caught sitting opposite her and being able to see her aunt's cards.

"Aunt Thelma, where is your mind tonight? I have never seen you miss so many numbers before," Kami asked in between games.

"I don't know." She sighed.

A few more games passed, and in the middle of the four-postage stamp game, Thelma jumped up and ran for the office without so much as a word to June or Kami. The sheriff was just leaving out the back door when Thelma flagged him down.

"I know who it is!" she claimed.

"What are you talking about?" the sheriff asked.

"The picture. The face in the picture. I know who it is."

"Well?"

"Think about the chin that you can just barely see in between the branches of the bush. The shape is very distinctive. The face is round, but the chin is extremely narrow and pointed. Add twenty-five years of aging, and who do you see?"

"Wayne Spikeman!"

"Exactly what I was thinking."

"So, if he was part of the kidnapping team, maybe the others thought he would be recognized from the picture. Maybe they thought they had to get rid of him to protect themselves," the sheriff summarized. "It still doesn't explain who sent the pictures."

"No, it doesn't. Agatha's attorney sent out the new copies of the files. I got mine today, and yours is probably at the station. I'm going to look them over when I go home tonight," Thelma replied.

"I have to run back to the station to write up the report on Betsy after I go to the hospital to interview her. I'll bring the files home with me."

"Good. I still don't know what to do about Kami. I'm afraid to leave her alone even for one night," Thelma said, frowning.

"Tell her to make sure everything is locked up tight. And she does have the dogs with her. I'm sure they would bark at any noise they hear which would warn Kami in plenty of time so she could react," the sheriff assured her. "And just to let you know, because of Agatha not trusting the police, I took the pictures home and locked them in my personal safe. My house is fully alarmed. I will do the same with the files."

"I'm glad they aren't at the station available for anyone to check out of evidence. Agatha must have had her reasons for not trusting the police, and maybe that reason is in the files somewhere. I will tell Kami what you said. Starting tomorrow, I will be staying with her until we get the place alarmed. One good thing is that she does have a can of mace to protect her."

"I have to get to the hospital," the sheriff stated, looking at his watch. "You actually left the bingo game? Who is watching your cards?"

"No one. It hit me out of the blue who was in the picture, and I just jumped up, right in the middle of my favorite game to catch you before you left."

"WOW! Thelma Frost ditched her cards. I have to mark this night on my calendar," he joked.

"Well, you can rest assured I won't do it again. You try and help someone, and all you get is grief," she stated as she squared her shoulders, then turned on one foot, and headed back to her table.

Sheriff Morse chuckled as he watched her red hair disappear through the door.

That woman has a good head on her shoulders. A bit of a nosy busy body, but a good heart. She may prove to be an asset in this cold case.

The night finished almost an hour later than usual because of all the delays with Lucy's faulty calling. The crowd being as big as it was, the three women didn't win a thing after Thelma's initial win in the early bird.

"Maybe I should have let Paul play my cards all night," Thelma stated as they were cleaning up their table. "At least he won."

"I know. I'm getting to the point that I like playing bingo in the offseason when the crowd is smaller. At least I have a chance to win then," June said, holding the door open for them to leave the building. "Did you notice how many games were won by multiple winners tonight? That one game had eleven people yell, and they only got five dollars apiece."

"No bingo for any of us tomorrow night. We need to attend Agatha's wake. I will pick you both up at six-thirty," Kami said.

"Remember what the sheriff said. Lock up tight and keep the dogs in the bedroom with you tonight. Do you have a baseball bat or something you can use as a weapon, need be?" her aunt asked.

"I do, and I have my mace that I'll put on the nightstand next to my bed. I'll be fine. Love you both," Kami said, walking away.

"Love you, too," her aunt replied.

"Homeward, James." June smiled, hooking arms with her best friend.

Zumbutt was curled up under the hallway table, waiting for Thelma to get home. Setting her bingo bag and keys on the table, she picked up the cat. He purred and tucked his head under her chin as she snuggled with him.

"You are such a good cat," she said, carrying him to the kitchen. "But I'm afraid you may have to sleep alone for a few nights. We have to protect Kami, and I know you don't want two strange dogs running around your house."

Setting the cat down, she refilled his dry food dish and gave him fresh water. Thelma glanced at the clock on the wall and decided that it was too late to start going through the files. She had the following day off from work. Besides a hair appointment in the morning, she would be free most of the day to study the information that Agatha had gathered.

"No wine for either of us tonight," Thelma said to the cat. "Time for bed."

The next morning as Thelma was getting dressed, she happened to look in the full-length mirror that stood in the corner of the bedroom. Standing in front of it, she fluffed her hair and then smoothed it down again.

"Thelma, it's time for a change," she announced to herself. "You've been a flaming redhead long enough. Maybe a light auburn with purple streaks? And let's go a little shorter this time."

While drinking her morning coffee, she opened her laptop and searched online for a shorter haircut that she liked. She found one that was long enough to cover her ears, which she was very self-conscious about but was still quite a bit shorter than what she was sporting now.

"Wait until they see the new me tonight," Thelma said to the cat as she hooked up the laptop to the printer so she could give her hairdresser a picture of what she wanted to have done.

Sissy's Hair and I Salon was on the outskirts of town. Thelma drove up the coastal road dodging cars that were trying to fit into parking spaces to spend the day at the beach. The weather was gorgeous. Every beach Thelma drove by was packed by eight-thirty in the morning.

She pulled into the parking lot at the salon and noticed the out of state plates there. There would be no friendly neighborhood gossip today. Too many strange faces would be filling the chairs instead of the usual locals that Thelma enjoyed spending time with each month.

"Thelma, give me about five minutes, and I'll be right with you," Karoline said from her station. "I'm running slightly behind."

"No problem," Thelma replied, grabbing a magazine and sitting down in the waiting area.

"Thelma, how's the summer treating you?" Sissy York, the owner of the salon, asked from behind the receptionist's desk.

"Okay. A little crazy here and there, but okay. How about you? Business looks to be booming," Thelma replied, looking around.

"It's been crazy here as well. Too bad about Agatha, huh?"

"Yes, it is. She still had many years ahead of her that someone stole from her."

"Have they figured out who did it?" Sissy asked.

"Not yet, but I'm confident that Sheriff Morse will find the person responsible," Thelma answered.

"Yea, just like he found my niece when she disappeared," Sissy said in disgust.

"Your niece? Who was your niece?" Thelma asked, believing she already knew the answer to her own questions.

"My niece was Amelia Bohannon. Her mother, Carol, is my older sister."

"I didn't know that," Thelma said. "It seems like everyone is related to someone else in this town."

"It's a small town. When Amelia disappeared, my sister had a nervous breakdown. Not long after that, her husband left. He sold out his half of the joint business he had with Agatha's husband and disappeared with all the money. No matter how much Agatha and I tried to help and support Carol, she couldn't deal with the loss of her child and her husband deserting her."

"What happened to her?"

"Carol always blamed her son for Amelia's kidnapping. He was crying because he fell and skinned his knee. She was attending to him when Amelia was taken from the stroller. I think deep down, she knew it wasn't his fault, but she couldn't get past the feelings that had built up over the two years after the kidnapping took place. She fell apart and couldn't cope with life."

"What was your nephew's name?" Thelma inquired.

"Jerry Bohannon."

"Where is he now?"

"When his mom began to ignore him completely, he moved away with his dad, and I haven't seen him in over twenty years. Shortly after he left, my sister left the area, too. She couldn't take the constant reminders of that day and moved to Massachusetts."

"Is she still there?"

"I think so. I talk to her every couple of years. Still, she withdrew from the whole family, even Agatha, who was her best friend," Sissy stated, sadly.

"Thelma, I'm ready for you. Come on over," Karoline called out over the buzz of the salon.

"Be right there. Sissy, do you have any ideas about who took the baby?"

"At first, I thought it was Hunter, Carol's husband. Personally, I think the marriage was already starting to crumble, and he didn't want to pay any child support if there was a divorce. He never wanted kids in the first place. He wanted to be free to travel and build his business," Sissy explained. "I even offered to take Jerry and raise him here. Hunter said no because he was afraid I would ask for support even though I said I would put it in writing that I didn't want or need any money from him."

"Do you know where they moved to?"

"No. I'm afraid I don't. I lost track of them after they moved five different times in one year."

"Thank you for your help," Thelma said, hurrying away before Sissy could ask what she meant.

"So, what are we doing today? I noticed you have a double appointment," Karoline asked, reaching out for the picture that Thelma was passing to her.

"We are going short and undertaking a dramatic color change," Thelma answered.

"This is a lot shorter than you have ever had it cut before. No more red hair? What color are you thinking about?"

"I want to tone it down. I am turning sixty in February, and I need a change."

"This is only August," the hairdresser insisted.

"I know, but I have had this bright red hair so long that I need to do this before I chicken out. I would like auburn colored hair with caramel highlights and a couple of purple streaks around my face. How's that for a change?" Thelma asked, smiling.

"Seriously? That's what you want done?" Karoline asked.

"Yes, now let's get started before I change my mind," Thelma insisted.

"Okay. Have a seat in the chair while I go mix the hair color," Karoline said, disappearing into the supply room.

Thelma looked in the mirror and started to have second thoughts about what she was doing. After all, she was known around town for her bright red hair, and now she would be just like everyone else. Her whole life, she had stood out for one reason or another. She had always been her own person. Why change now?

"Mommy, why does that lady have clown hair?" a small child asked, standing behind Thelma's chair. "It looks like my red crayon."

"Hush!" her mother said, shooing her away from Thelma's chair. "Sorry."

From the mouth of babes. I wonder how many other people thought my hair was too much but were afraid to say something. I guess a change is in order.

"Here is a sample of the color I mixed up for you. It may pick up on some of the red already in your hair, but I don't think it will be too much," Karoline said, returning with a small white bowl containing the hair dye.

"I like it, I guess," Thelma replied.

"Are you having second thoughts?" Karoline inquired.

"No, it's just for the last nineteen years my hair has been red, and people think it is my natural color," Thelma whispered. "And when I went red, it was to celebrate my divorce."

"If anyone says anything, just tell them you wanted something different. It's a woman's prerogative to change her mind, after all. And I think the purple streaks will be funky enough so that you won't be just like everyone else," Karoline assured her.

It was like her hairdresser had read Thelma's mind about being like everyone else.

"Shall we get started?" Karoline said, draping the apron around Thelma's neck to protect her clothes from the dye.

"Let's do this! Goodbye, red, hello purple!" Thelma said, smiling.

Over the next two hours, the two chatted about town happenings, what was happening in their own lives, and bingo. Karoline was excited to find out that Thelma and June were going on the bingo cruise in the spring and that she would know at least two other people on the ship.

The color of the dye looked a little dark to Thelma, but Karoline assured her that once it was dry, the color would lighten. She cut eight inches of hair off but left it long enough on the sides to cover her client's ears. She blow-dried the now short hair and explained to Thelma that she would add temporary purple streaks in her hair that would wash out over time.

When Karoline was done, she turned the chair around so Thelma could see her new image in the mirror for the first time. She had a long shag cut, and the color was perfect. Traces of the red had remained and blended with the caramel to become highlights in the auburn color.

The purple streaks were subtle and not in your face, but still stood out. A wide smile crossed Thelma's face.

"Well? You're not saying anything. What do you think?"

"I love it!"

"Looking good, Thelma," Sissy said as she passed Karoline's station.

"It's too bad that the first time that everyone sees the new me will be at Agatha's wake tonight," Thelma stated.

"Just smile and take any compliments that come your way. You made this appointment long before Agatha died," Karoline assured her. "Life has to go on."

"Wait until Kami and June see me," Thelma stated, still staring into the mirror.

"They will love it. I'll probably see you there tonight. Tim and I are going to pay our respects. I guess I can say something now that she is gone. Agatha paid for me to go to hairdresser's school," Karoline admitted.

"Really?" Thelma asked, shocked.

I was pregnant with my first child, and Tim and I were struggling. Agatha wanted my children to have a better life and knew I wanted to go to beauty school. She paid for the school and the babysitter that we needed while Tim worked, and while I attended classes. The one condition was that I promise to keep it a secret, and I did until just now," Karoline stated. "Not even Sissy knows."

"I am finding out more and more that Agatha had a kind side to her. She wasn't the gruff, mean woman that everyone thought she was," Thelma said, getting up from the chair and slipping a tip into Karoline's hand. "Thank you for a great job, and I'll make an appointment for next month for a touch-up."

"See you tonight," Karoline said, grabbing the broom to sweep up the cut hair to get ready for her next customer.

Thelma walked out into the sunshine, proud of what she had just accomplished. She felt better about herself and was glad that turning sixty was starting with this new hairdo. No more clown hair for Thelma ever again. She sat in the car, deciding what to do next.

I think I'll head home and check out the files. But first, I am going to stop at Café Beans and pick up a French toast bagel with maple cream cheese. I can show off my new do at the same time.

While Thelma waited in line at the café, several locals walked right by her, not recognizing her without her red hair. The ones who did recognize her were flabbergasted over her new image. Not many people in town would be able to remember Thelma from her pre-red hair days it was so long ago.

Zumbutt met Thelma at the door. He stopped and eyed her suspiciously. It wasn't until she spoke, and he knew her voice that he came near her. She picked him up and snuggled him.

"I guess I do look different." She laughed, carrying him to the kitchen. "How about a glass of wine to celebrate the new me? Which do you want? Red or Zin? Zin it is."

She ripped the envelope off the wall from behind the refrigerator, then sat down with the files and a glass of wine. The cat jumped up on the kitchen table, looking for his share of the poured wine.

"Get down off the table," she lectured the cat. "You'll get your share when I'm done. Go play."

The files dated back to the week of the kidnapping. The first thing that she studied was the original police reports that had been filed at the time. The report was twenty-nine pages long and contained the names of every witness that had been interrogated. Many of the people named had either died or moved away. There were some names Thelma didn't recognize at all.

One part of the report that particularly interested Thelma was the section about the recovered rental car that people had seen in the area of the park on the day of the kidnapping. The vehicle had been abandoned later and found in the woods near the dealership where it had been rented. The police assumed that the kidnappers had hidden another vehicle close to the area that they could escape undetected.

The car had been wiped clean of fingerprints. The only evidence left behind was the pink blanket that the baby had been wrapped in at the park.

The dealership where the car had been rented was listed as Sechuette Motors. A rumor had circulated around town that the family was somehow involved in the kidnapping because of the rental car. Nothing had ever been proven, but the distrust felt by the other locals killed their business. The owners filed for bankruptcy.

The Zender family drifted apart after they lost the business. Some stayed in town, and some moved away. Carl Zender, the father, had a series of strokes shortly after the business went under. He had started the dealership as a very young man and was devastated when it failed as he wanted to pass it down to his sons, Jake and Stephen, when he retired.

The building and property, still owned by the bank, stood vacant to this day.

Thelma had been so engrossed in her reading that she lost track of time. A knock on the door made her look up at the clock. Hurrying to the door, she saw June through the peephole, dressed in black and ready to go to the wake.

"Come in. I'm not ready yet. I lost track of time," she said when she opened the door.

June stayed put in the hall staring at her friend. Thelma had forgotten about her hair and suddenly realized why her friend was not moving. She burst out laughing and pulled June in the door.

"What do you think?" she asked, twirling around so her friend could see the whole hairdo.

"I never thought I would see the day when you didn't have bright red hair. What happened? Why did you change it?" June asked, dumbfounded.

"A small child at the salon asked her mother why I had clown hair. I had been wrestling with the idea of changing it for my sixtieth birthday. That comment made my decision to do it so much easier," Thelma answered. "You didn't answer me. What do you think?"

"I have to admit I am still in shock, but I really like it. The purple streaks are so you." June smiled. "Has Kami seen it?"

"No, just you so far. Oh, and a few people who walked right by and didn't recognize me while I stood in line at Café Beans." Thelma laughed.

"That's too funny. You do need to go get ready. Kami will be here in ten minutes," June claimed. "I'm going to say hi to Zumbutt."

Thelma hurried to the kitchen, returned the files to their envelope, and replaced them in their hiding place. She left June in the living room playing with the cat while she got ready for the wake. Dressed in a black pencil skirt, a dark gray blouse, and black heels, she clipped on black pearl earrings and checked herself in the full-length mirror.

"I'm ready," Thelma said, coming out of the bedroom. "Be a good cat while I am gone."

They didn't have to wait out front too long before Kami arrived to pick them up. She stared out the car window, not believing her eyes.

"Aunt Thelma! I love it," Kami said as her aunt climbed into the front seat. "I love the purple streaks."

"It's going to take some getting used to, but I like it," Thelma admitted.

"I forgot to thank you both for going with me tonight. I didn't want to go by myself. I hate wakes and funerals," Kami admitted.

"When you get to be our age, you tend to be used to them," June replied. "We don't have to stay long. Just pay our respects and move on."

"Good. Those places give me the creeps," Kami said, turning onto the road that led to the Thurman Funeral Home.

"It's not even seven o'clock yet, and the place is mobbed," Thelma said.

11

There was nowhere to park in the funeral home parking lot, so Kami drove a short way up the street and pulled into the high school parking lot, which was already filling up with parked cars.

"I had no idea that so many people would be here," June said as they walked back to the funeral home.

"Agatha had a lot of business associates as did her husband," Kami stated.

"I'm finding out that she had more family than people knew, too," Thelma added.

The line to pay respects extended out the door and around to the back of the building. The three women took their place at the end and slowly crept along toward the entrance. Many people stopped and commented on Thelma's hair, telling her how wonderful she looked.

"It's a good thing it's not raining," June said, looking at her watch. "We've been in line for almost an hour."

The trio finally stepped inside the front door into the foyer. They signed their names in the guest book and proceeded into the main room. The only family member standing in the receiving line was Jimmy. Agatha's brother was nowhere to be seen.

Hanson Beckworth, Agatha's attorney, was standing next to Jimmy. He looked up and smiled as the women approached. Thelma found it amusing that his smile was directed at her niece.

"Good to see you again," he said, shaking her hand. "Did you get the package I sent you?"

"Yes, I did, and I have already started to read through it," she replied.

"You look like a new woman, Thelma," Beckworth said. "Nice to see you again, June."

"Nice hair," Jimmy said as Thelma shook his hand.

"Has your father showed up?" she asked.

"No, and I didn't think he would," Jimmy answered, frowning. "He is her only living relative, and he couldn't even make an effort to be here. Sad, really."

"You hang in there, Jimmy. You are representing your aunt and doing a fine job at it," Thelma assured him. "I will see you tomorrow at the funeral."

She looked back and noticed that Kami was still talking to the attorney. She didn't know if their conversation was about the newspaper or something more personal. Still, it seemed that her niece was doing an awful lot of smiling.

June had gone around her and already paid her respects. Thelma walked up and knelt in front of the casket. She said a small prayer and wished Agatha peace in the afterlife. She also reaffirmed her promise to do the best she could to find Agatha's goddaughter. Kami walked up behind her and put her hand on her aunt's shoulder.

"Do you think she is with her husband now?"

"I think she is, and she's happy," her aunt answered, standing up. "Are you okay?"

"People didn't really know the real Agatha. I feel bad that I used to make fun of her at bingo, and then she goes and trusts me with her newspaper," Kami said with tears in her eyes. "She treated her employees well and was a decent human being behind the scenes. I will never understand why she had to be so nasty in public and wouldn't let people like her."

"Maybe somewhere in her past, she was hurt by someone she trusted and was close to. Or maybe it's from losing her godchild and husband and not wanting to let anyone else in out of fear of losing them, too." Thelma offered. "There could be many reasons, and we'll never know why she chose to be like she was."

"I guess, but I still feel bad about the way I acted," she said, wiping her eyes. "I'm going to find the bathroom and splash some water on my face."

"I'll be with June over in the corner," her aunt replied.

June was standing with Karoline and her husband. Sissy had joined them along with several other local business owners from the area. Thelma, on her way to the group, often stopped to look at the flowers and read the cards displayed with them.

One beautiful arrangement of white roses and pale pink lilies caught her eye. 'You didn't win' was printed on the card. Thelma waved one of the funeral home directors over to where she was standing.

"Do you know who sent this by any chance?" she asked, pointing to the flowers in front of them.

"All the flowers are delivered by the local florist. We just spread them around and stick the cards on holders so they can be read," he replied.

"You don't read the cards before you display them?"

"No, I am sorry. The only deliveries that we pay special attention to are the arrangements with ribbons that say they are from close family and must be displayed near the casket. Is there something wrong?"

As Thelma opened her mouth to answer, a loud commotion sounded from the front foyer. The director ran to the area to see who or what was causing the disruption. Thelma glanced around to see if anyone was looking in her direction, but all eyes were on the foyer. She took a tissue out of her purse and carefully folded the card in question into it and slipped it into her coat pocket. Satisfied that no one saw her, she wandered over to join her friends in the corner.

"What is going on out there?" June asked over the noise.

"I don't know, but there goes Jimmy and Beckworth to find out," Thelma answered.

"You can't tell me that I can't go in there," a loud voice boomed. "Agatha is my sister."

People were stepping through the door, trying to clear the foyer area. A man, swinging a whiskey bottle in his hand, came charging into the room and headed right to the casket. He set the bottle on the pillow near his dead sister's head.

"Come on, Dad. You don't want to do this right now," Jimmy lectured, standing behind his stepdad.

"Don't call me Dad! I am not your father," he yelled, turning to face Jimmy. "Leave me be. My sister and I have business to attend to."

"Not here and not at this moment you don't," Beckworth informed him.

"Well, look here if it isn't Agatha's big wig attorney. How much did she pay you an hour to tell her what to do? Sorry buddy, but you can't tell me what to do, so bug off," Tommy Hill screamed, slurring his words.

"If you insist on having this conversation with your sister, you can do it privately after the public wake," Beckworth insisted.

"And why would I do that? You don't want all these so-called friends to know the real Agatha? She was always so good at hiding everything," he said, picking up the bottle and taking another swig. "Did you all know that Amelia Bohannon was my dear sister's goddaughter. The only thing that mattered to her was that kid. She threw all the rest of us away, family or not."

"That's not true," Jimmy argued. "You were the one who threw your family away, not Aunt Agatha. What are you even doing here? You haven't talked to your sister in years, and now you want to talk to her when she's dead? What is wrong with you?"

"It doesn't matter. I won, and she didn't. I beat her, and she died before she could do anything about it," he muttered. "If she had just loved me, I would have helped her."

Sheriff Morse and two of his deputies approached Agatha's brother. He saw them coming and grabbed onto the handles of the casket.

"Let go of the casket, Tommy. You need to come with us," the sheriff ordered. "You're holding up all these nice people from saying goodbye to Agatha."

"Why didn't she love me?" Tommy asked, a tear sliding down his cheek. "I loved her."

"She did love you. Let's go talk about this at the station," the sheriff replied. "Let's go get coffee and some supper."

"Why didn't she love me?" Tommy sobbed as the sheriff led him out of the funeral parlor. "She ruined everything."

"Well, now I know who sent the flowers," Thelma mumbled under her breath.

"Were you talking to me?" June asked.

"No, just to myself again," Thelma replied.

Jimmy and Beckworth took their place near the casket, and people started to file by as if nothing had happened. Kami came out of the back hall and stopped to talk to the attorney before she rejoined her aunt.

"Do I detect a 'thing' happening between you and Mr. Beckworth?" June inquired.

"Not a thing, just a cup of coffee later at the wake's conclusion." Kami smiled. "He seems to be a very nice man."

"I knew it! I could tell by the way you were smiling at each other," Thelma declared.

"He came by the office to check on Betsy and me to make sure we were all right after Wayne disappeared. We talked for a couple of hours before we realized how much time had passed," Kami said. "Hanson is so pleasant and easy to talk to."

"Wouldn't a relationship like this be considered a conflict of interest on his part?" June asked.

"Number one, it's not a relationship yet, but I did ask him that when he asked me out for coffee just now. He said that because Agatha was his client and not me, it would be okay," she replied. "But you know how people in a small-town gossip. That's why we are keeping it under wraps until after the reading of the will."

"Smart girl. They can talk around here," June agreed. "Where are you going to have coffee? Everyone knows you at Coffee Beans."

"My house," Kami answered, blushing.

"I have to admit, it is nice that you have a man around for protection," Thelma said. "And an attorney to boot."

"Aunt Thelma, don't let your mind go crazy. It's just a cup of coffee," Kami said, rolling her eyes. "To listen to you, you already have us married."

"You never know, my dear, you never know." She smiled.

The ride back to their apartment complex was filled with good-natured ribbing about Kami's new love interest. She turned red several times but tried just to laugh it off. Leaving the two women at the front door, she drove home to clean up her kitchen before Hanson got there.

"It's only six-thirty. Do you want to come in for a glass of wine?" Thelma asked June as they walked to the elevator.

"Not tonight, thank you. I have a meeting at the college early in the morning to go over the new state rules for financial aid in September."

"But it's Saturday. Are you going to be out in time for the funeral service?" Thelma inquired.

"Phillip, the other financial aid assistant is going to pick me up at eight and bring me home by ten. The funeral is at eleven, so I think it will be okay."

"I'll be driving us. Kami is speaking at the service, so she must be at the church early. Meet you in the lobby at ten-thirty?"

"Sounds good. See you then," June replied as Thelma stepped off the elevator.

"Zumbutt, where are you?" Thelma hollered as she stepped inside the apartment.

Entering the living room, she spotted the cat looking down on her from on top of the bookcase.

"What are you doing up there? How did you even get up there in the first place?"

The cat stretched and closed his eyes again. He was in no mood to end his nap and stayed put where he was.

"I need to move the breakables from up there before you send them flying," Thelma acknowledged, taking down the three vases. "I guess I'll have to drink my wine all by myself."

She threw a single-serve lasagna in the microwave and poured herself a glass of red wine to go with dinner. Not having to get up early in the morning, she decided to spend a few hours going through the files and grabbed them from behind the refrigerator. Finishing up with the police report, she moved on to the other private agencies and what they found.

The first one had nothing more than what the original police report contained. It was almost like they had read the report and changed the wording around. Thelma felt that Agatha had been taken for a ride paying all that she had for work that wasn't done.

The alarm on the microwave signaled that her dinner was done. She peeled back the cellophane and stirred the lasagna. Setting the timer for another three minutes, she grabbed the salt and sat back down at the table.

When she picked up the second report, a small piece of paper fell out from in between the pages. Putting the other papers aside, Thelma stared at the small hand-drawn object at the center of the paper. The drawing resembled the shape of a single angel wing. She turned the paper over, but the backside was blank.

She quickly scanned through the other paperwork to see if there was an explanation for this item, but there was nothing. The microwave buzzer sounded. Thelma set the paperwork aside to eat her supper.

A loud cry for help came from the living room. Thelma dropped her fork and went running. Zumbutt was hanging from the top of the drape, his claws entangled in the material and unable to free himself.

"So that's how you got up there. You climbed up the drapes," she said to the cat as she freed his claws. "It didn't work so well on the way down, did it?"

She set him on the floor, and he took off to hide in the bedroom.

"That will teach you. When you calm down, come out and get your supper," she yelled up the hallway.

Twenty minutes later, the cat returned to the kitchen, looking for his supper. Thelma fed him, refilled her wine glass, and took the files to sit more comfortably in her recliner while she continued to peruse the files.

The little piece of paper kept drawing her back. Why was it in the files, and what exactly was it supposed to be? She made a mental note to call the agency on Monday and talk to the detective who worked on the case.

Zumbutt jumped up in the chair, meowing for his share of the wine.

"You don't deserve this climbing up my drapes like you did," Thelma lectured but gave him some wine anyway.

"I totally forgot what the date was," she said, patting the cat who had settled in between her leg and the chair. "I'm on vacation next week. It's the third week in August, and I always take this week off. Can you stand it if I'm home more than usual?"

The cat set his head down and closed his eyes.

"I can see you're really excited about me being home next week," she said, laughing. "Don't get too comfortable. It's almost time for bed."

Thelma finished reading through the second agency report and called it a night. Instead of taping the files back in their hiding place, she took them to the bedroom with her. Zumbutt was already on her pillow when she came out of the bathroom. She crawled in bed, and the cat started to purr.

"I am so lucky to have you," she said, kissing the cat goodnight. "So lucky."

Thelma puttered around the apartment the next morning. She read through a few more of the files and cooked herself what she called a vacation breakfast. It was the kind of breakfast that you would order at a restaurant if you were eating out—two eggs over easy, wheat toast, bacon, home fries, and a big glass of pulpy orange juice.

"This is the way to start a vacation," she said to the cat who was eating his breakfast, too.

Zumbutt would take a few bites of wet food, and then his nose would go up in the air sniffing the bacon that had been cooked. He jumped up in the empty chair next to his owner and waited patiently for something to fall his way. When Thelma was full, she took the last piece of bacon and crumbled it up, placing it on the wooden chair next to the cat. The bacon was gone in seconds.

At ten-thirty, she told the cat to behave and left for the lobby to meet June. Her friend was already there, and they left for the funeral service.

"I hope Agatha's service goes smoothly," June said as they rode to the church.

"Me, too. Hopefully, Tommy Hill has sobered up and will stay away," Thelma agreed.

"Another big crowd," June stated as they pulled into the church parking lot.

A cruiser pulled in behind them and parked next to them. Sheriff Morse got out escorting Tommy Hill, who had cleaned up and was in a suit. The two men walked into the back door of the church while Thelma and June went around to the front. The doors were still closed, and people were whispering among themselves, waiting for them to open.

"I bet the sheriff wanted to give Tommy some time with his sister now that he's sober," Thelma whispered to June.

"The sad part is I believe he truly loved Agatha and that something came between them."

"You mean someone, don't you?" Thelma asked.

"Ahh, would you be referring to Amelia?"

"That's what Tommy stated last night. Some say that when you are drunk, you have more tendency to tell the truth about how you really feel. I would like to talk to him and ask him what he meant about beating Agatha."

"Do you think he had something to do with Amelia's kidnapping?" June whispered.

"I think we have been friends far too long. You know exactly what I am thinking most of the time." Thelma laughed. "It would make sense. If he felt threatened by her, he would remove the threat."

The doors opened, signaling that people could enter the church. Tommy Hill and the sheriff were sitting in the front row with Jimmy. Hanson Beckworth and Kami were standing to the right of the pulpit, deep in discussion. June and Thelma took their seats and read through the service program.

The picture on the front of the memorial flyer was a beautiful picture of Agatha and her husband taken many years ago. She looked so happy back then.

Tommy took the podium and spoke about his sister and apologized for how he had acted the previous night. Other business partners told funny stories about events with Agatha. Jimmy gave the eulogy. Kami spoke on behalf of the employees at the paper and finished with a reading of the twenty-third Psalm. The service was over in an hour, and everyone was invited to go down to the rectory hall for a buffet and social hour.

Thelma filled her plate, and while she ate, she searched for Tommy. Both he and the sheriff must have left after the service as neither were in the hall. People were still coming up to Thelma to tell her how nice her hair looked, and she loved the attention. June joined her friend after making the rounds and had a full plate of desserts, stacked so high that it could have rivaled the Eiffel Tower.

"Really? Could you have fit anything else on that plate?" Thelma laughed, watching June balance the rest of the plate as she slipped a brownie out of the bottom of the pile.

"What? Can I help it if I have a super active sweet tooth?" she replied, taking a large bite of the chewy brownie. "Besides, I can take the rest home for later."

Kami joined them, and she was beaming. Thelma had never seen her niece looking so happy.

"So, how was the date last night?" her aunt asked.

"It wasn't a date. It was just a cup of coffee," Kami insisted. "But it was fine. We talked until one this morning."

"Sounds like you're getting kind of chummy to me," her aunt teased.

"Well, as a matter of fact, we have a date tonight. He's taking me to the Lincoln Room in Portland for dinner," Kami gushed. "Do you know how hard it is to get reservations at that place?"

"Wow! That restaurant is super fancy," June admitted. "What are you going to wear?"

"I don't know yet. I'm going shopping when I leave here for a new dress," Kami stated. "I was going to ask you to go with me so I could get your advice on what would be proper to wear to a place like that but still be pretty."

"I have nothing going on," June answered. "How about you, Thelma?"

"I'm on vacation. I can do whatever I want for the next week."

"Great. I will pick you up at two-thirty, and we'll head to the Sechuette Dress Shop. I'll see you then," Kami said, rushing off.

"First, the newspaper and now a new guy in her life. Kami's whole life is about to change and for the better," her aunt said, tearing up.

"Come on, softie, let's head home," June said. "First, I need to make one more stop at the dessert buffet for a few more of those mini eclairs."

The Sechuette Dress Shop was empty of customers even though it was a Saturday. Everyone was at the beach trying to cool off. The clerk told them to look around and that she would be at the register if they needed any help.

"What size are we looking for?" June asked, browsing through the rack closest to her.

"I wear a size ten, but I really should try anything on that we select," Kami said, pulling a mint green summer dress off the rack.

"Too beachy," her aunt stated, shaking her head no at Kami's choice.

"I don't want to look like a frump," Kami laughed.

"What about something like this?" June asked, holding up a black and white panel dress with white lace sleeves.

"He'll think he's going to court and not out to dinner," Thelma replied, flipping through the rack. "Now, this is perfect."

She held up a tea-length, deep purple halter dress. It had several layers of flowy chiffon over the satin skirt and rhinestones dotted the halter top.

"That's pretty," her niece agreed.

"And, of course, it has to be purple." June laughed.

"We have that dress in many different colors," the clerk advised from the register.

Kami picked out the dress in three colors: purple, seafoam green, and royal blue. She disappeared into the dressing room while June and Thelma wandered around the shop.

"I think a nice shawl would finish off her look, don't you?" June asked.

"Yes, and some simple rhinestone jewelry to match the ones on the dress," Thelma added.

Kami walked out of the dressing room. She chose to try on the sea foam green dress first but complained that with no time to get a good tan this summer, it made her skin look washed out. The others agreed.

Her second choice was the royal blue dress. Kami stood in front of the mirror, twirling around. It was obvious that she really liked this color choice. She turned from the mirror.

"What do you think? I really like this one," she said, her eyes twinkling.

"I think you look stunning," June answered.

"It's perfect for the Lincoln Room." Thelma sighed. "Is it the one you want?"

"This is the one," her niece answered, turning back to the mirror.

"Okay, now we need to complete the look. Step right this way to the jewelry area, and then we need matching heels," her aunt instructed.

Thelma stepped back and watched June help her niece try on the different necklaces. She choked up as she stood there. Never having any children of her own, she loved Kami like a daughter. She was incredibly proud of the woman that she had become and how beautiful she was.

Kami turned to ask her aunt what she thought about a simple teardrop necklace and matching earrings that she had picked to go with the dress and saw the tears. She rushed over to see what was wrong. Thelma wiped away the tears and smiled.

"I just love you so much," she told her. "You're so beautiful, and I'm sure Hanson will think so, too."

"I love you, too. More than you will ever know," her niece echoed, hugging her aunt.

Kami's parents divorced when she was eight years old. Her mother, a realtor like her dad, couldn't take the competition in the small town after the divorce. She moved to Boston, took a job with a large real estate company, and never looked back. Over the years, Kami heard from her mother a handful of times, but the bond between them was gone. Her aunt had become her substitute mother. Thelma was always there for her as Kami grew up. Now, they were inseparable.

"These heels would go beautifully with that dress," the clerk advised, holding out a pair of royal blue satin heels for Kami to see.

"The color is a perfect match. Do you have them in size eight?"

The clerk hurried off to get the requested size. June had picked out a pale blue chiffon shawl to finish the look. Once the shoes were in place, the young woman stood in front of the mirror, looking at her full ensemble.

"Beautiful." The clerk smiled.

"I think you are ready for tonight. A simple updo with a few hanging curls, and you will put everyone else in the restaurant to shame," her aunt bragged. "Hanson won't be able to take his eyes off you."

"I am so lucky to know two women that have such good taste," Kami stated, heading to the dressing room to change.

"I am paying for this," Thelma told the clerk after her niece disappeared behind the curtain. "Can you have it all rung up before she comes back out?"

"We can use the tags on the samples," she answered, getting to work on the sale.

When Kami exited from the dressing room, all that was left to do was to bag her items. She protested how her aunt had paid for everything, but Thelma stood her ground and shooed her out the door, and then thanked the clerk for her help.

"What say Kami goes home to get ready for her date, and you and I walk to the pier and have an early supper?" Thelma asked June.

"What about bingo?"

"It's almost the end of August, and neither of us has attended an outdoor concert on the town green. They have a group that plays blues and country performing tonight, and I hear that they are really good."

"One condition. We need to stop at the drugstore and get some bug spray. Last year I got eaten alive by the mosquitoes, and I itched for a week from the bites," June insisted.

"Deal! You run along, Kami, and have a great time tonight. Call me tomorrow and let me know how it went," her aunt requested.

"Love you both," Kami yelled out the car window as she drove away.

The pier was a short walk away from the dress shop. Families were starting to leave the beach, and the sidewalks were crowded. A couple of times, the women almost got beaned by a beach umbrella or tripped up by a cooler. Even the pier was more crowded than usual. They waited in line to order their supper and then had to wait for a table to empty.

"Why don't you stay here and watch for a table, and I'll run across the street and get the bug spray," June suggested.

Not long after June left, a table became available. Thelma had to scramble to get to the table ahead of another family who was looking for somewhere to sit, too. The mother gave her a dirty look, and Thelma just smiled back at her. The food arrived before June got back from her errand. Thelma had a lobster roll that should be eaten cold, but June had ordered seafood chowder and a scallop roll, both of which would be better eaten hot.

Where is that woman? How long does it take to buy bug spray?

June rushed up to the table and plunked down in her seat.

"Wait until you hear what I just overheard," she gushed excitedly.

"It must have been good," Thelma said, setting down her lobster roll. "Tell me."

"You know how you are working on Amelia's kidnapping? Well, Jake Zender was in the pharmacy waiting to pick up his daughter's prescriptions, and he was talking to someone I didn't recognize. I heard kidnapping and rental car, so I edged a little closer, pretending I was waiting for medicine, too."

"And?"

"Jake was saying that his dad still goes to work every day at the car dealership even though it's not open. Apparently, his mind is going, and he believes he still runs the place. His house is right up the street, so he walks to work with a packed lunch and comes home at the end of the day."

"I wonder if all the dealership's records are still on the property," Thelma replied.

"I don't know, but Jake was telling this man that he himself rented the car and everything was on the up and up. He insisted his family had nothing to do with the kidnapping, as was suggested in the newspaper at the time."

"I wonder who this man was that he was talking to."

"I don't know, but he was taking notes in a little notebook as Jake spoke. But that wasn't the good part," June replied.

"Don't keep me in suspense. What good part?"

"The car that was used in the kidnapping is still parked in the woods behind the dealership."

"Really? I wonder if the sheriff knows that the car is still around," Thelma pondered.

"Why would he be interested? Didn't they process the car when they first found it?" June inquired.

"Yes, they did. But think about the progress that has been made in the last twenty-five years in the field of forensics. Maybe there is still skin flakes left on the steering wheel for DNA testing. There could be other new evidence that they could collect and process using today's advances," Thelma explained.

"True. But wouldn't the evidence have been lost if the car sat in the woods that long?"

"It depends. Are the windows still intact and rolled up? Was the car a rental, and had it been driven again after the kidnapping, or did it sit unused after the kidnapping?"

"I'm sure if they find DNA evidence, it would probably belong to the Zender family. Can skin or body fluids be tested after twenty-five years?" June asked, dipping her scallop in ketchup.

"I don't know. I don't work in a forensics lab, but I am sure the sheriff would know the answer to that question," Thelma said, popping a piece of the lobster claw in her mouth. "I think I'll do a little hiking in the woods tomorrow and check out the condition of the car before I talk to the sheriff. I don't want him spending time or money if the car has been exposed to the elements all this time."

Thelma's cell phone rang.

"It's Kami face-timing us," Thelma stated. "I bet she is ready for her date and wants to show us the completed look. Hello, sweetie. Are you excited?"

"I am. What do you think? Is my make-up too much?"

"It's perfect. You're perfect from head to toe," Thelma replied, holding the phone out so June could see the screen.

"If he doesn't fall in love with you tonight, he never will." June smiled.

"I'm not looking for a proposal, maybe just a steady boyfriend to do stuff with when I'm not working."

"I think you have already won him over," her aunt assured her. "The way he looks at you is evidence of that."

"He just pulled in the driveway. I have to go. I'll call you tomorrow. Love you both, and thank you again for this afternoon."

The screen went blank, and Thelma let out a big sigh.

"She's a beautiful girl." June smiled. "You should be very proud of her. Who knows? Maybe you'll be planning a wedding before too long."

"You never know," Thelma replied. "Okay, back to the car."

"Never mind the car. See that guy standing at the front of the line at the ice cream window? That's the guy that Jake Zender was talking to," June announced.

"Guard our table. I'll be right back," Thelma said.

"Can I help you with something?" he asked as Thelma approached him.

"Yes, you can. Your conversation with Jake Zender was overheard by a friend of mine in the pharmacy. Will you please tell me what your interest is in the Amelia Bohannon kidnapping?"

"And I need to explain myself to you, why?"

"I am working this cold case with the Sechuette police department," Thelma said, trying to sound as official as she could. She was glad she didn't have her red clown hair anymore and would be taken more seriously. "We need to know who is asking around town about the kidnapping."

"My name is Drake Perkins, and I work for the *Portland Times*. My editor wanted me to do a follow-up story on the kidnapping for its twenty-fifth anniversary. Amelia Bohannon was never found, and stories circulated at the time was that someone on the police force was in on it," he answered, extending his hand. "I didn't know that the police had reopened the case."

"Just recently," Thelma mumbled, shaking his hand. "Would you care to join us at our table?"

"I'll be right over. Let me get my supper, and I'll join you."

"You're having ice cream for supper?"

"Yes, but don't tell my wife," he answered, smiling. "I'm supposed to be on some new diet, but she's back in Portland, and what she doesn't know won't hurt me."

"We are at the table closest to the stairs that lead down to the slips. By the way, my niece owns the *Sechuette Gazette*. I'm sure she would love to talk to you as they were considering running the same kind of story," Thelma informed him, walking away.

"Who is he?" June asked when her friend sat down.

"His name is Drake Perkins, and he's a reporter. He's coming over to talk to us as soon as he gets his food."

"I wouldn't count on it. He just took off in the opposite direction," June said, pointing toward the ice cream shack.

"What a snake! And he seemed so nice," Thelma replied, mad at herself for trusting him.

She pulled out her cell phone and searched for reporters' names that worked for the *Portland Times*.

"There is no Drake Perkins listed as an employee at the paper. How could I be so stupid and gullible?"

"You're not. He obviously had something to hide, and he turned on the charm to get away," June assured her. "You're not a trained police officer, remember?"

"I know. It's just aggravating. At least you got the information about the car, and I can check that out tomorrow."

"Let's finish our supper and walk home. I'm not much in the mood to listen to music tonight," June claimed.

"Me neither. Right now, pajamas, fuzzy socks, and a glass of wine sound so much better. Do you want to come over and read through some of the files with me? Two sets of eyes are better than one."

"Not tonight. I think my bed will be calling my name early. After all, I do need my rest if I am going to be traipsing around in the underbrush out in the fresh air tomorrow," June said, smiling.

"You are the best friend ever," Thelma said, taking a big bite of her lobster roll.

"I know," June agreed.

It was a pleasant walk home. Twenty minutes later, both women were safe in their apartments. Before they parted ways for the evening, they agreed June would be at Thelma's place at eight the next morning for breakfast before they left for the dealership.

"What are you hoping to find?" June asked, pouring coffee while Thelma cooked.

"I don't know. Reading through the police report, it seems to me that they didn't really pay much attention to the car. Maybe Agatha was right about someone on the force being in on the kidnapping."

"Who was in charge of the investigation?"

"Our own Captain Evan Brewer. At the time of the kidnapping, he was the first deputy. Sheriff Carson was out on medical leave, and Brewer was in charge. Carson died from a heart attack while out on leave. Sheriff Morse won the next election and has been sheriff ever since."

"Weird. Wouldn't you assume that Brewer would have been elected sheriff being the next in line?" June asked.

"From what I remember, he wasn't very well-liked, and he still isn't to this day. He may be second in command at the police station by climbing up the ranks. Still, he was never popular enough to be elected sheriff. Ready for a five-star breakfast?" Thelma boasted, setting two plates of food on the table.

"Oh, I forgot to tell you. I'm not very hungry this morning, so I'll pass on breakfast," June claimed, picking up her coffee mug. "Just coffee for me, thanks."

Thelma stood there looking at her friend in disbelief.

"I just spent all this time cooking breakfast, and you're not going to eat?" Thelma asked, upset at her friend.

"Got ya!" June chuckled, picking up her fork.

"Sometimes, girlfriend, I could just hit you." Thelma laughed.

An hour later, they were pulling up in front of the abandoned car dealership. The open area where the cars used to be parked was overgrown and unrecognizable as a car lot. The building was still standing, but most of the windows were broken, and nature had taken it over.

The two women walked up to the front door, which was still intact. Sechuette Motors was still visible in black letters on the top half of the door. Thelma caught movement inside the building out of the corner of her eye. She cautiously pushed the door open and stepped inside with June right behind her.

"Good morning! How can I help you today?" a man said, walking toward them.

"Isn't that Carl Zender?" June whispered to her friend.

"Yes, I believe it is," Thelma whispered back.

"Are you interested in purchasing a new car?" he asked, shuffling a pile of papers from one arm to the other to shake hands.

"Carl? Carl Zender?" Thelma asked.

"That would be me. And you are?"

"Thelma Frost."

"You're not Thelma. Thelma has bright red hair that you can see from a mile away." He snickered, walking to a desk that had been placed in the middle of the showroom. "Thelma has red hair—Bozo hair. You are not her."

June stifled a giggle.

"Not funny," Thelma whispered, giving her a dirty look.

He sat at the desk, shuffling papers and talking to someone who wasn't there. File cabinets lined the back wall, some drawers intact, and some missing. At his feet, vines and dead leaves covered the floor. Tree branches had grown through the cracks in the ceiling, vines had blanketed the walls, turning them green in color, but Carl didn't seem to notice any of that. He was attending to business just as he had twenty-five years ago.

"The story is true. Carl thinks the place is still open," Thelma whispered.

"I kind of feel bad for him," June acknowledged.

"Mr. Zender, is it okay if my friend and I look around?" Thelma requested.

"Help yourself. If you have any questions, I'll be happy to help. Buying a car is a wonderful feeling, especially if it's your first brand new car," he said, returning his attention to the folders in front of him. "Brownie, bring that rental around. I need it now!"

"Excuse me. You do rentals as well as car sales?" Thelma asked, trying to steer what was left of Carl's mind to the rental used for the kidnapping.

"Yes, we do. Rentals are parked around back. We rent them by the day, week, or month."

"May we look at the rentals?" June asked.

"Funny thing. No one wants rentals, and then two people in one day ask about them," Carl replied.

"Who else asked about your rental cars?

"A nice young gentleman was here just ahead of you. He left not more than ten minutes ago. At least I think it ten minutes ago."

"Thank you. We will get back to you if we need help," Thelma stated. "Come on, June. I have a feeling that nice young gentleman was our fake newspaper reporter, and he might be out at the car right now."

They ran around to the back of the building and could see the blue rental car through the trees. Approaching as quietly as they could, sneaking from tree to tree, they managed to get within ten feet of the vehicle. The man claiming to be Drake Perkins was so intent in his search of the car he didn't realize that the two women had walked up right behind him until Thelma tapped him on the shoulder.

Startled, he stood up before his head was clear of the car, and he whacked it on the door frame. Holding his head, he started to run away, but June, thinking quickly, stuck her foot out and tripped him. He landed with a thud, and the women surrounded him.

"Who are you? This time I want the truth," Thelma demanded, holding out her phone for him to see. "Before I call the sheriff and you can tell him who you are."

"Fine. I'm not Drake Perkins," he replied, sitting up.

"No kidding," June muttered.

"That's a name I use when I am on a job and don't want people to know who I really am," he informed them. "My real name is Dylan Peterson, and I do work for the *Portland Times*."

"I think I remember that name on the list of reporters for the paper," Thelma said. "Why did you lie, and why did you run from us?"

"Look, I didn't want to be scooped, so I ran after you told me that your niece owned the *Sechuette Gazette*."

"That's why you ran?" You didn't want to be scooped by my niece's paper?"

"And, I didn't know the police had reopened the case, and I thought you were a cop. The tip we received involved a dirty cop, but I don't know which one. It could have been you."

"Technically, the original case hasn't been reopened, but other more recent cases may be tied to the kidnapping. I am not a cop, but I am working on behalf of Agatha to find Amelia. What exactly was the tip that you received?"

"And why should I tell you?"

"You can either tell me or tell the sheriff," Thelma stated. "Or be charged with obstruction of justice."

"Fine! I can't protect my source if I don't know who she was in the first place. The paper got a call saying one of the police officers on the force at the time was involved in the kidnapping. The caller wouldn't give us the name of who it was, but she told us to take a better look at the rental car."

"She? The caller was a woman?" June asked.

Yes, it was. Apparently, someone in Tram's attorney's office leaked the story that they were looking for Amelia Bohannon because she was the goddaughter of Agatha. She was set to inherit a lot of money if they could find her. This woman didn't want to turn herself in, but she felt terrible that she had participated by driving the get-a-way car. She said she was forced to do it, or the others would have killed her. And now she is afraid that the real Amelia is in danger because of the inheritance."

"How did this woman even know that the rental car was still here?" Thelma pondered.

"I don't know, but she did."

"This doesn't make any sense," June said. "Why would the kidnappers have left the car here if it contained evidence that could point to them?"

"Didn't Jake tell you that the car had never been rented again?" Thelma asked Dylan.

"Yea, he said that his dad never wanted the car to be used again, so they junked it out here in the woods."

"What if the kidnappers did have a cop on the inside and were confident any incriminating evidence found would have been destroyed? The police report said the only thing found in the car was the pink blanket that was in the stroller with the baby at the time of the kidnapping. So, if they were sure the car would be wiped clean, they wouldn't have cared if the car was left here or not," Thelma said, thinking out loud.

"Makes sense," the reporter agreed.

"Wouldn't it also make sense that the one in charge of the investigation would be the one who covered everything up?" June asked. "Brewer had the perfect opportunity to do so."

"Not necessarily. I need to go back to the files to see who was in charge of the car after it was found," Thelma stated.

"You have files on the kidnapping?" Dylan asked. "I went to the police station to view the police records in the archives, but they conveniently had disappeared. There was no sign of them being checked out. They were just gone."

"That's because the sheriff has them. He also knows about the theory of a dirty cop and wanted the files protected," Thelma replied.

"Are you sure he's protecting them or just hiding them from everyone else?" Dylan asked.

"I already have copies of the report, and so does Agatha's attorney. He's definitely not trying to hide anything."

"He was on the force when the kidnapping occurred. Just how much do you know about him, and do you really trust him?" the reporter asked.

"I have known the sheriff since grade school. I trust him explicitly," Thelma stated. "He's never given me a reason not to."

"If you say so. I never trust anyone, and that keeps me safe," Dylan replied.

"I would assume it also makes you a very lonely person," June commented. "You're not really married, are you?"

"No, that's just another part of my cover story," he admitted.

"Have you found anything in the car yet?" Thelma asked.

"Nothing but lots of dirt and dust. The windows were up, but it's been unlocked all this time. So anyone and everyone had access to it."

Thelma moved to the opposite side and started to pull away some of the vines that had climbed the side of the car. June worked alongside her, and soon they had enough cleared away that they could open both passenger side doors.

"Put these on," Thelma instructed the other two, pulling rubber gloves out of her purse. "We don't want our prints on anything we may find."

The trio searched every inch of the car. An hour passed, and the only thing they had to show for it was being dirty from head to toe.

"I think this woman led us on a wild goose chase," Dylan said, sitting on the ground to give his back a break from stooping over.

"There has to be something here. Why would she take a chance to expose herself by making the call to your paper?" Thelma insisted, running her hand along the inside roof of the car.

"There's a bump here in the roof next to the light dome," June noticed.

"Here, take my pocketknife and slice the lining open around it," Dylan said from the front seat.

"There's something hidden here!" June exclaimed.

As she cut, several pictures and a lump of plastic wrapping fell onto the back seat. June reached for the items just as shots rang out above their heads.

They dove out of the car, taking refuse on the ground behind the vehicle. Thelma called 911 and reported that they were being shot at and where they were. Two more shots were fired in their direction. They appeared to be coming from the vacant car lot.

"Who is firing at us?" June stuttered.

"I wonder if this was all a set-up. Maybe somebody wanted us to do the work, and then they would take whatever we found," Thelma stated.

"Do you really think so?" Dylan asked as more shots rang out.

"Yes, I am still here, and they are still firing at us," Thelma said into her cell phone.

"She sounded so sincere on the phone," Dylan claimed.

Two more shots rang out as several branches behind them snapped and fell to the ground. They covered their heads and flattened themselves on the ground as the shots were coming closer. It hit Thelma that what they found was lying on the seat of the car. She pulled herself along on the ground toward the open back door.

"Thelma! Are you nuts? What are you doing?" June asked.

Thelma pulled herself up on the floor of the back seat as two more shots rang out. Stopping where she was and tucking her head behind the hump on the floor, she waited for them to stop firing. When they did, she quickly grabbed the items that had been found and retreated to the safety of the ground. She tucked them in her purse that was lying next to her.

They could hear voices coming from the direction of where the shots had been coming from. Several minutes of silence made June extremely nervous.

"We can't see anything," June whispered, her hands shaking. "Thelma what if they are coming up behind us in the woods?"

"Just stay put, but keep your eyes open," her friend advised.

"THELMA! Thelma Frost! It's Sheriff Morse. Where are you?" a familiar voice yelled.

"Over here behind the car," she answered, sitting up.

"How do you know it's really the sheriff?" Dylan asked, not moving.

"It's him. I know his voice," she replied. "You can get up off the ground now, Dylan."

"Thelma, June, are you okay?" Morse asked as he came around the corner of the car.

"We're fine. Did you get who was shooting at us?"

"Speak for yourself," June answered, still shaking.

"It was Carl Zender. He thought you were trying to steal his car."

"Why does he even have a gun in his possession with his mind going the way it is," June asked, brushing off her clothes.

"According to Carl, he's had the double-barreled shotgun for years, but he won't have it any longer. I confiscated it. I'm going to call his sons to see if he owns any more guns that are hidden around the dealership or at home. Up until now, he has been alone on the property, living in his own little world, never bothering anyone."

"What if it had been kids playing in the woods? June insisted. "They just built those new residential apartments a short distance down the road."

"I know, but Carl won't be here too much longer. The bank sold the property to a developer who is going to build another senior apartment complex on the site."

"Can't say that it's not needed," June replied.

"Who are you?" Morse asked, looking at the reporter.

"Your real name," Thelma advised.

"Real name?" Morse inquired, giving Thelma a funny look.

"Dylan Peterson. I'm a reporter for the *Portland Times,*" flipping out his credentials for the sheriff to see.

"Now for the million-dollar question. What are you doing out here, Thelma?" Morse asked.

"This is the rental car from the kidnapping," she started.

"I know," he replied. "And?"

"My paper received a tip that something was hidden in the car. June overheard me talking to Jake Zender, and we all ended up out here to find what was left behind in the car," Dylan answered.

"Did you find anything?"

"Not yet," Thelma piped up quickly before anyone else could offer an answer. "We were interrupted by the shooting."

"If you do make sure you let me know," he admonished the group. "I have to go. I left Carl locked up in the back of the cruiser, and he was none too happy."

"Why did you lie to someone that you trust?" Dylan asked when the sheriff was out of earshot.

"Because I haven't even had a chance to look at what we found, and I know he would have taken it with him as evidence. After we look it over, I will turn it in to him, stating that we found it after he left," Thelma said, reaching for her purse. "Don't you want to see what she hid?"

"Sure, I do, but why are you in charge of what happens to it? It was my tip, to begin with," Dylan questioned.

"You are both forgetting that I discovered it," June claimed. "Let's just quit this stupid bickering and take a look at what I found."

Thelma pulled the items out of her purse. Three, black and white pictures, were the same type that Agatha had entrusted

Thelma with. The first one was another shot of the face in the bushes. The second one featured the man that was running away with the blanket, except this time, his face was a full-frontal shot. The third was a wide shot of the park. They took turns passing them around.

"This is almost identical to the picture I had. It is a shot of Wayne Spikeman hiding in the bushes. Sheriff Morse and I think he might have been a lookout for the kidnappers," Thelma stated.

"You have a picture?" June asked.

"Agatha sent me two pictures that had been sent to her to use in finding Amelia. She asked me to guard them and not tell anyone that I had them. I guess she figured that all we did was fight when we were in public, and no one would ever suspect that she sent them to me for safe-keeping."

"Where are the pictures now?" Dylan inquired.

"Sheriff Morse has them locked away somewhere. These pictures are much better than the ones I have or had," she said. "In this one, we can see his full face. In the one I have, you can only see his face from the side. I don't understand the third picture at all. I'll have to go over it with a magnifying glass."

"So, the same woman must have taken all these shots, "June stated. "I wonder why she hid some and mailed the others."

"She said she was afraid for her life. Maybe she hoped that if something did happen to her, the pictures would surface, and the kidnappers and her killers, which would be one and the same, would be found and held accountable," Dylan suggested. "What's wrapped in the plastic?"

Thelma carefully peeled back the piece of tape that held the package together. She unrolled the plastic, and a single key fell out. The number one-two-six was etched into one side of the key.

"It looks like a key for a safety deposit box," Dylan commented. "But there is no bank name on it."

"Let's all go back to my apartment and check out these pictures more closely," Thelma suggested. "I'll make us some lunch, and if you're nice to me, Mr. Dylan Peterson, I might even let you look through Agatha's files. Maybe I should call Kami to join us as she might have something to add due to her and Betsy's research."

"I'm shocked she hasn't called you yet to let you know how last night went," June said as they walked back to the car.

"Is this Kami the one who owns the paper?" Dylan asked.

"Yes, she and Betsy Lee inherited it from Agatha."

"The *Sechuette Gazette* has a good reputation. The articles are precise and always based on facts. Except for that social column that Agatha Tram wrote. My editor and I always had a good chuckle when we read that," Dylan smiled. "You could tell who was not in her good graces that week."

"That is the first change Kami and Betsy are making at the paper. Agatha's social agenda is going to disappear forever," Thelma laughed, taking out her cell phone. "I think I'll give her a call right now."

"She might still be sleeping if they got in late," June stated. "She doesn't get many days off anymore."

"Hmm, it went straight to messages. She never turns her phone off because of the paper," Thelma said. "I think I'm going to stop at her house and check on her on the way home. We have to go right by it anyway."

"Is it okay if I tag along? I'd like to meet the owner of the paper," Dylan admitted.

The two cars pulled up in front of Kami's house. When they got out of their vehicles, they could hear the dogs barking in the back yard.

"She must be up, the dogs are out," Thelma stated. "Let's go see them."

The gate was closed, and the back slider was wide open. The dogs were running in and out of the house in a frenzy.

"Kami, are you in the kitchen?" Thelma yelled loudly.

No answer.

"Something's wrong. She wouldn't let the dogs outside on their own without being close by because of the red-tailed hawks in the area. Come on," she said, going through the gate.

Wags and Wiggles met the trio at the slider. They continued to bark and could not be comforted. Thelma closed the slider to keep the dogs inside.

"Where's Kami?" she asked the dogs.

They ran to the cellar door, scratching and whining.

"Hold the dogs," Dylan suggested. "I'll go down and check for your niece."

He disappeared down the stairs. All was quiet for a few seconds, and then a loud crash could be heard coming from the far end of the cellar.

"Dylan! What's happening?" Thelma yelled.

A few minutes later, Dylan ran up the stairs, blood dripping from the side of his head.

"He ran out the bulkhead with Kami over his shoulder," he yelled as he opened the slider and was gone.

"June call 911," Thelma ordered and ran out the door in the same direction as Dylan.

She could hear Dylan yelling for someone to stop and ran in the direction of his voice. From a distance, she saw him tackle the man who had Kami hoisted over his shoulder. They both hit the ground, but the kidnapper quickly recovered and responded by kicking the reporter square in the face. Stunned by the kick, Dylan fell backward and landed to the ground next to Kami. He wrapped his arm around her to protect her from being taken again.

"Kami! Dylan!" Thelma yelled, hoping to scare the intruder away.

The masked person ran up the path, and they could hear a car drive off on the other side of the tree line. When Thelma reached them, Dylan had managed to sit up but was covered in blood that was pouring out of his nose. Kami was still unconscious.

"Are you okay, Dylan?" Thelma asked, checking out his nose. "I think it's broken."

"You think? Just give me a minute to recoup, and I'll carry your niece back to the house," he said, laying back down in the grass.

"Just rest. The sheriff should be here shortly, and he can carry her back," Thelma stated. "You know you saved Kami. If you hadn't gone down cellar and seen them leaving, he would have gotten away with taking my niece."

"All in a day's work in the life of a reporter," he joked.

"I'm serious. You saved my Kami. She is my whole world, and I will be forever thankful for what you did today," Thelma said.

"You're welcome," he said sincerely, patting the back of her hand.

Sheriff Morse and two deputies ran up the path calling out Thelma's name. He stopped short when he saw the two bodies on the ground covered in blood.

"Are they...?"

"NO, they are not. Kami is unconscious. The blood on her is from Dylan. He threw his arm over her to protect her so the intruder couldn't pick her up and take off with her again. Dylan's nose is broken, and he received a nasty blow to the side of his head," Thelma replied. "They both need to go to the hospital to be checked out."

"Dylan, can you walk back to the house?" Morse asked, and Dylan nodded yes. "Elder! Pick up Kami and head back to the house. I'll steady our young hero here as he walks."

The ambulance was waiting at the house when they arrived. Kami was still out. They checked her vitals, and they were stable, so they strapped her to a gurney and loaded her into the ambulance.

"Elder!" Morse yelled.

Both deputies answered.

"Carleton. Accompany Kami in the ambulance to the hospital and stay with her. I want a twenty-four-hour guard on her room," the sheriff ordered. "I'll drive Mr. Peterson to the hospital after I ask him a few questions."

"Cameron. Go back out to the tree line and see if you can find any tire tracks. Bring the plaster kit in case you do."

Dylan sat on the couch with an ice pack on both his head and his nose. The dogs jumped up next to him as they could smell their owner on his clothes. He spoke to them in a quiet voice, and they settled down lying next to his leg. He closed his eyes as the sheriff started to question him.

"Did you recognize anything about him?"

"No, but I'm not from around here, so that doesn't mean too much."

"What happened down in the cellar?"

"I walked down the stairs and could smell the faint odor of chloroform. There was a body on the floor near the bulkhead door, but before I could reach it, I got cracked over the head with a lamp. It stunned me momentarily. The guy in the black ski mask leaned over me and growled that nobody was going to get his money."

"What money?" Morse asked.

"I don't know, that's all he said. He opened the bulkhead, picked up the body, and took off. It took me a second to regain my composure, and then I ran up the stairs to tell Thelma what had happened."

"Dylan ran out the slider, and I followed close behind," Thelma added. "He tackled the guy but got kicked in the face. As I said, Dylan threw his arm around Kami to protect her from being taken a second time. By that time, I was only thirty feet away, and the guy decided to run."

"Can you describe him at all?"

"He was about my height, slim and athletic. His voice sounded like a regular guy voice. Other than that, I can't help anymore," Dylan said.

The deputy returned to report that a park was on the other side of the trees, and there were far too many tire tracks to isolate just one set.

"Let's get you to the hospital, Mr. Peterson," the sheriff said. "Elder, go down in the cellar and see if you can find anything that was left behind that might have fingerprints on it."

"I'll take my car," Dylan insisted.

"You'll do no such thing. The sheriff will drive you to the hospital, and I will pull your car into the driveway here. I'll bring you back later to pick it up," Thelma stated. "I have to bring Kami home to get some clothes and pick up the dogs. She will be staying at my apartment from here on out."

"I'll pull my car in, thanks."

"Lock up when you're done, Cameron. I don't want anything more to upset the dogs," Thelma requested.

"Sheriff, do you think that the intruder will return?" June asked.

"No. He screwed up, and there is too much of a police presence. He wouldn't dare to," the sheriff replied.

"If you are sure he won't come back, I will stay here with the dogs until you come back from the hospital," June offered.

"Are you sure, June? It may take several hours before we return," Thelma replied.

"I'll stay, but I would really like to go to bingo tonight," June admitted hesitantly.

"When I find out about Kami's condition, I will call you. If they release her, I will get her set up in my apartment, and we can go," Thelma promised, knowing it was June's birthday but playing dumb to the fact.

Okay. Kami is more important than my silly old birthday," June sighed.

Thelma followed Dylan out through the slider, pretending that she didn't hear what June had said. The sheriff looked shocked at Thelma's snub of her best friend.

"Happy Birthday, June," he said, hugging her. "I think Thelma is worried about Kami and not hearing much else right now. She'll come around."

"At my age, I shouldn't make a fuss about my birthday, but they give you free cards at bingo if you are registered in the birthday book," June replied. "I know, stupid, right?"

"Not in the least. Everyone should celebrate their birthday no matter what their age," he answered with a smile.

Thelma was at the top of the driveway, watching Dylan pull his car in. The sheriff walked up next to her and cleared his throat.

"What?" she asked, looking at him.

"You do know that today is your best friend's birthday, don't you?"

"Of course, I do. I'm playing stupid because I have a surprise party already planned for her at bingo tonight."

"I should have known better. She thinks you forgot about what day it is."

"I purposely didn't say Happy Birthday to her this morning to make her think I forgot. It's all part of the plan," Thelma said, smiling. "You're welcome to join us at five-fifteen before bingo gets underway."

"I'll still be at work, but thanks anyway," he acknowledged. "Are you ready to go, Mr. Peterson?"

"Please, call me Dylan. Yes, I think I'm all set," he said, alarming his car.

"I'll follow you," Thelma stated, heading for her car.

Once at the hospital, Thelma went to find the cubicle where Kami was assigned. Deputy Elder was sitting outside the curtain, playing a game on his phone. He stood up as Thelma approached.

"She came to a little while ago and has been waiting for you to get here. Her dad is in there with her right now," he informed Thelma.

"Thank you for staying with her, Carlton."

"My pleasure, Ms. Frost," he said, sitting down again at his post.

"Hello! Can I come in?" Thelma asked, peeking around the curtain.

"Come on in, sis," her brother said.

"Hi, Aunt Thelma," Kami whispered. "Are the dogs okay?"

"That's my daughter. More concerned with the animals than herself." Her dad frowned.

"Wags and Wiggles are fine. June is staying with them as we speak," her aunt assured her. "How are you feeling?"

"I'm okay. I got a wicked headache, and I'm bruised and sore, but other than that, okay."

"What happened to my daughter, Thelma? Why would someone want to kidnap her? Does it have something to do with the paper?"

"We're not sure yet, Allan. The sheriff is looking into it."

"She can't stay at the house by herself anymore until this person is caught."

"No, Kami and the dogs are going to stay at my apartment for now," Thelma informed her worried brother.

"I can't give in to this person. I will be staying at my own house, but thank you anyway, Aunt Thelma," Kami stated.

"I don't think that is such a good idea, sweetheart," her dad replied. "What if he comes back?"

"I'll cross that bridge when I come to it. Maybe I can get someone to stay with me. The dogs have been through so much, and they are just getting used to their new house. I don't want to uproot them again. Besides, I don't know how well Zumbutt would like two dogs in his space," Kami commented.

"I have an idea. There is a young man that stepped up and saved you at the house today. He's in the hospital right now getting treatment. He is a reporter from the *Portland Times,* and his name is Dylan Peterson," Thelma said.

"I've heard of him. He's an investigative reporter, and some of his stories that I have read have been quite good. Why is he here in Sechuette?" Kami asked.

"He is following up on a tip his paper received regarding the Amelia Bohannon kidnapping."

"And you said that this young man saved my daughter?" Allan asked.

"He did. He took a crack on the head and a kick to the face to protect Kami," Thelma stated. "So, I was thinking..."

"Thinking what?" Kami asked.

"Maybe we could show him our thanks by offering him a room at your house instead of the local bed and breakfast where he is currently staying. Maybe you could work together on the story and share the by-line if we solve the whereabouts of Amelia Bohannon. It would be a second person in the house," Thelma suggested. "And he's already proved how brave he is."

"Number one, you don't even know if he would want to stay at the house after what he went through today. Number two, I just started dating Hanson, and I'm not sure he would like it if a strange man was spending nights at my house," Kami protested.

"Even if it was someone there to protect you?" her dad asked.

"It was just a thought," Thelma mumbled.

"I guess you will be staying at either my house or your aunt's house then," her dad stated. "Can I suggest that you have the same company that alarmed the paper come and do your house, too?"

"Hello," the emergency room doctor said as he pushed back the curtain around the cubicle. "Kami Frost?"

"I am Kami," she answered.

"I am Doctor Kane. After reviewing your head x-rays, there are no fractures. I do feel, however, that you may have sustained a concussion from your head slamming into the ground. You also have a hairline fracture of your right wrist."

"That must have happened when I punched the guy and tried to rip off his ski mask," Kami concluded. "Right before he pushed that white thing over my face."

"A girl after my own heart," Thelma chuckled.

Allan threw a dirty look his sister's way, and the doctor continued.

"We need to set your wrist. I will release you if someone stays with you tonight. If not, I must insist that you stay here overnight where the nurses can watch you."

"I think if there is a chance you have a concussion, you should spend the night here," her dad insisted. "Tomorrow, we can make arrangements for someone to stay with you."

"I have work tomorrow," Kami replied.

"It wouldn't hurt for you to take an extra day off and take it easy at home," the doctor advised.

"I will tell Betsy at bingo tonight that you won't be at work on Monday," her aunt offered.

"June's birthday party is tonight," Kami protested.

"You wouldn't be going to bingo even if you were at home," her dad said. "Get her a room, doc. She'll be staying here tonight."

"Fine. I'll go make the arrangements."

"I'm not happy about this," Kami complained.

"Happy about what?" Sheriff Morse asked, walking up to the open curtain accompanied by Dylan Peterson.

"Kami is staying here tonight," her dad answered.

"I will arrange for a deputy to be outside your door while you are here," he replied.

"I really don't think that's necessary," Kami replied. "This is a public place, after all."

"Public or not, people have been known to disappear from hospitals, so, yes, it is necessary," the sheriff stated.

"How's your nose, Dylan?" Thelma asked.

"It's broken in two places. They snapped it back in place, and that hurt more than getting kicked in the first place," he complained. "Head's fine, though. My dad always said you couldn't hurt a rock."

"Are you Dylan Peterson?" Kami asked.

"Yes, I am. It's nice to talk to you finally," he answered with a big smile.

"Thelma here tells me that you saved my daughter from the kidnapper. Thank you so much," Allan said, extending his hand.

"Right place, right time. Nothing more," he replied.

"There were no fingerprints on the can of ether or the lamp," Sheriff Morse told Thelma.

"He had on black gloves," Kami offered. "I saw them when he held the white cloth over my face."

"How did he get in the house?" Sheriff Morse asked.

"I was outside with the dogs, and the hawk flew over. I reached through the open slider to get the small bat off the counter that I keep just inside the door, and I got tackled from behind. The person sat on my back while putting a rag over my face. The last thing I remember is the dogs barking like crazy," Kami answered.

"He must have heard me calling from the backyard and brought Kami down cellar to hide, but the dogs gave him away by scratching at the door," Thelma said.

"And I really ruined his plans when I went down to check out why the dogs were going nuts," Dylan added. "He had no choice but to clobber me one and then escape through the bulkhead."

"Did you recognize anything about your attacker, Kami?"

"It all happened so fast. He didn't say anything, and he hit me from behind, so I never saw him," Kami admitted.

"Coward," her father mumbled.

"I agree, Allan," the sheriff replied. "Once they assign Kami a room, there will be someone sitting outside it guarding her throughout the night. This creep isn't going to get a second chance."

"Now that I know my niece will be protected, I have to run. I need to drop off the cake at the hall and decorate our table before I go pick up June from Kami's house. Oh, crap. I just thought about something. Who's going to stay with the dogs tonight with Kami here in the hospital?" Thelma asked.

"See, Dad, I need to go home," Kami insisted.

"I'll stay with the dogs for the night. We get along really well," Dylan offered.

"What a great idea! The dogs snuggled on the couch with Dylan while the sheriff questioned him and was quite content," Thelma agreed.

"I don't know..." Kami hesitated.

"The man spilled his blood for you. You don't think you can trust him with your dogs?" Thelma said. "Really?"

"I guess it wouldn't hurt for one night," Kami relented. "But I'll be home tomorrow morning."

"Come on, Dylan. I'll drive you back to the house after we make a stop at the bingo hall," Thelma offered. "Kami, I'll pick you up. Give me a call when they are going to release you."

"Maybe we can discuss the Bohannon case when you feel up to it," Dylan suggested, smiling at Kami. "I'll take good care of the dogs, I promise."

"Don't let them outside after dusk and never by themselves," Kami lectured. "And the refrigerator is full. Help yourself."

"I know. Coyotes and red-tailed hawks," Dylan replied as they exited the cubicle. "Don't worry."

"I love the nose bandage," Thelma joked as they walked to her car.

"I think it makes me just that much more handsome being a hero and all." Dylan chuckled, puffing out his chest. "I wish I had looked a little better when I met your niece, though."

"You look like a hero in my book, and I'm sure in hers, too," Thelma replied.

They pulled into the All Sliced Up cake shop to pick up June's cake. Thelma had ordered it weeks ago as a special surprise for her best friend. The full sheet cake, chocolate cake, frosted with vanilla buttercream was covered with bingo cards and fake fifty-dollar bills. In the center was an exact duplicate of June's new bingo bag made of cake and surrounded by new mini daubers.

"That is one awesome cake," Dylan exclaimed as he slid the box into the back of Thelma's SUV.

"I think she'll like it. Now, let's get to the bingo hall and then run by the bed and breakfast and pick up what you'll need for the night."

One of the volunteers let them through the back door of the kitchen. Thelma spread a birthday tablecloth over half of their lucky table, and Dylan placed the cake near where June would be sitting. A tiara was placed at June's seat and her gift's next to the cake.

"Look's good to me," Thelma said. "People will be bringing other gifts to add to the pile. Let's get your stuff and pick up the birthday girl. Remember, not a word. She thinks that I have forgotten her birthday."

"I won't breathe a word. I am looking forward to staying in a house and having room to move around," Dylan admitted.

"Maybe I can talk you into staying there until the guy is caught," Thelma suggested. "I know you got whacked, and I wouldn't blame you if you said no, but Kami does need someone to stay with her and protect her when she's home at night."

"I think that should be Kami's decision, but if she wants me to, I will," Dylan replied. "That would give us some extra time to work on the kidnapping case together."

"When I pick up my niece from the hospital tomorrow, I will bring you a copy of Agatha's files. Then you can look over them together," Thelma added, sweetening the pot a little. "Here we are. Remember, not a word."

The dogs ran to the slider barking. June was right behind them to unlock the door and let them in. Dylan threw his overnight bag on the kitchen table and patted each of the dogs.

"We're going to be roomies tonight," he told them, smiling.

"Are you planning on going anywhere tonight, Dylan?" Thelma inquired. "I'll leave you my key if you are."

"No, but thanks anyway. Kami said I could help myself to food, and it will be nice to cook something instead of eating fast food."

"You cook?" June asked.

"I was an executive chef before I quit the long, stressful hours to become a reporter," he replied. "One of my sous chefs was murdered when I was working in New York City. I helped to find his killer, and the investigating bug bit me. I quit my job and moved to Portland, where I was hired at the *Portland Times*."

"Wow! Impressive," June stated.

"Not really. My nerves were shot working as an executive chef. This job I have now allows me to work at my own pace and use my brainpower for something other than if a plate of food looks appealing enough to be sold at outrageous prices."

"That's why I don't eat out much," Thelma agreed. "Too expensive."

"Not to be pushy, but we really need to get going if we are going to get our lucky seats," June stated. "I forgot. Hanson stopped by to take Kami out for dinner and was terribly upset to learn what happened. He said he was heading to the hospital when he left here."

"Who is this Hanson guy?" Dylan asked.

"Hanson Beckworth. He is or was Agatha Tram's attorney. He took Kami out on their first date to the Lincoln Room in Portland last night."

"Wow! The Lincoln Room! He is either super rich or has connections," Dylan stated.

"He's an attorney and has his own firm in Portland," June replied.

"Beckworth. I think I have heard of his firm," Dylan muttered. "The paper was looking into several of their cases some years ago."

"Something bad?"

"No, just background research," Dylan replied quickly.

"Whew. Glad to hear that. Have fun with the dogs and enjoy the kitchen privileges," Thelma said, heading for the slider. "We'll see you tomorrow."

The parking lot was just beginning to fill up at the community center. From here on out, things would start to slow down in the town as it was getting closer to Labor Day when all the families would be returning home to get ready for the beginning of school.

Thelma walked in the door ahead of her friend. Sheriff Morse's wife was standing near the inner door and signaled to Thelma that everything was good to go. Thelma walked into the hall and stepped aside for June to go ahead of her. A dozen or so of her bingo buddies yelled surprise as June cleared the door.

"You didn't forget," June said, hugging her friend. "You're the best."

"Go open your presents. I ran a little later than I expected getting you here. We can cut your cake at intermission." Thelma smiled. "Now, you will understand why we didn't have to go home to get your bingo bag."

At the table, June was opening one present after another. She was laughing at the joke gifts and admiring the nicer ones. Paul, one of the volunteers, handed her a packet of free cards to play for her birthday. Thelma watched from across the room, enjoying her friend's happiness.

"I think she was surprised," Amy Spikeman said, in passing.

"I think so, too," Thelma agreed. "Amy, do you have a second?"

"Sure, what's up?"

"You told Kami that you were adopted, right?"

"Yes, I was. My biological mom gave me up at birth. Uncle Wayne gave his sister, my mother, enough money to pay the adoption fees," she replied.

"I was wondering if you know who your biological mother is or what agency you were adopted through at the time," Thelma inquired.

"It was a closed adoption, but I do know that it was an attorney in Portland who handled it. By law, once I turned eighteen, I could ask to open the records, but I have no interest in the information contained in them."

"Not even with your adoptive mother gone now?"

"No. She raised me as best she could as a single mom, and that's all I need to know," Amy stated. "She is my mom, and no one else."

"How old are you?" Thelma asked.

"Kami told me that you were helping to find Amelia Bohannon. I am a year older than Amelia and have already been questioned quite extensively by the sheriff, and so was my mother way back when it happened. I am not her," Amy stated. "I was adopted months before Amelia disappeared."

"Thank you for talking to me," Thelma said, smiling.

"Did you really think that she could be Amelia?" Ellie Morse asked as Amy walked away.

"I wasn't sure, but I can definitely cross her off my list now," Thelma replied. "I still need to buy my cards. I'm going to go see some of June's gifts and then get in line before it gets too long."

"Good luck tonight," Ellie said, going to get in line.

"You, too," Thelma answered, heading toward the party table.

"I love my new bingo bag!" June exclaimed as her friend drew near. "And all the little doodads that filled it."

"I am so glad you like it. Now, you can throw that other thing away." Thelma smiled. "I'll look at your gifts at intermission. Unlike some people who received free cards tonight, I have to go stand in line."

"Eat your heart out." June laughed, holding up her free card packet.

"We set up a table for your cake near the coffee area. I'll have Paul come move it so I can sit in my lucky seat when I get back," Thelma said, grabbing her wallet from her purse.

Wendy Small and Mandy Benson joined Thelma in line. Since the first night that they introduced themselves, they had been sitting at the table with the group and had become friends.

"How are Tucker and Tommy doing?" Thelma asked.

"They are so happy to be at home again," Mandy said, smiling.

"Sometimes they disappear, and we can't find them. I don't know where they go to, but they always show up in time for supper."

"The first few days they meowed constantly. I think they were looking for Mrs. Greystone," Wendy stated. "Now they have accepted us and snuggle in our laps. They are the best cats ever."

"You will never know how grateful I am that you took them in. No one ever wants to adopt older cats. They all want kittens. How's your new business going?"

"We only opened a week ago. We missed most of the summer business, but we have several large orders from schools and local sports teams, and that is helping us to get our name out there," Mandy answered.

"I'm glad things are picking up. It's always good to have new businesses open in town," Thelma replied, turning around as she was next to pay the cashier. "Make sure you have some of June's cake at intermission."

Thelma noticed that the woman from the pier was several people ahead of her in line. She finished paying for her cards and was returning to the same table in the back corner where she had been sitting before.

She seems so lonely. I think I will invite her to sit with us.

"I'll be right back," Thelma told June, throwing her cards on the table.

"Hello. Do you remember me?" Thelma asked the woman as she approached her.

"I do," she answered, smiling.

"We were wondering if you would like to sit with us. It's June's birthday, and we are going to have cake at intermission, and you are welcome to join us," Thelma offered. "You don't have to sit by yourself."

"Oh, I don't think so, but thank you anyway," she replied.

"I can't believe you are still here. You must be really enjoying your stay here in our little town," Thelma smiled.

"I love it here. The outer harbor is so 'picture perfect' and peaceful.

I love the small motels right on the water," she answered, staring directly at Thelma. "The people are so nice, too."

"My name is Thelma Frost. And you are?"

"Shirley Potts."

"Are you sure you wouldn't like to sit with us?"

"Maybe, I will. It would be nice to have someone to talk to for a change." She smiled.

"Great! I will go clear the space across from me, and you can sit there," Thelma said.

Thelma went back to her table and cleared a spot for their new friend. A loud commotion broke out at the back of the hall. Thelma looked up and saw Shirley's husband from the pier trying to drag her out of the hallway, and it was quite clear that she did not want to go.

14

"Hey! Get your hands off her," Thelma yelled out, running across the hall.

Shirley Potts was doing her best to break free of his grasp, but he held on tight, continuing to drag her closer to the exit door.

"Let me go," she pleaded with him. "I just want to play bingo."

"I said you're leaving!" he demanded of her.

"I don't want to leave," she begged, still trying to release herself.

Thelma stepped right in between the couple and the door. Paul stood next to her, and together they blocked the exit.

"Get out of my way! NOW!" he ordered.

"Ellie, call your husband," Paul requested.

"Ellie's husband is the sheriff. We'll let him decide if you can continue to treat your wife like you are and drag her out of here," Thelma threatened him.

"You'll pay for your interference." He snarled at Thelma.

"Is that a threat?" Thelma challenged, stepping closer to him and showing no fear.

"Play your stupid bingo," he said, glaring at his wife and releasing the hold he had on her wrist. "You'll pay for your defiance later."

He stormed out of the hall, and Shirley broke down in tears. Thelma guided her to their table and had her sit down so she could compose herself. June offered to go collect Shirley's belongings from the table where they were left before the commotion broke out.

"I'll get you a cup of tea," Thelma offered.

"That would be nice." Shirley sighed.

"Here you go," Thelma said, setting the cup in front of her new friend. "Are you going to be okay?"

"Someday, I guess I will be. I should never have married him twenty-six years ago." Shirley sobbed. "I don't know how much more of his abuse I can take."

"You have been living like this for that many years?" June asked, setting down the collected items. "Why didn't you leave him?"

"I guess I'm afraid of what he will do if I try to," she replied. "Besides, I have no money and no way to support myself."

"There are all kinds of help out there for women in your situation," June advised. "Thelma here was in almost the same situation when she left her husband and look how she turned out. Strong, feisty, and independent."

"If I could do it, anyone can," Thelma said, smiling and taking hold of Shirley's hand.

"He'll be waiting at the door when halftime rolls around. He won't let me stay any longer than that," Shirley stated.

"Why?"

"I can't... Just suffice it to say he doesn't want me to make any friends," she replied. "After tonight, I won't be able to go to bingo anymore, either."

Sheriff Morse walked up to the table, and fear took over Shirley. She started shaking and crying all over again.

"Drink your tea," Thelma told her. "I'll be right back."

"Ellie called me and told me what happened. What do you want me to do?" Morse asked.

"I need your cruiser parked outside the front door at the start of intermission and you to be standing at the front door. Her husband will be back to get her, and I am terrified for her. She defied him, and things will not go well for her."

"Kind of hits home, huh?" the sheriff asked.

"Yes, and I am hoping that I can talk her into spending the night at my house until he cools down a bit," Thelma replied.

"Are you sure you want to get involved?"

"I have to. I see myself in her and can't stand idly by. And, she said something to me earlier, and I need to know what she meant," Thelma added.

"What did she say?" Morse inquired.

"Shirley used the term picture-perfect in describing the harbor. It wasn't her use of the words; it was how she said it to me. She stared right at me and enunciated the two words," Thelma said. "I think she was trying to hint to me that she is the one who sent the pictures."

"Why don't you just ask her straight out?"

"Because she is afraid, petrified, and probably would not admit to it here at bingo," Thelma answered. "That's why I would like to get her away from her husband for the night. She might feel empowered enough to confide in me if she was safely tucked away at my apartment."

"Just be careful, Thelma. I will be here at intermission as you requested, but I think I will have Deputy Elder stick around for the whole evening. I'll return as back-up. We can also escort you home at the end of the night if Shirley decides to go home with you," the sheriff confirmed. "You better go. They are going to start."

"Darn. I don't have my early birds marked," she said, running off.

"You're all set," June said as Thelma plunked down in her chair. "Shirley and I marked your cards and put them in the right order."

"Thank you very much, nice ladies," Thelma replied, picking up her green dauber. "Now, let's play bingo and win!"

The first couple of games passed, and Shirley hadn't said a word. June won the double bingo in the early-bird game and attributed it to her birthday luck. She passed the cash around the table for everyone to touch for good luck, and it worked. Shirley won the first regular game and smiled for the first time since she had sat down with them.

"It is so nice to see you smile," Thelma said, taking Shirley's winnings and rubbing herself all over with the cash. "I sure hope this helps me win."

"You win more than anyone I know," June teased her friend. "You don't need any more help at winning bingo. Now me, on the other hand..."

"You have a new bingo bag, new daubers, and a new lucky elephant with his trunk up. How much more help do you need to win?" Thelma laughed.

Shirley chuckled at the banter between the two friends. She looked up and saw the deputy standing guard near the door, and her somber mood returned. Most of the first half was gone, and it was almost intermission. Thelma decided to speak up and make the offer of sanctuary at her apartment to Shirley.

"I know you are worried about what will happen later when your husband returns to pick you up. If you are serious about trying to break away from your situation, I am offering you the safety of my apartment tonight. The sheriff will escort us home and see us in," Thelma offered. "My apartment at the Falling Leaves Complex is a secured building, and your husband would not be able to get to you once we are inside."

"I can't do that. It would be worse than ever when he finally does get his hands on me if I defy him any more than I have already," Shirley answered. "I just want you both to know that you have given me one of the most enjoyable nights of my life, and I thank you for that."

"It doesn't have to be for only one night. Just keep that in the back of your mind. We have a great town full of good people who would step up and help you in any way that they can," June added.

"I'm not so sure about that, but I do thank you, and I do know what is best for everyone," Shirley commented. "It's not just me who would be in danger."

"I'm not afraid of your husband if that's what bothering you,'" Thelma advised.

"You have no idea how mean he can get. I don't want you to be on the receiving end of his horrible temper," Shirley replied.

The caller declared it was intermission. Voices at the front door caught everyone's attention. The sheriff and deputy were restraining Shirley's husband from entering the bingo hall, and he was not a happy person.

"I have to go," Shirley said, collecting her things.

"I really wish you wouldn't," Thelma insisted.

"I know, and I appreciate your concern, but this is best," she replied.

"You sent the pictures," Thelma bluntly stated as Shirley stood up to leave.

"I did, and thank you for such a fun night," she announced loud enough for her husband to hear. "Happy Birthday, June."

"Get out of the way," Shirley's husband ordered the sheriff.

"It's okay," Shirley said to them, and they stepped aside to let her leave.

"Let's go," he ordered as he grabbed Shirley by the back of the neck and herded her to the car.

"Are we just going to let them go? Look at the way he's treating her!" Deputy Elder asked, furious as to what he was witnessing.

"I'm afraid there is nothing we can do if she goes with him willingly," the sheriff replied.

The sheriff looked at Thelma, and she shrugged her shoulders. She had done all she could to prevent what she knew was going to happen due to her own experiences in the past. It was now time to return her attention to her best friend and her birthday celebration.

All the bingo players sang to June as she cut her cake and passed it out to anyone who wanted some. Thelma grabbed some ice cream and coffee for both her and June and returned to the table, waiting for her friend to return.

"I need to go to the bathroom and wash my hands. I'll be right back," June said, hurrying by the table to get back before the second half started.

"I'm going to be leaving now," the sheriff said. "I'm also going to pull the deputy seen as Shirley is gone. If you need anything later, call me. You have my cell number, and I am on the overnight tonight."

"She sent the pictures," Thelma stated.

"And you didn't tell me so I could stop her at the door," he said, angrily.

"If you had stopped her at the door and questioned her, you would be finding a dead body in the morning. He would have killed her for what she did."

"How are we going to question her? We don't even know where she is staying."

"I have an idea. She told me how nice the outer harbor was and how she enjoyed the small motels right on the water. I have a feeling she was trying to tell me that's where they are staying," Thelma commented. "I may have to take a walk tomorrow morning to see if I can find her."

"I can send an undercover car to cruise the harbor road, and maybe we can spot her that way. I just hope she makes it through the night. He was a mean one. He had no fear of the law what-so-ever," Morse replied. "If we find her, I may take her into protective custody for her own good."

"With all the danger she was in herself, she was still looking out for everyone else," June said, returning from the bathroom. "She was afraid for Thelma and went willingly with that monster to protect her. To me, it sounded like she's given up on her own life."

"We need to find her. If she gets in touch with you again, don't take it upon yourself to question her. She is a suspect in a kidnapping and needs to be brought in," Sheriff Morse said. "Did you hear me, Thelma?"

"I heard you. If she did participate, I don't think she did it willingly."

"It doesn't matter. She still needs to be brought in because she might be able to lead us to Amelia. Happy Birthday, June."

"Thank you, Sheriff," she said, taping her strips together.

Two hours later, Thelma and June arrived at home. They were standing outside the car, gathering June's birthday presents together to take inside when a faint voice called out to them. June jumped, and Thelma stood up, looking around for where the voice had come from. A figure stood up behind the big Rhododendron bush at the front of Thelma's car.

"Help me."

"It's Shirley," June stated.

The two women ran to their new friend. They sat her down in the grass and realized she was hurt, really hurt.

"June call 911. I'll call the sheriff," Thelma said.

"Yes, she's conscious," June said into her phone. "Hurry, please."

"Sheriff Morse, Thelma here. You need to come to my apartment as fast as you can," she said, brushing the hair off Shirley's face. "It's Shirley, and she's not in good shape. We are out in the parking lot, and I am afraid her husband may have followed her and could be near us."

"The ambulance is on its way," June announced, remaining on the phone with the dispatcher.

"So is the sheriff," Thelma replied. "You stay here with Shirley. I'm going to look around and make sure her husband isn't anywhere in the area. First, I need to get my bat out of the car."

Jimmy spotted Thelma walking through the parking lot, holding the bat from the reception desk. He locked the door behind him and joined Thelma in her search. The sheriff arrived, lights flashing with two other cruisers. The ambulance pulled in right behind him.

"Elder! West! Check the perimeter for any activity," the sheriff ordered.

June stepped back so the paramedics could take over. They took Shirley's vitals and hooked her up to several machines. The sheriff approached them and asked them for a status update.

"She's stable for transport, but I think she may have broken ribs and she's in shock. We have to get her to the hospital as soon as possible," the paramedic stated. "Do you know who she is?"

The sheriff looked to Thelma to answer the question.

"Her name is Shirley Potts. She's not from around here, and I don't know where she lives. Whatever you do, don't let her husband anywhere near her in the emergency room no matter what he says. I am quite sure he did this to her," Thelma replied, tearing up. "I knew this was going to happen if she went with him."

"At least she is still alive," the sheriff stated. "We will have a full-time guard on her door at the hospital. If her husband shows up, he will be arrested."

"Can I go to the hospital and stay with her," Thelma requested. "She has no other friends in the area. Shirley needs to have a friendly face that she knows in the room with her. She needs to feel safe."

"That actually sounds like a good idea," the sheriff agreed.

"Come on, June. I'll walk you into the building," Jimmy said.

"I'll call you in the morning and let you know what's happening," Thelma told her friend.

The ambulance was parked behind Thelma's car, so she stood with the sheriff while they finished loading Shirley for transport.

"How did she know where to find you?" Morse asked.

"I told her where I lived and that it was a secured building where she would be safe. She must have remembered what I told her," Thelma explained. "I can't believe she walked all the way from the outer harbor to here in the condition she's in."

"When survival mode kicks in, people can accomplish amazing things. I forgot to tell you earlier that Wayne was sighted in Portland yesterday. I have the Portland police following up, but they haven't called with any information yet."

"Does that mean he wasn't kidnapped?" Thelma asked.

"Maybe he just made it look like he was kidnapped so he could hide out."

"Do you really think Wayne is that smart?" Thelma mumbled.

"At this point, I can believe anything," Morse answered.

"The big question is, do any of these people that are involved know where the real Amelia is? And it seems to me that our suspect list is growing each day. Don't forget that we also must find Kami's abductor and who the crooked cop was at the time of the kidnapping."

"If there really was one. I hope Shirley will press charges against her husband after this latest episode. I have many questions to ask that woman," Morse said, watching her being loaded into the back of the ambulance.

"There has to be more information contained in those new pictures that I am not seeing," Thelma stated. "Have you had a chance to go through Agatha's files that Hanson sent you yet?"

"Wait a minute! What new pictures?"

"Oh, umm, after you left this morning, we found more pictures hidden in the car," Thelma replied. "And a key."

"And you're just telling me about them now?" the sheriff fumed.

"Well, a lot has happened today. First Kami, then the events at the bingo hall and now this. I forgot that we found them," Thelma insisted.

"Forgot? Where are they?" the sheriff demanded.

"They are locked in my car. I was going to look them over tonight and bring them to you in the morning," she admitted.

"I should charge you with interference in an ongoing investigation," he stated, staring her down. "How many times do I have to tell you that you can't pull stunts like this?"

"I'll turn them over to you at the hospital. I just want a quick look at them," she insisted, avoiding his stare.

"And to answer your question, I just started looking over the files last night. I have them with me and was going to finish going through them tonight at the station."

"Let me know what you think of the little piece of paper with the drawing on it. I think it looks like an angel wing, but I have no idea why it is in the file. There's no other writing on the paper to say what it is."

"I'll check it out. Don't try to change the subject. I want those pictures when we get to the hospital, understand? I should make you get them right now, but I don't want the ambulance arriving at the hospital with no one there to guard it."

Thelma shook her head in agreement as the deputies returned from their search.

"There is no one around the property," West announced.

"Maybe her husband didn't know she left, and she got far enough away before he discovered her missing," Thelma replied. "I don't think she would have told him my full name or where I lived."

"The ambulance is leaving, and I don't want Shirley left alone for even a minute," the sheriff stated. "West, you follow me, and you will take the first shift guarding our patient."

"I'll be right behind you," Thelma commented, searching her purse for her car keys.

Twenty minutes later, they all arrived at the hospital together. The sheriff had arranged for a private cubicle far away from any other patients admitted to the emergency room. Thelma stayed with Shirley behind the curtain, and West sat outside guarding the area. The sheriff took up his post in the waiting room, watching for Shirley's husband if he dared to show up.

"Let's get those ribs x-rayed," the doctor said.

"Thelma, will you come with me?" Shirley asked. "I don't want to be alone in case James shows up."

"You are safe at the hospital. Nothing will happen to you here," the doctor assured her. "Try to relax."

"I'm sure by now he knows you are gone and that you went for help. He wouldn't dare show his face here," Thelma insisted. "You have friends who will protect you now."

"You don't know James..." Shirley started.

"I know him, and others like him. The deputy is outside your cubicle, and the sheriff is staking out the emergency room entrance. I will go with you wherever you need to go while you are here. Try to relax like the doctor said," Thelma said, holding her bruised hand.

"The nurse will come get you when x-ray is ready for you. I'm going to make arrangements for a room for you to spend the night," the doctor said as he was leaving. "I'll be back when I have seen the x-rays."

"I don't have any insurance to stay here tonight. I don't even have any money to pay for all they have already done," Shirley claimed.

"Don't you worry. We will work something out financially with the hospital," Thelma replied. "Are you going to press charges this time?"

"Yes, I am,' she stated, hesitating a bit.

"Then you need to tell us where you were staying so the sheriff can arrest James," Thelma stated.

"We were staying at The Starfish Motel, room fourteen, down at the end closest to the jetty," she sighed. "They won't find him... he's probably long gone by now."

"Deputy West, would you go tell the sheriff that James Potts is at the Starfish Motel, room fourteen and that Shirley is going to press charges this time," Thelma said, pushing the curtain back to talk to the deputy.

"I'm not supposed to leave my post," he insisted.

"Then, please call him or do whatever you need to do to get the information to him."

"Will do," he said, talking into his shoulder radio.

"I don't deserve this. I don't deserve your help or anyone else's," Shirley mumbled, closing her eyes.

"Why? Because you helped kidnap Amelia Bohannon twenty-five years ago?" Thelma blurted out.

"You figured that out already?" she whispered as if the words stung.

"Did you personally take the pictures?"

"I did. I was the driver. Those pictures kept me alive all these years."

"What do you mean?"

"I hid them for over twenty years, but someone found out I had them and told James. I told him that if my body showed up dead at any time, there were instructions to send the pictures to the FBI. He couldn't take the chance, so he would beat me to the point where I couldn't function but never killed me."

"Do you know who told him?" Thelma asked.

At first, I thought it was Wayne Spikeman, but it wasn't. That day, the day of the kidnapping, he hid in the bushes because he was afraid. He witnessed the kidnapping and was threatened by someone on the Sechuette police force to keep his mouth shut or his niece would be the next one to disappear."

"Agatha said that she didn't trust the police, and it looks like she was right," Thelma noted. "So, Wayne kept his mouth shut all these years to protect his niece."

"James found out that Wayne was in one of the pictures and he was afraid he would break down and tell the police everything when they questioned him, so he forced Wayne to leave his job that day. I think he has him hidden somewhere nearby to keep him quiet until they finish what they have to do."

"And what is it that they have to do?" Thelma inquired.

"I don't know. James never told me anything. He was very secretive."

"The police have the pictures that you sent to Agatha. I have the pictures that you hid in the car. What is the key to that was wrapped in the plastic wrap?"

"The key is to a safety deposit box. It holds six more pictures and a journal I kept regarding any information I overheard about the kidnappings. And a letter requesting the contents be turned over to the FBI upon surrender of the box," Shirley explained.

"Kidnappings? There were more than one?"

"There were many. James was not the only one involved. He worked with a team of people from all over Maine."

"Do you know any of their names?"

"No, I didn't know who to trust and who not to trust, so I kept my mouth shut and minded my own business to stay alive."

"Why didn't you leave James after the first kidnapping?"

"He threatened to kill my parents and my sister if I left him. I knew he would do it or one of his team would, so I stayed to protect them. As of last year, they are all deceased, and James has nothing to hold over my head anymore. That's what we were fighting about that day on the pier."

"Why did you come back to Sechuette?"

"James came back every summer to reinforce his threat to Wayne that he would kill his niece. This year was different, though. Something bigger is happening, but I don't know what. All the attention to the anniversary of the kidnapping was making James extra jittery. He was constantly on the phone with someone who is calling all the shots. They argued a lot."

"Are we ready to go to x-ray?" a nurse asked, pushing the curtain back.

"We are so ready. Let's go see what needs to be fixed," Thelma said, standing up, smiling at Shirley.

"I'll be close behind," Deputy West told them as they left the cubicle.

Twenty minutes later, they were back with the deputy returning to his post. Shirley had dozed off due to the pain medication that she had received, and Thelma needed something to do to keep herself awake. She pulled the pictures out of her purse that they had found in the car earlier that day.

She now realized that the man running with the blanket was a younger James Potts. She had already figured out that it was Wayne in the bushes. The third picture was the one that she had to concentrate on. It was a wide-angle picture of the park. In the upper left corner of the photograph, Thelma spotted a police car parked at the edge of the park entrance. Someone was sitting in the front driver's seat watching the area.

That cop had to be able to see the kidnapping as it was taking place. This picture must be of the inside person that was on the Sechuette Police at the time, but the picture is too blurry to tell who it is.

"Ah, the pictures," the sheriff said, entering the cubicle and holding his hand out. "Hand them over."

"This picture is just another picture of Wayne hiding in the bushes," Thelma said, handing him the first picture.

"You mean being the lookout," the sheriff corrected her.

"No, I mean hiding. Shirley told me that he was a witness and not a participant in the kidnapping."

"I asked you not to question Shirley," the sheriff replied.

"I didn't. We just had a casual conversation. If you look at the new picture of the man running with the blanket, you can tell that it is a young James Potts," she continued, ignoring how mad the sheriff was getting. "It's the third picture that is the most interesting."

"Look at the upper left corner and tell me what you see," Thelma requested, handing it to him.

The sheriff frowned when he acknowledged what Thelma had seen.

"There *was* a Sechuette cop sitting at the park who witnessed the whole thing and didn't stop it. Agatha was right. I need to get this picture to the lab to see if they can clean it up so we can make out who it is that's sitting in the driver's seat."

"Yes, they have police in their pockets everywhere,' Shirley acknowledged, opening her eyes. "But, unfortunately, I don't know who any of them are."

"You will need to tell the sheriff everything that you have already told me," Thelma said.

The sheriff's cell phone rang, and he stepped outside to answer it.

"That was Deputy Palmer. There is no sign of James Potts at the hotel. He cleaned out everything except his wife's suitcase."

"Thank goodness he left that behind." Shirley breathed a sigh of relief.

"We could have bought you some new clothes," Thelma insisted.

"No, you don't understand. I hid copies of some of the fake birth certificates in the lining of the suitcase."

"Was one of them Amelia's, by any chance," Thelma asked before the sheriff could.

"No. Her kidnapping was very well guarded, much more so than any of the others, and I could never figure out why," Shirley answered.

The doctor entered the crowded cubicle.

"Well, Mrs. Potts. You have two bruised ribs on your right side. I'm amazed that none of them broke. There is a hairline fracture on your right cheekbone. You are a fortunate woman. You are going to be very sore for quite some time. I have arranged for a room for tonight, and I will reassess your case tomorrow to see if you can be released. At the request of the sheriff, you have a private room. I have put you next to Kami Frost's room, so there will be two deputies in the same area."

"Thank you, Doc. I appreciate all your help," the sheriff told him.

"I will see you in the morning, Mrs. Potts," he stated, leaving the cubicle.

"Thelma, I did check in with Elder before I came down here. He said Kami was sleeping peacefully, and the only visitor she had was Hanson Beckworth, her boyfriend. He stayed for a couple of hours, ate supper with her, and left at the close of visiting hours."

"If this keeps up, we will need a whole floor of this hospital." Thelma sighed.

"Let's hope not. Shirley is there anywhere that you could think of that your husband would hide here in town. Does he know anyone?"

"The only person he knew was Wayne, and they weren't friends by any means. He only came back to threaten Wayne each summer like I told Thelma," she replied. "And he always used stolen credit cards to register wherever we stayed. He never uses the same card or name twice."

"And being a tourist area, it would take us a week to check each hotel or motel in the area," the sheriff admitted.

"What bothers me the most is that Shirley said something big is going to happen. What if they have planned another kidnapping? We do have a lot of celebrities and their families vacationing here," Thelma said. "And most of the houses out on the outer harbor are owned by very well to do people, and that is where James Potts chose to stay. What if he was watching a specific family?"

"It's not about another kidnapping. They stopped doing that about ten years ago. They had made a lot of money from the previous kidnappings and lived it up for a while. No, this is something different."

"There are just too many unanswered questions. Shirley Potts, I am placing you under arrest and putting you in protective custody. You cannot leave the hospital, do you understand?" the sheriff asked. "I know you are uncomfortable because of your injuries, so I will not handcuff you to the bed if you promise not to leave your hospital room."

"I will not go anywhere, I promise. I am afraid that James would find me, and I need to tell you everything I can to help you to find your answers."

"I will take you at your word," the sheriff said. "Thelma, can I see you outside a minute?"

"I'll be right back, I promise," she said to Shirley, patting her shoulder.

"I didn't want to say anything in front of Shirley, but now that I have seen the picture with the cruiser stationed at the park, I think I am right," Morse started.

"Right about what?"

"Remember I said that I started to look over the files? As you know, I have the original police files locked in a safe at my house because I was afraid that if Agatha was right. We did have a dirty cop still among us that the files would conveniently disappear."

"And?"

"The police files that are in the packet that Agatha's attorney sent us don't have the complete police files. Many pages are missing of witness testimony and pictures of the crime scene the day it happened."

"Maybe Agatha didn't trust anyone at all, including her own people, and kept some of the files for her own investigations," Thelma suggested.

"Could be. There was nothing important missing from the files. Just the same sort of statements from witnesses saying they didn't see anything," Morse said. "The pictures were general pictures of the crime scene, no people in them. It's just strange, that's all."

"Nothing Agatha did was normal. She must have had her reasons for what she did," Thelma insisted.

"I was going to spend the night chained behind my desk going over the files, but I think I will ride around town and see if I can spot Potts anywhere. I'll talk to you tomorrow."

Thelma returned to the cubicle. Shirley had dozed off again, so Thelma turned on the television and muted the voice. The news was on every channel, so there wasn't a lot to choose from to watch. A car accident had taken place on the outskirts of town near Sissy's Hair and I Salon. As the cameraman was panning the area around the accident, a familiar face appeared exiting the Burger Palace.

Thelma sprang from her chair to get to the deputy outside the cubicle.

15

"Call the sheriff. I just saw James Potts coming out of The Burger Palace at the edge of town," Thelma instructed him. "A car accident was being covered live on the news, and the cameraman caught Potts carrying a to-go bag. He covered his face with the bag, but I saw him before he could react."

West got on his shoulder radio and passed on Thelma's message.

"He's only two minutes from there. He was already heading to the accident," West told Thelma.

"I hope they catch him," she said as a nurse walked up to the pair.

"Mrs. Potts' room is ready."

"She's sleeping, but I'm sure she'll wake up as you move her," Thelma replied.

"There is a second bed in the room for you, per order of the doctor," the nurse said, pushing the curtain back so the bed could be moved. "And a chair outside the room for you, Deputy West."

"Great! I'm going to grab some coffee out of the vending machine, and I'll be right behind you," Deputy West stated.

"There's free coffee at the nurse's station upstairs. The other deputy has been helping himself to it all night," the nurse said, unlocking the wheels and moving the bed forward.

Shirley stirred as the bed moved, but never woke up even after they got to the room. Thelma stopped to look in on her niece, who was asleep also. The two deputies took up their posts, and Thelma settled in on the extra bed and fell asleep. The rest of the night passed uneventfully.

The next morning the doctor told Shirley that she would be staying at least another twenty-four hours as she was still using large amounts of pain killers. Thelma assured her before she left to bring Kami home that she would do all she could to talk to the sheriff so Shirley could stay at her apartment in a secured building instead of a jail cell. Shirley closed her eyes to rest, feeling better that she might have somewhere to go.

Kami was sitting on her bed, dressed and ready to go when her aunt entered her room. Hanson was standing near the windowsill, collecting her flower arrangements, and placing them in a box that he had brought with him.

"Wow! Look at all the flowers," Thelma commented. "You were only here for one day."

"Most of them are from Hanson," she acknowledged, smiling. "There's one from Betsy and Henry, too."

"Well, now I feel pretty cheap. Thanks for showing me up so badly, Hanson." Thelma laughed.

"I didn't mean to. I'm just showing my girl how much I care about her," he shot back defensively, picking up a vase of orange roses dotted with white baby's breath and adding it to the box.

"I'm joking, Hanson. Lighten up," Thelma replied. "Why are you here? Didn't Kami tell you that I was taking her home?"

"Yes, she did. I just came to give you these notices. All Agatha's paperwork cleared the courts earlier than expected, and the reading of the will has been moved up ahead of the original date. The meeting is now scheduled for this Thursday."

"I can make it. I'm still on vacation," Thelma replied, taking the envelope.

"I have also discussed it with Kami, and she has approved having the reading at the paper. It is much easier for one person to travel here than make everyone drive to Portland," Hanson stated.

"Sounds good to me," Thelma said. "Why did the paperwork go through the court system so quickly?"

"There was no one to contest the will. The bulk of the estate will be held in a trust until Amelia Bohannon is found," the attorney answered.

"And who controls the trust?"

"I can't see why that is any of your concern, but my law firm will be in control of the trust. My dad was good friends with Agatha and her husband for many years. He was their attorney until I took over the firm when my dad died," Hanson stated. "She trusted my family explicitly."

"I'm glad that Agatha had someone that she could turn to all those past years," Thelma said, holding the wheelchair while her niece climbed into it. "We need to relieve Dylan of his dog-sitting duties."

"Whose Dylan?" Hanson asked, glaring at Kami.

"He's a reporter that works for the *Portland Times*. Our paths crossed, and he happened to be free to watch Kami's dogs while she was here at the hospital," Thelma replied.

"So, you just let anyone stay at your house? You don't even know this guy," Hanson demanded.

"My aunt trusts him, and that's good enough for me," Kami stated. "Speaking of the dogs, I really want to get home to see them. Can we leave now?"

"I'll put the box in your car, Thelma, and then I have to deliver the rest of the notices," he said, picking up the box and wincing from the weight of it.

"Thank you for everything, Deputy Elder," Kami said as he stood up. "Go home and get some sleep."

"Are you sure you don't want me to follow you home?"

"No, thank you, anyway. Aunt Thelma is with me, and Dylan is at the house. I'll be fine," Kami answered.

"Be careful and if you need anything, call us," Deputy Elder said as he walked away from the group.

"Just set the box in the back," Thelma instructed, opening the hatch of her car. "Dylan can carry it in when we get to Kami's house. Thank you for bringing it out to the car for us, Hanson."

"Is this Dylan staying at your house tonight while you are there?" Hanson asked Kami before she climbed in the passenger side front seat.

"I don't think so," she replied. "He has a room at the bed and break-fast in town."

"Although, that would be a great idea. I don't like the thought of my niece staying there by herself after what happened yesterday," Thelma interjected.

"Maybe I'm old fashioned, but I am not crazy about a man you hardly know staying in your house with you. We did just start dating. What are people going to say?"

"You don't have to worry about a thing, Hanson. He's a reporter, and we are both working on the same story, nothing more, nothing less," she said, taking his hand. "You're my guy, okay?"

"Well, okay," he said, kissing her cheek. "I'll see you Thursday."

"Jealous or what?" Thelma commented as he walked away.

"Like he said. He's very old fashioned and set in his ways," Kami defended him. "He's very guarded. His finance left him a week before they were supposed to get married."

"Just be careful," Thelma advised her niece.

They pulled into the driveway at Kami's house, and the dogs were barking in the back yard.

"Music to my ears." Kami smiled, getting out of the car.

They peeked around the corner of the house and saw Dylan throwing a ball for the dogs. They ran across the yard, barking at the ball and each other, and returning to Dylan to throw it again. He laughed as he fought to get the ball from Wags.

"Aren't we all having a good time?" Kami spoke up.

Dylan spun around, and the dogs ran to the gate at the sound of their owner's voice.

"Some guard dogs you are." Kami laughed, kneeling to pat the dogs who were washing her face all over with kisses. "I was all the way to the fence before you even knew I was here."

"In their defense, I didn't hear you either." Dylan smiled. "We were having too much fun. How are you feeling?"

"Better, but still sore. How about you?"

"The headache is gone, but the nose still hurts. I did sleep better than I have in a long-time last night, though. I forgot the peacefulness of listening to the critters of the woods while dozing off at night," he replied.

"It is nice here on the edge of the woods," Kami agreed. "Except for…"

"The hawks and coyotes, I know," Dylan recited, finishing her sentence.

"I guess I'm not needed here," Thelma commented to the dogs.

"Did you bring the files with you?" Dylan asked.

"Yes, but I would rather go in the house before I remove them from my purse just in case someone is watching," Thelma replied. "Maybe the two of you could work together this afternoon and go over the files. I always say two sets of eyes are better than one."

"Is anyone hungry? I could make some lunch, and we could all look at them together," Dylan suggested, looking at Kami. "I am a good cook, you know."

"Great! Because I'm not." Kami laughed.

"I have to beg out. Things to do and things to do," Thelma insisted, following them into the house. "I know this is my niece's decision, but I would feel much better if you would continue to stay here at the house, so she's not by herself."

"I don't know…" Dylan said, looking at Kami.

"Look, it's not like you have to sleep together," Thelma stated. "There are two bedrooms in this place."

"Aunt Thelma!" Kami exclaimed. "Really?"

"As your dad said, it's either someone stays here with you or you come stay with me."

"You're not even giving Dylan a say in this. Maybe one broken nose is enough for the man," Kami protested.

"Do I get to cook?" he asked, cocking one eyebrow and crossing his arms.

"I guess so," Kami answered, looking at him funny.

"Then I'm in." He smiled. "You do have to promise me that we get an equal byline if we break this story."

"Deal!" Kami said, extending her hand.

"Good, then it's settled. I feel much better knowing you will be here," Thelma said.

"I have to run to the bed and breakfast and get my stuff and check out. Can you stay here with your niece until I get back? It shouldn't be any more than thirty minutes," Dylan requested.

"I can stay for a bit, and then I want to get back to the hospital and check on Shirley."

"I'll make it fast," Dylan said, heading out the slider.

"I'm quite sure that Hanson is not going to like this arrangement," Kami commented after Dylan left. "He's so strait-laced."

"Is he that afraid of what people will say? If he was that upset with the idea when I said something at the hospital, then he should have offered to stay here himself," Thelma pointed out.

"I know. I just hope he doesn't decide to stop dating me because of it," Kami said, dejectedly.

"If he stops dating you because of you looking out for your own safety, then he doesn't deserve to have you as his girlfriend," her aunt declared.

"It's just his parents had an arranged marriage and didn't meet until the day of their wedding. Hanson was brought up in a very strict household. His mother never left the house and never talked to other men, and now I am staying in the same house with another man. It's a wonder he's freaking out," Kami said, defending her new boyfriend.

"Does he think that you will never talk to another man now that you're dating?" Thelma asked. "He needs to get with the times."

"I hope he can." Kami sighed.

"It's so beautiful out. Let's get some wine and sit in the backyard and enjoy the sunshine," her aunt suggested, trying to change the subject.

"Sounds good. I have the day off, so I might as well enjoy it," Kami agreed.

The two women discussed some of the changes that Kami and Betsy were implementing at the paper now that they were in charge. They also talked about what may be in Agatha's will at the reading that was to take place this coming Thursday. It wasn't long before Dylan returned and joined them at the picnic table with his own glass of wine.

"You like wine?" Thelma chuckled. "I knew I liked you for some reason."

"Wine and cooking go together, hand in hand," he stated. "Now, how about we get to those files?"

"I'm going to head to the hospital. I left the files on the kitchen table. Please look them over inside," Thelma requested, standing up and taking her keys out of her purse.

"We will. I'll call you if we find anything out of the ordinary," Kami replied.

"I'm going to bingo tonight. It may be the last time I can go for a while if Shirley is released to my custody and stays at my apartment. Call me on my cell if you need to get in touch with me," Thelma stated, going through the gate to leave.

Sheriff Morse was at the hospital questioning Shirley when Thelma arrived. Shirley's suitcase was sitting on the windowsill, open. The lining had been removed, and the paperwork hidden inside it lay on the bed next to Shirley.

"Hi, Thelma." Shirley winced, trying to sit up higher in the bed.

"Well, don't you look one hundred percent better today." Thelma smiled.

"I'm still sore all over, but my conscious feels so much better," she acknowledged. "I've been helping Sheriff Morse with what I know about each of the birth certificates that I managed to copy without James knowing that I did it."

"I think we may be able to track down some of these children that were kidnaped with Shirley's help," Morse admitted.

"You have to remember that the adoptive parents didn't know that the babies they adopted were stolen," Shirley pointed out. "It's going to be a shock to all those involved."

"Can you imagine after all these years finding out that you were kidnapped and sold?" Thelma stated. "Their whole world will be turned upside down."

"I feel so badly that I didn't speak up before now, but I was terrified for my life, and they haven't taken any more children, at least that I know of, in a while."

"You're speaking up now, and that's what counts," Thelma replied.

"The big problem is that I don't know anyone in the inner circle. That's what James used to call his partners so he wouldn't use names," Shirley stated. "I do know that one person calls all the shots and has for a very long time."

"If we knew who that one person was, we could uncover files to help us reunite all the kidnapped children," Morse stated. "Shirley has given the bank permission to open her safety deposit box for me to collect the contents. That should help us also."

"Did you have a chance to go over the rest of the files last night?" Thelma asked, sitting on the bed next to Shirley's.

"I did when I returned to the station. We lost James among the crowd around the accident. He was on foot so we figured that he couldn't have got too far away from the restaurant. We checked the area lodgings but to no avail."

"What did you think of that drawing?"

"I went through the entire file twice, and there was no drawing in it," Morse answered.

"That's odd," Thelma replied. "I'll have to ask Hanson about it next time I see him."

"Shirley is going to be staying another night. Palmer will stay here until eleven, and then Elder will take over until seven tomorrow morning. Personally, I think she would be safer at the station. However, if you still are offering to put her up in your secure building, I will release her to your custody," the sheriff stated.

"I'm on vacation this week, so it's fine if Shirley comes to stay with me. I also arranged for Dylan to stay at Kami's house so that she won't be alone at night," Thelma said.

"That's great. I was worried about her staying by herself seen as we don't know why she was being kidnapped in the first place. I can understand Wayne's disappearance as he was a witness, but Kami was only an infant when the kidnapping happened. It doesn't make any sense," Morse commented, standing up and collecting the paperwork spread on the bed. "I need to go home and get some sleep before my next shift."

"June and I will be at bingo tonight if you need to get in touch with me."

"There's a shock! I'm sure my wife will see you there."

"I haven't been going half as much as I usually go with all that has happened around here this summer. I think I deserve a nice quiet night at bingo," Thelma defended herself and her bingo playing.

"Whatever excuse you need, Thelma Frost, to feed your need to get that elusive bingo," he said, smiling as he walked toward the door. "And now I understand that you have talked my wife into going on the bingo cruise with you and June in the spring."

"I don't NEED to go, I just like to go," she hollered after him not knowing if he heard her or not. "And Ellie wanted to go on that cruise. I didn't talk her into anything."

Shirley laughed.

"What's so funny?" Thelma inquired, plopping into the chair the sheriff just vacated.

"You two are. I love the way that you get along, but don't get along. And I can see through it all there is a great trust between the two of you," Shirley replied.

"I guess so. Sheriff Morse has never let me down," Thelma admitted. "So, I was thinking last night about what you said about multiple kidnappings over the years. Just how long has this been going on?"

"When I married James, he was already working for the kidnapping ring. I would venture to guess at least thirty or so years, maybe even more."

"So, the person running the ring would have to be up there in years, probably middle-aged, if it has been running as long as you think it has," Thelma pondered.

"One day, I managed to glance at James's cell phone, which he left on the coffee table while he went to the bathroom. He guarded that thing with his life, so I figured it must have been a trap to see if I would go through it."

"Did you go for it?"

"I left it where it was and didn't touch it. He came back in the room, eyed me suspiciously, and picked it up. He told me I passed the test and went into the kitchen to get something to eat. What he didn't know was that I watched him unlock the phone, and I now knew the code. Later that day, when he took his shower, I opened the phone and saw that most of his calls were to someone in Portland. I tried to find a pen and paper to write down the most called numbers, but the water turned off, and I knew I needed to get out of there. He changed the code before I could get to the phone again."

"It's easier to work out of a big city like Portland or Augusta if you want to be able to get lost in the crowd," Thelma admitted. "Where did you live?"

"We had a small house in Westover, out in the sticks. It was easier for James to hide out there and to keep me isolated from any people. And we were only ten minutes from Portland where James spent most of his time."

"You never had any children?"

"James hated children. I think that's why he fit in so well in this ring. He had no regard for the children that they stole or for the families they stole them from." Shirley sighed.

"It must have been awful lonely for you in the woods."

"I had my sewing and my journals that I wrote in secretly and kept hidden," she replied. "I hope if the sheriff sends men to the house like he said he would, they will find the journals where I told him they were hidden. There is a lot of information in those journals that might be useful to the police."

"Like what?"

"I always wrote down bits and pieces of conversations that I overheard. Most of the time, it was just one-sided conversations by James while he was on the phone and didn't think I was close enough to hear him. Still, maybe Sheriff Morse and his men can get something out of the journals to help them," Shirley said, yawning.

"Get some rest. I'm going to bingo with June tonight, and I'll be back in the morning to get you when they release you from this place," Thelma said, standing up. "The deputy will still be guarding you, and besides, I think James is long gone from here. His face is too well known now."

"Whatever it is that they are planning will set them all up for life. James talked about heading to the Caribbean and living his life out in the warm sun," Shirley said, closing her eyes. "I hope the sheriff can stop them."

"Me, too. I'll see you tomorrow."

Thelma and June arrived at bingo in time to get their regular seats. The crowd had already reduced in size as families were leaving to get ready for the start of school. Labor Day was less than two weeks away, and Sechuette would be returning to its slower pace of living.

"Look who took over Agatha's spot now that she's gone," June said, snickering.

Thelma glanced over and saw the two girls who had fought with Agatha the week before until Wayne had stepped in and convinced them to move. Now they were sitting where they wanted to sit in the first place, and no one would challenge them for the seats.

"Too funny," Thelma replied, returning her attention to taping her paper strips together.

"I overheard they have a new caller training tonight. Wayne hasn't returned, and too many people were complaining about how long it was taking to play with Lucy that replaced him," June stated. "I don't know who it is, though."

"I don't care who it is as long as I have a nice, quiet, relaxing night of bingo," Thelma stated, opening her handful of rip-offs that she had purchased. "Look! I got a number for the drawing."

"If you win the twelve hundred, you are so buying lunch tomorrow." June laughed.

The two friends ordered supper, grabbed a cup of coffee, and settled in for an enjoyable night of bingo together. Neither of them won a thing the first half.

"It's the same winners all the time," Thelma complained.

"Do you include yourself on that list?" her friend asked.

"I win, I'll admit that, but not as much as Rachael over there. She wins at least three to four times a night. I have never seen anyone so lucky."

"Everyone goes through winning streaks and losing streaks. I'm sure she has her share of losing, too," June insisted.

"I've never seen it, her losing streaks, I mean."

"Are you going to get cake? I would love a piece of chocolate with vanilla frosting if you're going to stand in line," June requested. "I'll refill our coffee after I make a trip to the bathroom."

"Fine, I'll get the cake, and I'll meet you back here at the table."

Thelma stood in line, listening to the conversations going on around her. One conversation caught her attention. The woman was telling her friend about how strange it was that so many cars were going in and out of Agatha Tram's estate. She stated that even when Agatha was alive, she never had that many people visit her at home.

Who would be staying at Agatha's estate?

"Excuse me. Did you say Agatha Tram's estate?" Thelma inquired.

"Yes, I did. You're Thelma Frost, aren't you?"

"Yes, I am."

"I love your new hair, by the way. I am or was Agatha's neighbor.

She told me that you were helping to find Amelia, and she was incredibly grateful."

"You spoke to Agatha?' Thelma asked, surprised. "I didn't think she had any friends."

"Almost every day. We would meet out in her gardens at the back of her house. They were beautiful, and Agatha attended to them every morning. We would have coffee on her terrace and talk about her flowers."

"You said that cars were going in and out of the estate. Did you recognize any of the people driving the cars?"

"Only one; Hanson Beckworth, Agatha's attorney. I was in the garden one morning, and he came out and requested that I stay off the property from there on out. He said that they were preparing the property to close it down until Amelia Bohannon was found. I assumed that everyone going in and out were people doing the work."

"Thank you for your help," Thelma said, turning to pick out two of the largest pieces of cake she could find.

The caller announced that the drawings for the door prizes were about to start, and everyone should return to their seats. Thelma paid for two pieces of cake and sat down just as the numbers of the admission cards were being called.

"Guess what I found out. Agatha actually did have some friends, contrary to what most people believed. The next-door neighbor said she spent every morning having coffee with Agatha in her gardens out behind the estate."

"Appearances can be deceiving," June replied. "You just never know."

"I also found out that the estate has been a beehive of activity in the last week."

"Who has any right to be in Agatha's mansion?"

"Hanson Beckworth told the next-door neighbor that they are closing it down until Amelia is found. I guess that makes sense seen as no one will be living there," Thelma replied. "I'm going to have the sheriff check it out anyway and make sure things aren't disappearing from the mansion."

"Are you saying that you don't trust Hanson?" June asked, surprised.

"No, I'm not saying that even if he does creep me out a bit. It's just if people know the mansion is vacant, it would be an easy target."

"Make sure your even numbers are covered on your intermission strips," the caller announced. "We will be starting in about two minutes."

"This is our half," Thelma told her friend, dauber in hand and ready to play.

Thelma was right. She won twice, and June won once. They had a lovely night at bingo with no drama included and were home early enough to enjoy a glass of wine at Thelma's before June went home for the evening.

●16

Thelma stopped to check on her niece on the way to the hospital. Both Kami's and Dylan's cars were in the driveway along with Hanson Beckworth's.

"This can't be good," Thelma thought out loud as she looked through the sliders.

All three were sitting at the kitchen table, having coffee. Hanson gave Dylan a dirty look as he got up to go to the stove. Kami was pointing something out to Hanson in the files that were spread out over the table. He wasn't paying any attention to what she was telling him as he was too busy watching Dylan. Thelma knocked on the slider, and her niece waved her in.

"Just in time for breakfast," Dylan announced, smiling broadly. "Want some coffee?"

"I would love some," Thelma replied, sitting down at the table.

"Grand Central Station," Hanson muttered under his breath.

"Excuse me? Did you say something?" Thelma inquired, her eyes narrowing when looking at her niece's new boyfriend.

"No, nothing," he replied, frowning.

"Good. So, did you come up with anything new while looking over the files?" Thelma asked.

"We don't know if it's new or not because we hadn't had a chance to talk to you before now," Kami replied. "Do you have some time before I have to go to work?"

"All the time in the world for you," her aunt replied.

"Speaking of work, I have to leave," Hanson declared.

"I heard at bingo last night that you are shutting down Agatha's mansion until Amelia is found," Thelma stated.

"You must have heard that from that busy body neighbor of hers. I keep telling her to stay off the property, but she doesn't listen. She claims she loves to walk the gardens and that she and Agatha used to discuss flowers during their morning coffee. Personally, I think she's just nosy," Hanson replied. "And yes, I am shutting down the place."

"How long before you think Amelia will be found? If ever?" Thelma questioned.

"I have no idea. We are still working on it," Hanson answered nastily. "I'll be here to pick you up for dinner at seven, Kami."

"I'll be ready," she answered.

He went out the slider without so much as a goodbye to anyone. Thelma and Dylan looked at each other, each thinking what a jerk he was, but not saying anything in front of Kami.

"Whatever you are cooking, it smells good," Thelma said, breaking the silence that occurred after Hanson left.

"Southwestern omelets with homemade salsa, and they're almost done," Dylan replied.

"Did you have a chance to look at the drawing I was talking about yesterday?" Thelma asked, pouring herself more coffee.

"We only got halfway through the file, but I haven't seen any drawing, Have you, Dylan?" Kami asked.

"Let's find it now," Thelma suggested.

While Dylan cooked, the two women scanned the files for the hand-drawn picture. It was nowhere to be found.

"Well, that's weird. Maybe it fell out in my purse," Thelma

claimed, emptying the contents of her purse on the table. "It's not here either."

"When is the last time that you saw it?" Dylan asked.

"At the apartment. Maybe it fell out there, and the cat played with it, so I didn't see it on the floor," Thelma reasoned. "I'll check around when I get home."

"I didn't notice anything that stuck out to me when we were going through the files," Dylan said. "I'll finish going through the rest this morning, and then I have to run to work in Portland and pick up some of my additional files on the kidnapping. I'll be back before you get home from work."

"I'll be going out tonight, so don't hurry back if you have other things to do," Kami insisted.

"Who's ready to eat?" Dylan asked, standing next to the table with two plates in his hand. "Salsa's coming right up."

"I'm starving," Thelma said as Dylan set the plate in front of her. "It just seems to me that this investigation is going nowhere. They haven't found Wayne; we still don't know who the inside man was in the Sechuette police, and there is not even the smallest clue to tell us where Amelia is. She could be in Alaska for all we know."

"I don't think so. All these events would point to the fact that the ring returned here for a reason, a specific reason. My gut feeling says that they came back to make sure Amelia Bohannon is not found. Who exactly would benefit if she's not found?" Dylan said, setting the bowl of salsa in the middle of the table and sitting down with his plate.

"No one really. The will has been filed in court. It will be read on Thursday. The newspaper has been passed to the new owners with the bulk of the estate entered into a trust until Amelia is found," Thelma answered.

"Who is in control of that trust?" Dylan asked. "Look at the who, and you may have your answer."

"Are you insinuating that Hanson has something to do with all this?" Kami demanded, offended at Dylan's suggestion.

"I'm not suggesting anything, just following the clues," he stated. "That's what I do. I'm an investigative reporter and a good one."

"Kami, we have to look at all avenues," her aunt stated.

"For your information, Dylan, Hanson was only a teenager when the kidnapping occurred. His father had been Agatha's attorney until he died, and then Hanson took over the firm. You don't know him and have no right to judge him," Kami stated.

"Excuse me for saying so, but you don't know him very well either. You have only been on one date with him," her aunt replied. "And truth be told, I don't particularly like the way he talks to you."

"I don't have to listen to this. I'm going to work." Kami stormed off to her bedroom.

"I don't think I am welcome here anymore," Dylan said, putting down his fork. "I didn't mean to accuse Hanson; I was just working out a trail of clues, and it came out that way."

"Don't worry about it. Kami will cool off and see what you were doing. Between you and me, I don't like Hanson very much. He is very controlling, and he has a short temper. I'm afraid for my niece," Thelma admitted.

"Nothing will happen to her while I am around, that is if she lets me stay."

"She will. She can't stay with me because Shirley is coming home with me today, which means she would have to stay with her father. And believe me, that's the last thing she wants to have to do." Thelma chuckled.

"I'll be home later tonight. Dylan would you feed the dogs their supper so I can leave from work for my date, please," Kami requested, returning from her bedroom like nothing happened.

"I will be glad to," Dylan answered, picking up his fork again.

Kami walked out the slider after saying goodbye to her furry roommates. Thelma snickered and continued to eat.

"See, I told you," she bragged. "I know my niece all too well."

"Now that she's gone, just how much do you know about Hanson Beckworth?" Dylan asked.

"Not much. I do know that Sheriff Morse told me that when Hanson released the files from Agatha to me that almost half the original police report was missing. I can't for the life of me figure out why."

"You said that there was a crooked cop on the force at the time. Maybe that was all he released to Agatha, and she would have no way of knowing that she received an incomplete report," Dylan suggested. "The report was pieced together extremely well. I didn't even realize pages were missing."

"This whole investigation has turned into finding Amelia, but it all started with finding Agatha's killer who is still on the loose, by the way."

"I don't know anything about Agatha's murder. All I came to cover was the twenty-fifth anniversary of the kidnapping. I do know that Beckworth's firm had been under investigation before, but I can't remember for what. That's why I need to go to Portland today and gather up those additional files."

"I'd be interested in reading those files if you don't mind. Did Kami give you a key to the house, or do you need my spare?" Thelma asked in between bites. "This is so good. I can't believe you don't want to cook for a living."

"Yes, she did, and she gave it to me in front of Hanson, which didn't go over too well."

"Apparently, our Mr. Beckworth isn't very concerned with his new girlfriend's safety, only his own reputation," Thelma replied in disgust. "I know he's involved somehow, and I hope Kami doesn't get too hurt when this is all said and done."

"I'll keep a close eye on Hanson Beckworth and do everything in my power to keep your niece safe," Dylan stated.

"I know you will," Thelma said, reaching for the salsa. "I wouldn't have suggested you stay here if I didn't trust you."

They finished eating their breakfast on a lighter note discussing Dylan's future and Thelma's bingo obsession. She insisted on cleaning up the kitchen so he could get on the road to Portland. After letting the dogs out one more time so there would be no accidents, Thelma left for the hospital to pick up Shirley.

The sheriff was in the room when Thelma arrived.

"I was explaining the rules of this release to Shirley. She is not to leave your apartment for any reason, or she goes directly to jail," the sheriff said to Thelma. "I will ask you one more time. Are you sure you want to be responsible for Shirley once she leaves the hospital?"

"I only have one question. Can she go to bingo if she stays with either June or I and doesn't leave our sight?"

"I don't know. It might be too risky if James Potts is still in the area," he responded.

"We have your wife's birthday party planned for Thursday night. I promise that will be the only time we leave the apartment," Thelma insisted.

"Thanks, throw the old guilt trip on me." The sheriff frowned.

"I will be leaving on Thursday morning for a short time for the reading of Agatha's will. But I have made arrangements for Deputy Elder to come stay with Shirley while I am gone."

"I guess you have thought this thing out. All right, I guess you can go to bingo on Thursday night. I may pop in to see how things are going."

"And for a piece of cake." Thelma chuckled.

"We have started to trace the names you gave us, and so far, no luck," the sheriff said to Shirley, ignoring Thelma's cake comment. "While this ring operated, they left no paper trails and nothing to follow. They knew what they were doing."

"I tried to tell you that what I had to offer was only bits and pieces. I did the best I could gathering information without jeopardizing my own life," Shirley replied.

"I know you did. We will continue to work with what you have given us, and maybe we will catch a lucky break," the sheriff said, standing up to leave. "Thelma, I'll be in touch."

"You have my cell number," she said.

An hour later, they were entering the lobby of Thelma's apartment.

Jimmy was at the front desk.

"Hi, Thelma. Still on vacation?" he asked, smiling.

"Yes, I am. A friend of mine named Dylan Peterson will be coming over to drop some important papers off tonight. Other than him, don't let anyone else in no matter what they tell you," she insisted. "He works for the *Portland Times,* and I told him to show you his media ID for verification."

"What, no bingo?" He laughed.

"Not tonight, anyway. Tomorrow night we will be going. Are you ready for the reading of the will tomorrow morning?" It should be interesting," Thelma said.

"Oh, it will definitely be interesting. I can guarantee that," he replied. "I'll see you there."

"Who was that?" Shirley asked while they rode up in the elevator.

"That's Jimmy, Agatha's nephew by marriage. He's a good kid and a hard worker. I hope Agatha took good care of him in her will. He deserves a break," Thelma commented. "He would like to go to college but can't afford it."

"That's too bad," Shirley mumbled.

Once in the apartment, Thelma got her temporary roommate settled into the spare bedroom. After the trip from the hospital, Shirley was tired and wanted to take a nap. Thelma quietly wandered around her place, checking the floor for the missing piece of paper, the cat following her everywhere she went.

Zumbutt wanted some attention as his mistress hadn't been around much lately. He meowed loudly until Thelma picked him up and snuggled with him. She didn't want the meowing to disrupt her sleeping guest, so she carried him with her as she walked around.

"Did you play with the missing piece of paper?" she asked the cat who had tucked his head under her chin and was purring loudly.

After looking around the entire apartment except for the spare bedroom, Thelma found nothing except dust bunnies and a pile of milk caps that the cat had hoarded. She poured herself a tall glass of ice-cold root beer and settled in to watch some television. She dozed off in her recliner while watching a forensic show with Zumbutt contently tucked in next to her leg. She didn't wake up until the door buzzer went off, announcing that she had visitors.

The buzzer woke up her guest at the same time. Shirley wandered out of the bedroom, looking for the bathroom. Thelma directed her where to find it while she answered the buzzer. She let Dylan in the apartment a minute later.

"Do you have them?" Thelma asked.

"Hello to you, too." He laughed. "Yes, I do. I made copies for you so you could keep them here and look them over. I need to get back to the house to let the dogs out."

"So, what was the investigation for?"

"Embezzlement, but the charges were dropped. It's all in the files. After you read it, let me know what you think," Dylan requested.

"Embezzlement? How long ago?"

"Twenty-six years ago. It wasn't Hanson. It was against his father. A client of the firm accused him of stealing funds from the family trust. The money miraculously showed up in some other account and was returned to the family, so the charges were dropped. Hanson Sr. claimed it was just deposited in a wrong account. They pinned the mistake on some young clerk and fired her. She claimed she didn't do it but lost her job anyway. It's pretty interesting reading." Dylan claimed. "I really have to run. The dogs need to go out before dusk."

"I know, coyotes. Thanks for the paperwork," Thelma said, showing him to the door.

"Who is this Hanson guy?" Shirley asked as Thelma returned to the living room.

"Just someone my niece is dating and I, as the overprotective aunt, is checking him out," Thelma fibbed, not feeling like Shirley needed to know.

"I guess I would do the same thing," Shirley agreed.

"I ordered Thai food for supper. It should be here any minute. I hope you like Thai," Thelma stated.

"I don't know if I do or not. I have never had it." Shirley smiled.

The food was delivered to the desk downstairs. Thelma went to pick it up. As she was paying the delivery man, she happened to glance at the door. James Potts was staring back at her. Grabbing the phone on the desk, she dialed the sheriff. He ran when she picked up the phone.

"Did you see that man that was just standing at the door?" Thelma asked Jimmy.

"Yea, he's been loitering outside for a good twenty minutes."

The sheriff's car pulled up to the door. Another cruiser pulled up behind, and the two deputies jumped out and started to search the grounds.

"I'll let the sheriff in," Thelma said.

"And me out," the delivery man requested.

"Are you sure it was James Potts that you saw?" Morse asked.

"Oh, it was him all right," Thelma replied.

"He must have found out that Shirley is staying here. She may have to come down to the station for her own safety."

"Is that really a good idea? Especially if there is still someone on the inside. Somebody who told him where I lived, and that Shirley was here. Jimmy got a good look at him and knows who he is. He will call you right away if he sees him in the area again, won't you, Jimmy?"

"Yes, ma'am. My shift doesn't end until seven tomorrow morning. No one that I don't know will get in here."

"We'll check out the area. If he returns, Shirley will have to go to the station with a twenty-four-hour guard on her cell," the sheriff insisted. "Be careful, Thelma, please."

"I will. I have a triple lock on the apartment door, and I won't be leaving again tonight, for any reason."

"Okay. My deputy will be here in the morning to stay with Shirley when you have to leave for the reading of the will. Have a good night, and Jimmy, you be careful about who gets in or out tonight," the sheriff admonished him.

"I will, sir. May I talk to you a moment before you leave?"

"Sure. Thelma, I'll see you tomorrow night at bingo," the sheriff said, huddling with Jimmy and listening intently at what he had to say.

Thelma reported to Shirley that her husband had been spotted downstairs but told her not to worry as the sheriff chased him off, and Jimmy would be on the lookout for him. They ate their food, which Shirley thoroughly enjoyed, and went to bed.

It was a gloomy, rainy day when Thelma woke up the next morning. She drank her coffee, looking out her window at the drops forming on the windowpane. They looked like tears sliding down someone's cheek.

How appropriate is this weather? Gloomy seems to go with a reading of a will.

"That coffee smells great. It woke me up out of a sound sleep," Shirley stated as she entered the kitchen. "Wow! No one will be at the beach today, that's for sure."

"No, they won't," Thelma agreed, keeping her own thoughts to herself. "Help yourself to whatever you want for breakfast. I have to shower and get ready to leave."

Deputy Elder arrived right on time. Thelma couldn't help but notice how nervous Shirley was around the one who was supposed to be protecting her. Maybe she just didn't trust men anymore after what she had been through in her lifetime.

"I'll be home this afternoon. Rest up for bingo tonight," Thelma advised Shirley as she went out the door and listened for the deputy to lock the door behind her.

The paper was in full swing when Thelma arrived at ten-forty-five. Employees waved hi and bye to her as she entered the building and went to the second-floor conference room. There were already many people inside the room, many of whom Thelma didn't know. Coffee and pastries were on the table available to anyone who wanted some.

Kami, Betsy, and Hanson were in the far corner deep in a discussion. Jimmy, already seated at the table, waved to her. Sissy, Thelma's hairdresser, was also present. As it got closer to eleven o'clock, the room became more crowded. Hanson called the room to order, and Thelma took a seat next to Betsy at the table.

"I will now begin. Some of you have already received what you were left. To make the reading legal, all people mentioned in the will had to be present today. As your name is read, you may leave if you chose, and my office will be in touch with you in the coming week. Just give me a minute to get the paperwork in order."

"I love your watch, Betsy," Thelma said as they waited. "Purple is my favorite color."

"I am drawn to big, round, colorful watches. I must have thirty of them." Betsy smiled.

"I am ready to start," Hanson announced.

As the attorney read off the list of names and amounts received, Thelma noticed that Jimmy began to fidget in his chair. Even when his name was read with a good amount of inheritance that he could go to school with, he was frowning and extremely upset.

When most of the people in the room had left, Jimmy stood up and cleared his throat. Everyone turned to look at him.

"You, sir, are lying," Jimmy announced loudly. "That is not my aunt's real will."

"I don't know what you are talking about," Hanson stated, gathering the paperwork in front of him and shoving it in his briefcase. "If you think you have a more current will than the one that I filed with the courts, then you can send my office a copy, and we will look into the matter."

"You know exactly what I am talking about. My aunt didn't trust you, so she gave me a copy of her will that she drew up just three months ago with another attorney."

"Hanson! What is going on?" Kami demanded, standing up and knocking her cup of coffee all over her co-worker's arm and lap. "Betsy, I am so sorry. Let me get you some paper towels."

"It's okay. It was just an accident," she replied, taking off her watch and wiping it dry with the towels handed to her.

It was then that Thelma saw it, the angel wing birthmark that was hidden under Betsy's watch. Unfortunately, Hanson Beckworth spotted it at the same time. His eyes grew in size, and he bolted out of the room at top speed knocking several people over as he fled.

"What is going on?" Kami demanded again as Jimmy flew out of the room after the attorney.

"Betsy, you were adopted, weren't you?" Thelma asked, holding up the arm with the birthmark on the back of the wrist.

"I was, but no one knows that except my husband and myself. How did you know?"

"You, my friend, are Amelia Bohannon. This birthmark proves it."

"What are you saying?" Betsy stammered.

"I am saying that Agatha and Hanson Beckworth have been looking for you for all these years, and you were right under their noses this whole time," Thelma replied. "He knows who you are, too. He spotted the birthmark the same time that I did, and that's why he took off as fast as he did."

"He didn't get far," said a voice from the conference room door.

Everyone looked up and saw a furious Hanson Beckworth hand-cuffed and being held at bay by Sheriff Morse. Kami's eyes filled with tears. She had been played just like everyone else.

"How did you get here so fast?" Thelma asked.

"I have been hiding in the adjacent room. Jimmy told me what he suspected last night about the wills being switched and requested that I be on the premises if something happened. He was right," the sheriff answered.

"So, this is the something big," Thelma stated. "All these years just waiting for Agatha to die so they could steal her fortune. Your forged documents don't mean a thing now, do they? We have the real Amelia Bohannon right here in this room, don't we, Hanson?"

"You would never have known if I hadn't been so stupid and left that piece of paper in the file with the birthmark drawn on it," Hanson grumbled.

"What?" the sheriff said, pushing his prisoner down in a chair and looking around the room from person to person. "Who?"

"Sheriff Morse, meet Betsy Lee, the real Amelia Bohannon."

"If I hadn't been so stupid..." Hanson muttered.

"I totally agree with you that you were stupid and careless. That little piece of paper told me everything that I needed to know to find the real missing heir," Thelma announced. "You stole the drawing out of the file at Kami's house yesterday morning at breakfast. But it was too late. I had already seen it."

"If you hadn't spilled that coffee you stupid idiot, I would have been long gone with the money before anyone figured it out," Hanson growled at Kami. "You destroyed twenty-six years of planning with your one stupid accident."

Kami burst into tears and ran from the room.

"Why did you try to kidnap Kami?" Thelma quizzed the prisoner.

"I didn't," he argued.

"Yes, you did. I didn't put two and two together until just now. The next day at the hospital, you started to pick up the box of flower arrangements but dropped it again. You rubbed your shoulder after you put the box of flowers in the car. The same shoulder you landed on when you hit the ground when Dylan tackled you. You cringed again today when you swung your briefcase up on the table. I'll ask again, why Kami?"

"I don't have to answer any of your questions," he growled.

"Where is Wayne Spikeman?" Thelma pushed on.

Silence.

"That's all right. I think I already know. Sheriff, I am sure if you take a few men with you to Agatha's mansion, you will find Wayne somewhere on the premises. More than likely, James Potts will be there guarding him," Thelma suggested. "Agatha's neighbor told me that Hanson had been visiting the mansion quite a bit lately."

"Stupid, busy-body old women," Hanson stated, glaring at Thelma. "My people..."

"Your people what?" Thelma replied, glaring right back at Hanson, not wavering in the least. "From the way I see it, they're going to be pretty upset when they find out that your carelessness cost them millions of dollars and lots of wasted years. I'd be watching my own back if I were you."

Hanson lunged for Thelma, and the sheriff slammed him back down in the chair.

"One last question? Was it you or Potts who attacked Agatha at bingo? Did you want to speed up the timeline to get your hands on her fortune?"

"It wasn't me. I may be a lot of things, but I am no killer," he answered.

"Come on, Hanson. I have a nice cell waiting for you down at the station," the sheriff announced.

"Is that a smart thing to do? What happens if *someone* lets him escape?" Thelma asked.

"You don't have to worry about that anymore. We got our answers back from the crime lab about the picture. The cop sitting in the cruiser was Sheriff Carson, who was out on medical leave at the time. He's now deceased, so we can't question him, but as far as we can tell through our investigations, no one else was tied to him or the kidnapping ring."

"I've done my part and kept my promise. I found Amelia, and now you can find out who killed Agatha," Thelma said to the sheriff.

"I'm doing my best," the sheriff stated, yanking Hanson up out of his chair. "Let's go."

"I need to go find Kami," Thelma said, sitting down next to Betsy. "Will you be okay until I get back?"

"I'm fine. Just a little in shock, I guess," Betsy replied. "Go, make sure that Kami's okay."

Thelma scurried around the second floor, looking for her niece. She checked Kami's office, the other conference rooms, and all the bathrooms. Her niece was nowhere on the second floor. Checking out the window at the end of the hall, Thelma could see Kami's car still parked in her assigned space.

Hurrying to the stairs that led to the first floor, she stopped when she heard voices coming out of a small storage closet adjacent to the top of the stairs.

17

"**K**ami! Are you in there?" Thelma asked, knocking quietly on the door.

"Come in, Aunt Thelma," her niece answered.

Thelma opened the door to see Kami and Dylan sitting on some old boxes writing on notepads. Kami's tears were gone, and she was smiling.

"Are you okay?" Thelma asked, pulling up a box next to her niece to sit on.

"Yea, I'm okay, thanks to Dylan," she answered. "He made me see that I had only been out on one date with that jerk and that he was nothing to cry over, especially after last night. He assured me that I could do a lot better than a stuck-up, self-centered attorney."

"One date? I thought last night was your second date?" her aunt asked.

"It would have been if the slimeball had shown up for the date, but he didn't. He stood me up. So, Dylan and I spent the evening going over the files, and he made me a beautiful steak dinner," Kami said, smiling at Dylan. "We found out that we have a lot in common."

Thelma glanced at him and mouthed the words "thank you."

"We are working on a story together to let the world know that Amelia Bohannon has been found," Kami stated. "Dylan called his editor-in-chief, and we are going to run front-page stories in both papers with a shared byline when we know for sure that Betsy is Amelia."

"Who's going to cover the story about the kidnapping ring and the plan to steal Agatha's fortune?" Thelma asked, happy that her niece had moved on so quickly.

"Both of us," they answered at the same time.

"Another shared byline?" Thelma laughed.

"I hate to break this up, but I think Betsy would appreciate some friendly faces around her right now. Let's go give her some support while she attempts to deal with all this news that has just been dumped on her," Thelma suggested. "You, too, Dylan."

The trio arrived back at the conference room as a man unknown to them was talking to Betsy and Jimmy. As the man spoke, Betsy just kept shaking her head yes and wringing her hands. Jimmy waved the trio over to join the conversation.

"Thelma, this is Robert Owens. He was working with Agatha to regain control over her estate."

"Nice to meet you," Thelma said, extending her hand.

"Things are going to be quite a mess for the next few months until we see the total damage that has been done to Agatha's estate. We will be working closely with the police and private investigators to recover the parts of her estate that have gone missing. Once things are straightened out, and we do a DNA test on Mrs. Lee to make sure that she actually is Amelia Bohannon, we will file the correct court documents and have another reading of the will," Owens explained.

"I don't know where her mother is, but her aunt is right here in Sechuette," Thelma offered.

"Good to know, thank you," Owens stated.

"Do you want the money back that Hanson Beckworth has already passed out," Kami asked, worried that she had received a large check from the bogus attorney.

"We have everything on file. The attorney general's office and many others have been watching Beckworth and his firm for quite some time now. The amounts that he gave out were just to keep people happy and not ask questions. They only make up a tiny fraction of the estate," he replied. "He and his friends had made plans to steal the bulk of the estate."

"A tiny fraction?" Betsy asked.

"Aunt Agatha's estate is worth over seventy million dollars," Jimmy replied. "I was appointed the executor to work with Mr. Owens."

"And just like that, we will need a new desk person at our complex. Congratulations, Jimmy, you so deserve this," Thelma said, hugging him.

"What a story this is going to make," Dylan said, letting out a whistle.

"Anything to do with the estate can't be reported in the papers just yet. There are legal procedures that must be followed, and that may take some time to complete. You don't want to print anything unsubstantiated in your paper, do you?"

"We will sit on the story as long as we can. This is a small town, and I am sure word has already leaked out on Betsy. This place will be flooded before long with news crews from all over the place," Kami stated.

"True, but only two papers will have the exclusive on the story," Betsy smiled.

"I will be in touch with everyone concerned in the settling of this case," Owens commented. "As they say in the movies, don't leave town. Good day, all."

"As exciting as all this is, I have to get home to relieve the deputy of his watch over Shirley," Thelma said, slipping her arm around Betsy's waist. "Don't forget bingo tonight. We are having a birthday party for Ellie."

"I'll be there," Betsy replied.

Me, too. I may even drag Dylan with me," Kami said, laughing, poking him in the ribs.

"I need a cup of coffee. I also need to call Henry before he hears this from someone else," Betsy sighed.

"I'll make a new pot," Kami offered. "Why don't you ask Henry to join us here in the conference room instead of telling him on the phone? We all need to sit and relax."

Thelma looked back at she left the conference room and smiled. Her niece was going to be fine. She had a good circle of friends, and she was the co-owner of her own newspaper. There was a definite spark happening between Dylan, and her niece, and Thelma couldn't have been happier about it. Dylan was a good man.

When she arrived back at her apartment, Thelma went directly to her best friend's apartment to tell her what had happened at the reading of the will. June was shocked that the kidnapped girl had been right here in town the whole time and worked for her godmother to boot. They agreed to meet at four in the lobby to leave for bingo.

Shirley was in the kitchen, making two turkey sandwiches. Deputy Elder was sitting on the couch playing with the cat.

"Would you like a sandwich?" Shirley asked. "The deputy's stomach was growling so loud I couldn't hear the television."

"Sure, no onion on mine, please." Thelma requested, taking three glasses down out of the cabinet. "I would venture to say that you are now a safe woman."

"What do you mean?" Shirley asked, setting down the knife she was using to spread the mayo.

"Hanson Beckworth is in custody. I would venture to say your husband has already joined him in a nice jail cell, courtesy of the Sechuette Police."

"The man who your niece was dating?"

"He's the attorney that your husband has been working with all these years," Thelma replied. "You don't know the name?"

"I told you before. My husband was very secretive about who his associates were," she replied.

"I'm sure the sheriff will have questions for you after he talks to the two of them," Thelma said, pouring iced tea into the three glasses. "How does it feel knowing that you don't have to look over your shoulder for your husband anymore? He's going away for a long time."

"Truth be known, I hope he rots in jail for what he did to all those children and me," Shirley yelled. "I never want to see his horrible face again."

The deputy jumped up from the sofa and made his way to the kitchen when he heard Shirley yelling. Zumbutt took off down the hallway to hide under the bed.

"Is everything okay in here, Thelma?" the deputy asked.

"Everything's fine. Shirley just got a little excited when I told her that her husband had been arrested."

"Now that you're home, I need to get back to the station. By any chance, can I get that sandwich to go?"

"Let me wrap it for you," Thelma replied, pulling the plastic wrap out of the drawer.

Deputy Elder left, and the two women sat down to eat. Shirley played with the sandwich but didn't take a bite. Thelma watched her and wondered why she wasn't eating.

"Do you think I will go to jail, too?" Shirley asked quietly.

"I don't know," Thelma admitted, setting down her sandwich. "There are extenuating circumstances in your case, but I can't tell you how a judge or jury will think when presented with your case."

"I've spent the last twenty-six years in my own kind of jail. I just can't...." She sobbed.

"Maybe with all the information and evidence that you have given to the sheriff, they will go easier on you. You might end up with just probation," Thelma offered the distraught woman.

"I am helping, aren't I? Maybe they will find some of those children even though most of them are adults now."

"Let's just finish eating. We have to leave shortly as I need to pick up Ellie's cake before we go to the hall," Thelma suggested.

"I don't have any money to buy cards or my bingo bag to use,"

Shirley protested. "James probably took my bag with him as it had a false bottom, and that's where he kept all the stolen charge cards."

"You need to tell that to the sheriff. Tonight's on me. I don't have an extra bag, but we can buy you some new daubers when we get there."

June met the two women in the lobby at four. They picked up the cake and got to the bingo hall before the birthday girl did. Ellie's lucky table was set up with the cake, balloons, and several small gifts. Paul, the bingo worker, set a packet of free cards at her chair. They had just finished when Ellie walked in.

Everyone yelled *Happy Birthday* as she approached the table.

"Thank you, guys,' she said, setting down her bingo bag. "This is so nice."

"Another member of the bingo birthday club hits the big six-o," June joked.

"Shh! I'm thirty-eight and holding."

"Whatever you say, Ellie, we believe." June laughed.

"Did you hear? Betsy Lee is really Amelia Bohannon," Ellie whispered, looking around to make sure no one was close enough to hear her.

"I'm sure the whole town knows by now," Thelma commented. "This is a small town, and nothing stays secret for too long."

"They found Amelia Bohannon?" Shirley asked.

"Thelma found her. My best friend is one great detective," June said, proudly.

"Enough. We need to get to our seats and claim our territory. It's starting to fill up in here," Thelma recommended. "Happy Birthday, Ellie! Good luck tonight!"

The women returned to their own table and were setting out daubers to save Kami and Dylan's spots and their two new friend's spots, Wendy and Mandy, who sat next to Thelma. A round of applause broke out around the hall. Thelma turned to see Wayne Spikeman entering the door. He headed straight for Thelma and gave her a long hug.

"Sheriff Morse tells me that I have you to thank for him finding me," Wayne said. "I don't know what to say."

"I was right then. You were at Agatha's mansion, weren't you?"

"Someone they called JP brought me there when they took me from the mailroom. They thought Kami had seen the whole thing, so they went after her next. I was terrified for her, but I couldn't get away to warn her. But when they tried to kidnap her, some guy screwed it up by tackling Beckworth."

"Well, that answers the question why they tried to kidnap Kami," Thelma stated. "I'm glad you're safe, Wayne, and welcome back. We missed your calling skills."

"I'm calling tonight. I need to jump right back into things," he admitted. "Good luck! I have to go pick out my caller's choice games for the schedule."

"It's good to see Wayne back," June stated. "Maybe we will be out of here on time tonight for a change."

I'm going to get in line. June, if you want to stay here with Shirley, I will get everyone's cards," Thelma offered. "What color daubers do you want, Shirley?"

"I would love a green one and purple one if it's not too much to ask," she replied. "I love green. It's my favorite color."

"Mine, too, and fluorescent orange," Amy Spikeman said, coming up behind Thelma. "I just wanted to thank you for saving my Uncle Wayne. He means the world to me, and I don't know what I would have done if anything happened to him."

I'm glad I could help," Thelma replied.

"At least some people step up when someone needs help," Amy complained.

"I try," Thelma replied.

"I have to get in line, and thank you again," she said, waving goodbye with her admission card.

Thelma went to stand in line. Kami and Dylan joined her when they arrived, but the lady behind Thelma started to complain that they cut the line and that they needed to take their place at the end. Thelma rolled her eyes and grabbed Kami and Dylan's admission cards.

"I'll buy your cards. You can pay me back when I return to the table. Go," Thelma said, turning to the woman behind her. "There, now they're not cutting in line anymore."

"Boy, bingo is cutthroat," Dylan said as they walked away.

"Just wait until we start playing, and someone calls bingo that doesn't really have it. You haven't seen anything yet." Kami laughed.

The woman mumbled something under her breath but chose not to push the matter any further. While the line advanced, people approached Thelma to tell her what a great job she did finding the kidnapped girl and saving Wayne. The woman behind her listened wide-eyed as each person congratulated Thelma.

Thelma finally made it to the end of the line and started back to her table. She struggled to balance five packets of bingo cards, two daubers, and five sets of raffle tickets. Two feet away from the cashier, the daubers slipped out of Thelma's arms, and the raffle tickets fell to the floor next. Wayne rushed forward, setting his clipboard on the floor, and helped to pick up all the items that Thelma had dropped.

"Nice doodles," Thelma said as she waited for him to chase the daubers.

"I get bored sitting in the office," he answered, picking up his clipboard.

"Aunt Thelma, why didn't you call us for some help?" Kami asked as she took the items from Wayne that he had picked up off the floor.

"I almost made it back." Her aunt laughed.

Thelma passed out the card packets, collected all the money owed to her, and started to tape her early-bird strips together. Everyone was chatting happily. Kami told her aunt that Betsy wasn't going to attend bingo tonight as she was afraid of what would happen with the news that had just broke.

Shirley had thanked Thelma at least ten times for treating her to bingo. Turning her nightly program over to its blank white side, she opened her new green dauber and started to daub the head on the paper to make the ink flow through the sponge.

Thelma got lost in the green circles and the pattern they were forming on the paper. She watched Shirley open the purple dauber and go through the same routine that she had with the green one. She excused herself and placed a call to the sheriff.

"Bring the pictures taken of Agatha in the bathroom the night she was injured. I think I know who fought with her," Thelma announced.

helma waited at the front door for the sheriff to arrive.

"Did you bring the pictures?"

"Here is the file," he said, handing her a thick file.

"I only need the pictures taken of her face," she insisted.

The sheriff picked through the file and pulled out four pictures of Agatha's face.

"What is this all about?" Morse asked.

"Look at the pictures. What do you see?"

"I see Agatha's face covered with green circles. What am I supposed to see?"

"A pattern. There is a definite pattern across her face, and I have seen this pattern somewhere else tonight," Thelma explained. "Come with me."

She led the sheriff into the bingo hall and stopped at her table.

"Would you please get me a coffee for when I get back?" she asked June. "Thanks."

She left the table and knocked on the partially opened office door. Paul was counting money at the back table, and Wayne was sitting at the desk, counting out rip-off tickets and putting them in piles of twenty. Both men looked up.

"Hello, Sheriff Morse. Can we help you with something?" Paul asked.

"We need to speak with Wayne in private," the sheriff requested. "I won't let anyone near the money."

Paul left the room, and Thelma closed the door behind him. Wayne never moved behind the desk. He just stared straight ahead.

"Why did you do it, Wayne? What happened in the bathroom that night?" the sheriff asked.

"How did you know it was me?" he whispered.

"Where is your clipboard?" Thelma asked.

"On the desk."

"It was your pattern. When a person plays bingo for so many years, sometimes they develop a pattern when using daubers. I do it, subconsciously, without realizing I am daubing circles in the same formation," Thelma said, picking up the clipboard and showing it to the sheriff. "A line of three daubs, then one, then three again."

"It's the same formation of circles across Agatha's face that are on your clipboard," Thelma said, holding up the two together, side by side.

"What happened, Wayne?" the sheriff asked again.

"I tried to talk to Agatha in the hallway, but she brushed me off like she always did and entered the woman's bathroom, thinking that I wouldn't follow her," he started.

"But you did," Thelma said. "What was so important that it couldn't wait until you were at work the next day?"

"I'm losing my house. It is in foreclosure, and I had tried to talk to Agatha at work at least five or six times in the last month, but she would lock me out of her office and pull the blinds. All I wanted was a small advance to catch my mortgage up so I wouldn't lose my house. Carol has been sick, and the medical bills have piled up, but my heartless boss didn't care. It was under two thousand dollars, and with her millions, she wouldn't have even noticed it gone. I would have paid every cent back."

"So, you fought in the bathroom?" the sheriff asked.

"Yes, I reminded her that I had been a loyal employee for many years and had never asked for help before. She laughed at me and threatened my job. I got mad and shoved her because I couldn't take her laughter ringing in my ears anymore. She fell backward and hit her head on the pipe inside the stall."

"Was she conscious after she hit her head?" Thelma inquired.

"She was, for a short time anyway. She kept laughing at me and then added that she was now going to charge me for assault and battery on top of everything else. I lost it. How could anyone with so much begrudge and belittle someone who had been so loyal to her?"

"Then what happened?" the sheriff asked.

I saw a green dauber that someone had left on the windowsill in the bathroom. I grabbed it and started beating her face with it, and when I did, she stopped laughing. She tried to dodge the dauber and whacked her head again. This time she didn't wake up. I wiped my fingerprints off the dauber and tossed it on the floor. I grabbed her purse and bingo bag, knowing that she always carried large sums of cash on her, and ran out the back door."

"Why didn't you get some help for Agatha?" Morse asked.

"I was so afraid, not for myself, but my wife. She's sick and can't be left alone. I took the money to the bank the next morning. I paid the mortgage up to date, figuring before long Agatha would regain consciousness, and I would be going to jail. But at least Carol would have a house to live in." He sobbed into his hands. "I never dreamed that Agatha would die."

"I have to take you downtown, Wayne. I'm sorry," the sheriff stated

"It's okay, I understand. You know, I'm almost relieved that the truth is out. If I could take it all back, I would." He sighed. "A little too late, I know."

The sheriff opened the door and called Paul back into the office. He explained the situation and told him that Wayne would be leaving and not calling bingo for the evening. He also requested that he not tell anyone why. Paul agreed and said he would say that a family emergency arose and left to find Bob would have to fill in calling.

Thelma watched as the two men walked out the back door. He was right on one count. She didn't know if she felt worse for him or his wife. Bob was explaining that Wayne had left for the evening and that bingo would start in five minutes. Thelma headed back to her table with a heavy heart. She almost wished that she hadn't come to bingo.

"Your coffee is cold. Do you want me to get you a fresh cup before we get started?" June asked her as she sat down. "Are you okay?"

"Not really. I'd like everyone to meet at Kami's house after bingo. I have a lot to tell you." She sighed.

Thelma was quiet most of the night. She missed a bingo, which she never did and wasn't even upset about it. Everyone at the table could see how upset their friend was, but they respected her request to wait until later that night to find out why.

At intermission, they all gathered around Ellie's table to sing to her and have cake. Thelma passed out slices to the people at the surrounding tables. As she set pieces of cake down in front of people, she spotted something that made her gasp.

"Kami! You need to take June and Shirley to your house when bingo ends. There's somewhere I have to go," Thelma requested.

She grabbed her purse from the table and ran out the door. Her friends stared at each other.

"It must be something really important for Aunt Thelma to leave bingo," Kami stated.

Thelma entered the police station and requested to see the sheriff. The deputy went to find him.

"I should have realized this earlier," she chided herself, pacing back and forth.

"He'll be right out. He's in interrogation," the deputy said.

"Thelma, this better be important. I'm a little busy here," the sheriff stated, entering the lobby. "Whatever it is, can it wait until morning?"

"No, it can't. You have the wrong person. I need to talk to Wayne," she replied.

"What do you mean by the wrong person? You led us right to him, and he confessed."

"I know. You won't hear me say this very often, Clayton Morse, but I made a mistake."

"I don't get it,' the sheriff said, shaking his head. "He confessed."

"Yes, he did because he is covering for someone else. I need to talk to Wayne, please," Thelma pleaded.

"Okay. I have to stay in the room with you. You understand that?"

"That's fine."

Sheriff Morse opened the door to room three, and Wayne looked up, confused at what he was seeing. Thelma took the seat opposite him at the table where he was sitting.

"You know why I am here, don't you, Wayne?" Thelma asked.

"No," he mumbled.

"You didn't do it. I know that, you know that, and one other person knows that," she started.

"I confessed, now go away and let me be," Wayne ordered her.

"Your confession is bogus. You are protecting someone. Someone that you have protected your whole life."

He looked at Thelma with tears in his eyes but didn't utter a word.

"Amy went into the office and visited with you before bingo. I remember seeing her go into the office. She was the one who doodled on your clipboard while she was there," Thelma continued.

"No, you're wrong. I did it," he claimed.

"As I was passing out cake at intermission, I noticed Amy's admission card and program at her seat. The same pattern of ink circles was on both. They matched what was on your clipboard and what was stamped on Agatha's face."

"No...no. I did it, I tell you," Wayne yelled, slamming his fists on the wooden table.

"No, you didn't. The more I thought about that night at bingo, the more I realized that there wasn't enough time for you to have done it. You were in the main hall with me when Ellie screamed. You wouldn't have had time to fight with Agatha, go out the back door, rifle through her purse and bingo bag and get back into the hall up to the caller's podium. And, besides, you looked as shocked as I did when you first saw Agatha lying on the floor."

"Thelma, just leave this alone, please," Wayne begged.

"I can't. You have spent your whole life protecting your niece from that creep James Potts. I can't let you go to prison and leave your wife for something you didn't do," Thelma replied. "It's time you let go and let Amy stand on her own."

"She has her whole life ahead of her, and when my wife is gone, which will be soon, it won't matter if I go prison or not." Wayne sobbed.

"Tell us the truth this time, Wayne," the sheriff requested.

"I can't, I mean I already have," he stated.

A knock sounded on the door. The sheriff excused himself and stepped outside. When he returned, he had Amy Spikeman with him. She stood next to her uncle and sighed.

"I can't let you do this, Uncle Wayne. You have looked out for mom and me my whole life. When mom died, you stepped in and helped me whenever I needed it. It's my turn to look out for you," she said, placing her hand on his shoulder.

"Amy... don't," he whispered.

"Sheriff, I will make a full statement. I was the one who fought with Agatha. I followed her into the bathroom with the full intention of telling her off for not helping my uncle. The argument became physical. She fell backward through the swinging stall door and whacked her head on the pipes," Amy stated. She laughed at me, calling my family pitiful, and I lost my temper and took the dauber I had in my hand and continued to daub her face with it the more she laughed at me. The whole thing was a terrible accident."

"Can't you see? This happened because of me," Wayne claimed.

"I stole her purse and gave the money to Uncle Wayne so he could pay the bank. I didn't tell him where the money came from until after he had already made the mortgage payments. That's when I broke down and told him what happened and that the money wasn't really from my savings account," Amy continued.

"We had an agreement," Wayne protested, looking up at his niece.

"An agreement that I can't keep," Amy told him, wiping a tear away from his cheek. "You need to be home with Aunt Carol. Spend all the time that you have left with her together, and not from a jail cell. Hold her hand, take her out to dinner, and make all her remaining time with you special."

"Amy, you need to come with me," the sheriff ordered. "Wayne, you are free to go for the time being, but don't go far. There may be other charges pending against you."

He led Amy out of the room, and they disappeared down the hallway.

"Come on, Wayne, I will drive you back to hall so you can get your car," Thelma said, helping him to stand up.

"Do you think if I can figure out how to pay the money back, they will go a little easier on Amy?" Wayne asked as they walked to the front door of the station.

"I'm going to let you in on a little secret, but you didn't hear it from me." Thelma leaned over and whispered near his ear. "You are in Agatha's will, and when they get the correct papers filed in court, you will be able to pay the money back and hire a good attorney for both of you."

"Sad."

"What's sad?"

"That Agatha would help me in her death but not while she was alive. It doesn't make any sense," Wayne replied.

"Not a lot of things in life make sense," Thelma agreed. "Now, let's get you home to Carol."

The hall was in total darkness when they pulled into the parking lot. Wayne's car was the only one left in the employee parking lot. He waved to her as he drove away. She sat there for several minutes, trying to imagine what his life was going to be like in the next few months. He was a good man who had tried to do things the right way his whole life. He deserved a break, and hopefully, he would get one.

Thelma pulled into Kami's driveway. She decided on the way into the house to give them the quick version of tonight's events. It had been a long week, and suddenly she was exhausted. An hour later, she climbed into bed with Zumbutt curled up in a ball next to her head on the spare pillow.

"This is my life, and you are all I need," she murmured to the cat, closing her eyes.

Almost two weeks had passed, and the busy summer had transformed into a quiet offseason. It was Labor Day Monday, and most of the locals were gathering on the town green for the annual parade that celebrated the end of the summer.

Thelma and June were sitting on a large blanket, waiting for the rest of their crew to arrive. A large picnic basket filled to the brim with lots of homemade goodies was sitting on the blanket, waiting for everyone's arrival.

"I love Labor Day," June said, stretching out on the blanket so the sun could shine on her face. "I thought Shirley was going to join us."

"She finished her depositions, and the sheriff got her into the witness protection program earlier than planned. Shirley has a new name and a new life, and I really wish her well," Thelma replied. "Here come Kami and Dylan."

"Hi, Aunt Thelma. Happy Labor Day!" she said, planting herself on the blanket next to her aunt.

"You brought food, too?" Thelma asked, watching Dylan set another picnic basket next to the other one.

"You didn't think a full-fledged cook would show up without any food, did you?" Dylan smiled, taking his place next to Kami.

"You just wanted to show me up with your fancy cooking." Thelma laughed. "I guess my potato salad just isn't good enough anymore now that you are around, but people will eat my food again when you go back to Portland."

"About that," Kami replied, smiling. "Dylan's not going back to Portland. I mean, he is to give up his apartment and turn in his two-week notice at the *Times*."

"Excuse me?" June replied, sitting up.

"You are looking at the new head investigative reporter for the *Sechuette Gazette*," Dylan announced. "I start in two weeks."

"That's wonderful," Thelma exclaimed. "I knew that you two would work well together."

"He's renting the small house two doors down from my dad," Kami told her aunt.

"I doubt he'll spend much time there," Thelma whispered to June.

Wayne Spikeman and his wife walked up to the blanket. They were holding hands and smiling at each other like newlyweds. Carol was carrying a bottle of wine and Wayne two glasses.

"I just wanted to say thank you for bringing my husband back to me," Carol said to Thelma. "He's a changed man."

"Betsy is going to loan me the money against the inheritance that I am supposed to receive so I can pay the money back and hire an attorney for Amy. She is also going to pay for a new treatment for Carol to see if we can beat this thing," he said, looking at his wife lovingly.

"We'll all keep our fingers crossed," Thelma replied. "Happy Labor Day!"

"See you at work tomorrow, Kami," Wayne said, walking away.

"He seems so happy now," June noted.

"Betsy's attorney has completed his investigation and filed the real will with the court. He had to do a lot of extra paperwork because Betsy has decided to keep her current name instead of going back to

Amelia. She and Henry are moving into Agatha's mansion next week," Kami announced.

"Great news. I wasn't sure whether I should call her Betsy or Amelia the next time I saw her." June chuckled. "I hope they were able to recover everything for Betsy."

"Close. The attorney said that he couldn't account for about four million dollars. He thinks it's either hidden in an offshore account somewhere or spent. Beckworth did like flashy cars and nice suits. According to the legitimate will, the trust has over fifty million in it. I think Betsy can live on that for a while." Kami laughed. "And she keeps hinting that people are going to be incredibly surprised when the will is finally read. But that won't be for another couple months or so."

"If Agatha was good to me, maybe I can retire from my job and become a professional bingo player." Thelma laughed. "What do you think, June? Travel all over and play bingo?"

"Sounds good to me," her best friend agreed. "I was hoping for just enough to pay for the bingo cruise in the spring."

"I might even join you on that cruise," Kami stated.

"I'm hungry?" Thelma said, opening the two picnic baskets. "Who wants wine?"

June broke out the plastic glasses, and Thelma poured the wine. She held her glass up in the air to make a toast.

"To great food, old friends and new friends, and the official start of offseason. Life just doesn't get any better than this," she announced. "Unless, of course, you are playing bingo."

THE END